COSMIC LOVE & STARDUST

AVA WIXX

Cosmic Love & Stardust
Cosmic Love & Stardust © 2023 by Ava Wixx

All Rights Reserved. Except as permitted under the U.S. Copyright act of 1976, no part of this publication may be reproduced, distributed, or transmitted in any form or by any means, or stored in a database or retrieval system, without the prior written permission of the author.

The characters and events in this book are fictitious. Any similarity to real persons, living or dead, is coincidental and not intended by the author.

First Edition: August 2023
Published in the United States of America by
Wicked Wixx Press.
The Wicked Wixx Press Logo is a trademark of
Wicked Wixx Press.

Cover Art, Ava Wixx Logo, Wicked Wixx Logo, & Interior Book Graphics by Lindsay Tiry of LT Arts
Edited by Melissa Ringsted of There For You Editing

Print ISBN: 978-1-955950-09-1
Kindle ISBN: 978-1-955950-10-7
EPUB ISBN: 978-1-955950-11-4

For more information visit: avawixx.com

For everyone who gets frustrated when I don't answer the phone or respond to texts ... or emails. This is what I was doing.

Ashes to ashes, Dust to dust ...

... IN HER VEINS BURNS STARDUST.

Introduction

Once upon a time, humans thought they were alone in the Universe.

They were wrong.

Hundreds of thousands of species existed that weren't indigenous to Earth. So many, it was thought that no one would ever discover or catalogue every species and subspecies out there in the big, wide open.

Humans also used to think they were at the top of the food chain.

They were wrong about that, too.

Sexual, racial, religious discrimination ... it all stopped mattering once humans realized they were the only ones who saw the difference. A human was a human, no matter their creed, and the rest of the Universe didn't have high opinions of the natives of Earth.

Long story short ...

Introduction

Humans had been long overdue for an awakening, and they'd been scrambling to survive ever since they got one.

In hopes to compete with alien races that were superior physically and mentally, humans began to splice their genes to create hybrids. New humans were born, and the rules changed yet again.

Battles waged and large casualties were amassed, including the loss of entire planets. So an alliance was formed, simply known as the Unified Galactic Federation of Stars or UGFS. It would govern all so chaos would no longer reign supreme.

Of course, that's when things really got complicated…

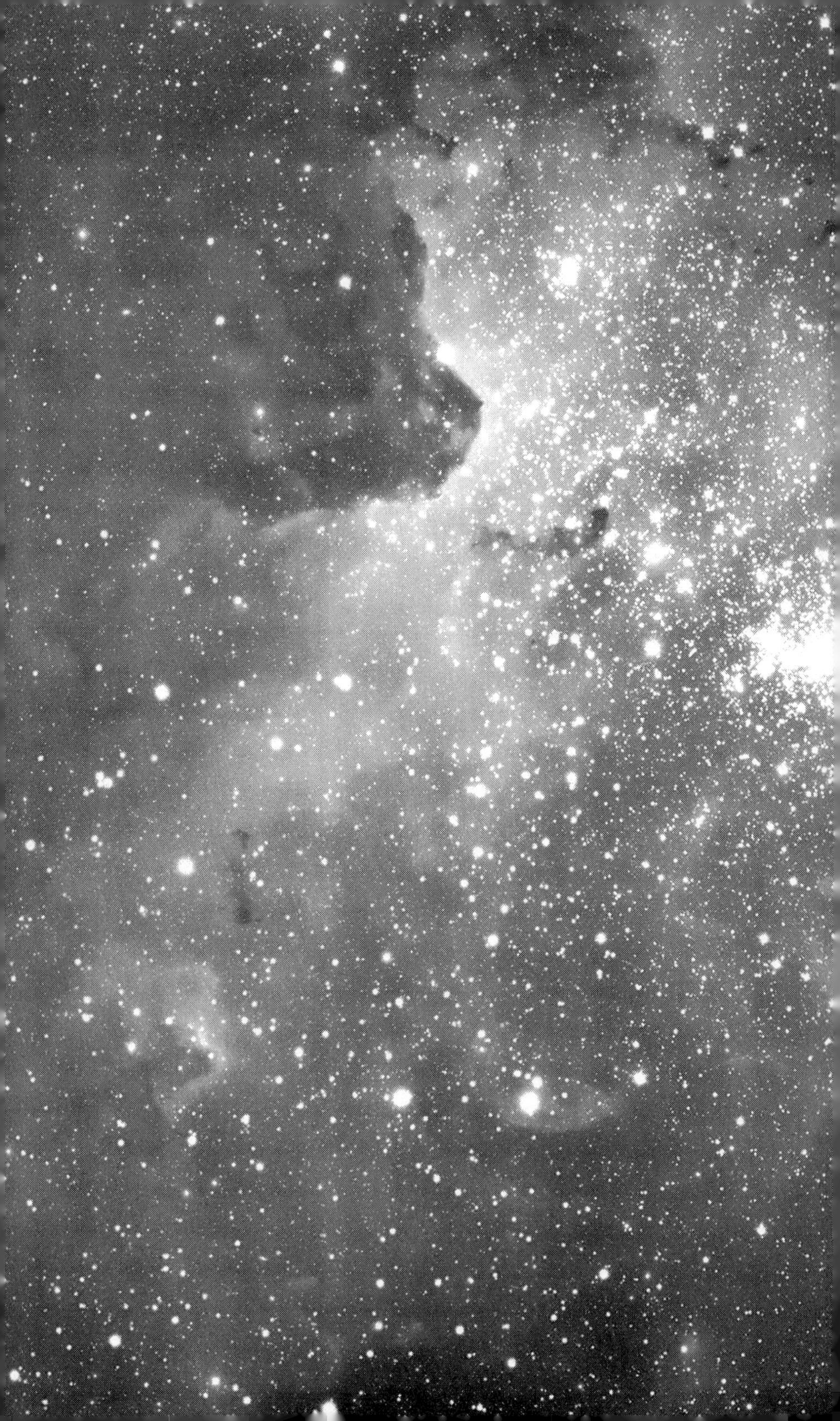

Chapter 1

"Anyone good?" I asked, leaning over Zula's shoulder.

She snorted. "I'm pretty sure my definition of good and yours differ greatly." She continued to flip through images of potential bounties on our ship's central computer.

I stabbed my finger against the screen. "Oh! What about that one?" Pictured was a large humanoid male—red skin, shaved head, Species Class 4. *Could be interesting.* He was last seen not too far from our current location. *Possible easy money. My favorite kind.*

Zula sank back into her seat, the worn leather creaking as she heaved a huge sigh. "Allow me to jog your memory about what happened the last time you went after a Species Class 4."

I raised my hands into the air, backing up a few steps. "Hey, hey now. Everything turned out fine."

"After you spent two weeks in a coma."

My mind flashed to the little incident Zula was referring to.

"Put your hands up and turn around nice and slow," I growled, hopefully loud enough for tall, green, and scaly to hear me. I eyed my laser handgun to make sure I had the safety off, wishing I hadn't let Tamzea talk me into the stupid contraption. I missed my vintage 9mm Earth gun, but unfortunately it was useless against some species, especially the kind with armor-like skin. I had that lesson beaten into me the hard way.

Lizard-man, as I'd dubbed him in my head since I'd already forgotten his name, turned around slowly to face me. "Are you talking to me, hu-mutt?"

Oh no he didn't! I knew I shouldn't let it get to me. I'd heard the term so many times I couldn't count it anymore. It shouldn't, but it definitely did get under my skin when I was referred to by the derogatory slang for genetically spliced humans. Hu-mutt ... not even the tiniest bit clever if you asked me. Obviously, no one ever did.

I demonstratively tapped my left ear, where one of my interpreter implants was located. "I'm sorry, one or both of my interpreters must be malfunctioning. I know you didn't just call me a hu-mutt," I spat, the word bitter on my tongue.

A slow smile spread across Lizard-man's face, revealing razor-sharp teeth. I stifled a shudder. He was seriously ugly. "They're working just fine."

As my trigger finger twitched, I reminded myself that Lizard-man was wanted alive, and I wouldn't get paid if I killed him. I bared my own teeth in a mock smile. "I'm really going to enjoy taking you in. I'll try not to spend—"

I sucked in a breath. Soft light shimmered around him, building steadily in intensity. I fumbled my left hand for my PAER—Psychic And Energy Reader—which was hooked onto my belt. It would tell me exactly what was going on with the light show, and how potentially dangerous it was for me. As soon as I pointed it at Lizard-man, it flashed a bright red.

"Oh shit," I muttered.

A moment later, my world exploded into a kaleidoscope of colors before everything went dark.

"Don't be such a downer. Danger goes with the job. And I was fine ... after I woke up. No harm no foul." I crossed my arms over my chest, scanning the details of the potential bounty. Species Class 4 could mean anything. Zula hated the unknown, which was exactly what that classification translated to.

"I just don't like—"

"I know, I know ... anything unpredictable, which rules out *all* Species Class 4s. But let *me* remind *you* that they are always worth the most money."

"I don't like it."

"Of course you don't. You're a Galvraron. You like everything planned and plotted out," I singsonged, my tone mocking. "Not knowing what we're going up against gives you a panic attack."

Narrowing her eyes, Zula tucked one side of her chin-length flaxen hair behind her ear. "Galvrarons have the highest IQs of any species. Our brains—"

"Yes, yes, you're a genius. You're all geniuses. But none of you know how to have any fun ... Smurfette." I grinned, waiting for her reaction.

A low growl vibrated in Zula's throat, her knuckles going white as she clenched her fists. She hated when I called her Smurfette. It couldn't be helped, though. I mean, Zula did have blonde hair and blue-ish-tinged skin. "Stop using archaic Earth references around or referring to me. You weren't born on Earth. It was destroyed decades before you were even—"

"It's my heritage! I'm human!"

"Part human. And what does that have to do with your obsession with Earth culture? Everything you can get your hands on you—"

I slammed my palms down on top of the computer screen, the image wavering for an instant from impact. *Hunk of junk needs replaced soon. Which is why I need to pull in some easy money.* "Message whoever has the claim out for the Class 4. Let them know we're interested and get the rest of the details."

I spun on my heels, stalking from the control room. As much as I loved my crew, none of them understood my attachment to Earth culture. I may not be one hundred percent human, but I didn't know what my mixed genetics were. I simply wanted to feel like I was from somewhere, like I belonged to some kind of rich history, instead of the failed science experiment I really was. Other species took pride in their heritage. What was wrong with me doing the same thing? *Nothing, as far as I'm concerned.*

My gaze roamed over the dark metal corridors of my ship as I trudged along. Although more than some of The Pittsburgh's equipment needed to be replaced or an overhaul, the bones of my baby would always take me where I wanted to go. I ran my fingertips over an oblong dent in the center of my door. *I don't remember what happened here. Huh. Did I do this on one of my firejuice benders?* I shrugged, punching the unlock code into the worn keypad.

Once inside my living quarters, I hurled myself onto my bed face first, groaning. The scent of stale, fading fabric softener assaulted my nose. *When was the last time I washed these? Ugh. Who cares?* I was getting antsy, focusing on inane things. I needed an exciting hunt in my life soon or I would have to jettison myself out into space to die. *I know, a bit dramatic, but I blame my unknown genetics.*

I didn't know much about my DNA. The only clue I had to my other half was that I could withstand any level of fire without injury. *Very helpful at times, especially against flamethrowers.* I'd also found that out the hard way. Or in the end, it had been a lucky discovery, although a bit too late in my life. One of the reasons I'd been rejected from any kind of training program on New Earth was because I'd never shown any useful abilities. No one wanted a *normal* human anymore, not even my parents. It was fine with me, though. I was happy as captain of my own ship, hunting down the scum of the Universe for money. Actually, I didn't care if they were scum or not, I'd haul in almost anyone for the right price tag.

My door buzzed, sliding abruptly open. *Should've locked it.* Scowling, I sat up as Tamzea strode in, her lavender eyes narrowed, and her pale skin flushed. "I heard you were planning on going after another Class 4?" She stopped in front of me, her hands on her hips. "Are you insane?"

"We could use the money. The ship needs maintenance. Lots of maintenance."

"There are plenty of other options in the database, Jane."

Rolling my eyes, I flopped back onto my bed. Tamzea worried about me too much. She was a Mazatimz, a species of healer who appeared human, except for their lavender eyes and hair. Most of them ended up as some kind of doctor somewhere. They also drove everyone insane with their constant worrying and overprotectiveness. Or at least that was my theory.

"I'm a bit bored, too," I muttered, tracing the pattern of flowers on my sheets with my index finger.

Tamzea was silent as she moved around my quarters touching various objects ... dolls, knick-knacks, baubles I didn't even have names for. I trailed her movements with only my eyes. She picked up one of my human history books, flipping through it without actually looking at it. "I don't want you to be injured again. One day I may not be able to heal you. My powers can only do so much."

"We all know that day will come, no use worrying about it," I retorted. "You know I'd rather live a short, exciting life than a long, boring one. Just as long as it stays uncomplicated and drama free."

"*That* is the human in you." Tamzea slid my book back on its shelf and came to stand in front of me again. She absently fiddled with her signature crown of braids piled on top of her head, the lines on her face deepening. "So there's *nothing* I can say to change your mind?"

I grinned. "Nope."

She shook her head slowly while studying me. "It's a wonder purebred humans lasted as long as they did. I don't know how any of them lived past infancy. To think that hybrids like yourself are thought to be an improvement. It truly boggles my mind."

"Hey," I snapped. I knew what she was trying to do, but I wasn't going to fall for it. "I'm not changing my mind no matter how much you insult my human side. Now get out of here so I can get some shut-eye."

Tamzea frowned, and then scuffled for my door, pausing before exiting to peer at a black light poster depicting a prowling panther. "Where do you find this stuff?"

I shrugged. "It's pretty easy to come by actually. It's surprisingly not that much in demand."

Tamzea snorted loudly before muttering, "That should tell you something." She ducked out into the corridor without another word, shutting my door behind her.

As soon as she was gone I locked the door and flicked off the lights. Settling in for what promised to be another restless night, I hoped I could at least get a few hours of sleep.

I really do need some excitement in my life before I go insane. If it's not already too late.

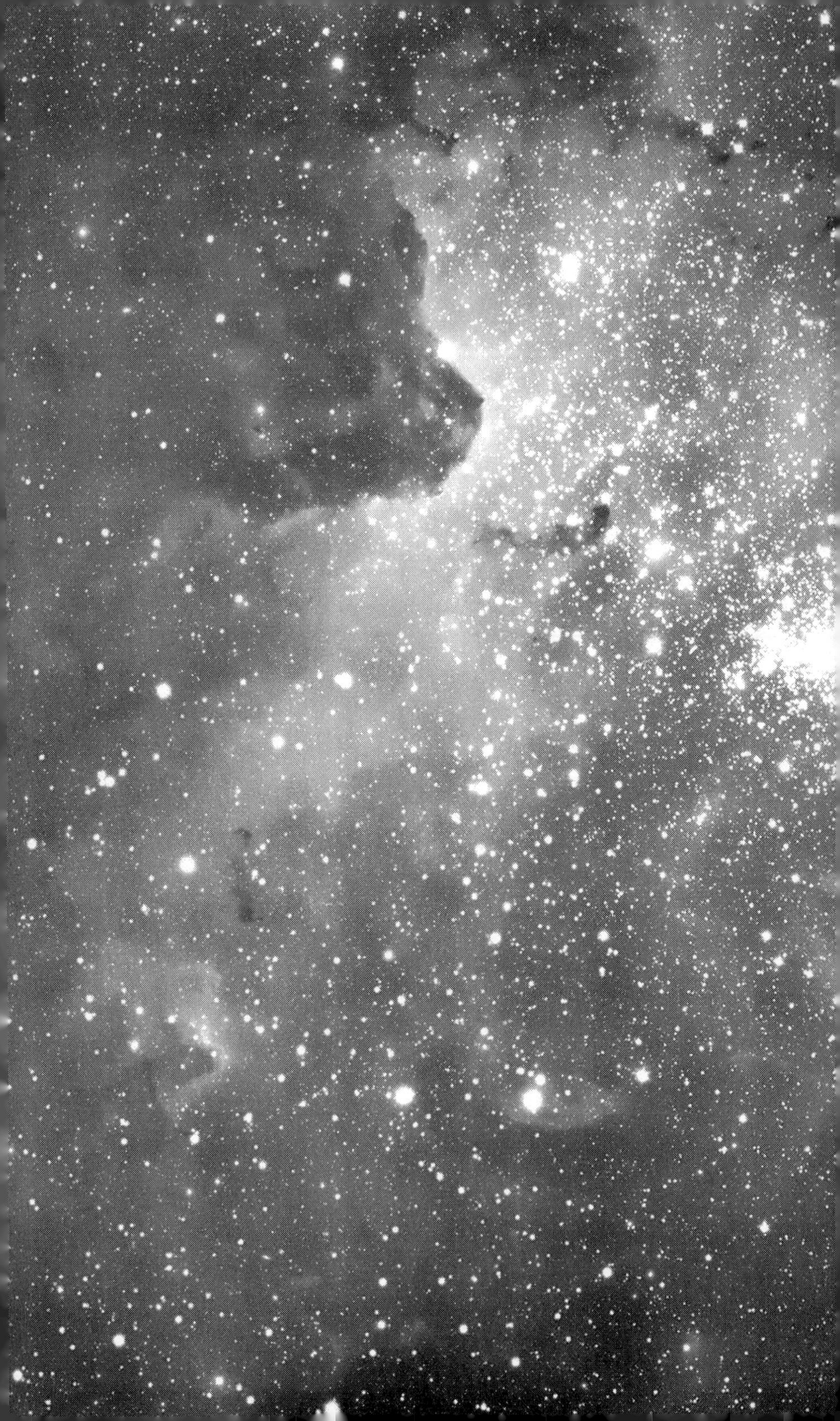

Chapter 2

"Fuck me," I groaned. My PAER flashed red, the light reflecting eerily off the freshly cleaned metal corridor walls of the supply space station. "Not again."

If I lived to tell the tale, I was never going to hear the end of it from my crew. Tall, big, and bald had seemed like he was going to be an easy takedown. I tracked him to a nearby supply space station in practically no time at all. I'd thought it was a sign that it was meant to be. *I hate when I'm wrong.*

Even as my PAER kept flashing red, nothing was happening. Frowning, I craned my neck forward. "Umm … whatcha doin' there?"

My paycheck gritted his teeth, his hands rubbing together in a circular motion. The entire situation was a bit confusing, and because of it, I was utterly transfixed. I should have run, yet I continued to linger, the choice fueled by nothing short of stupidity. After all, I wasn't a cat and I only had one life, so if curiosity killed me ... I was screwed.

"He's trying to build fire." A smooth baritone voice tickled my senses, causing the tiny hairs on the back of my neck to lift. Something in my stomach fluttered, but I chose to ignore it.

I blinked rapidly but didn't take my eyes off the scene in front of me. "What?" I muttered.

"I said he's trying to build fire. You might want to leave before he turns you and your ... *interesting* outfit into ashes."

"What?" I repeated, annoyance causing my ears to heat. "Did you just insult my clothes?"

I always dressed carefully when on a job. I had a reputation to uphold, after all. Nice clothes meant I was pulling good bounties, which garnered respect. I'd worked my ass off to get where I was, and now I had access to top-grade bounties. Only a few of my peers had the same level of street cred and connections in the UGFS that I did. Considered the best of the best, I secretly thought it had a lot to do with how I dressed.

In preparation for this gig, I'd carefully selected one of the new outfits I'd recently purchased from an Earth Museum that was permanently closing. The curator had assured me that the pristine pieces were legitimate nineteenth-century Earth clothing, called Steampunk. I was already attached to the vibe, especially the leather pants with all their adornments, and thought I looked pretty damn good, too.

A grunt met my ears. "I just warned you about your imminent demise, and you're worried about your clothes. Well there, sweetheart, I'm thinking you might want to stop—"

I whirled around to face my tormentor, my bounty temporarily forgotten. "Oh, dear God," I murmured, unable to contain my reaction. *Because of course he's attractive ... of course.*

His eyes were what caught my attention first. They were like molten-gold, warm and bright, ringed with a deep amber shade. Set behind long, inky lashes, they gazed at me with a palpable arrogance that had me grinding my teeth.

Continuing my perusal, I noted the way his midnight hair had a slight wave to it, a rogue curl sweeping across his bronzed forehead. My fingers itched to touch that silky scrap of hair, to push it off his face before running my hands down the scruff on his chiseled jaw. I idly wondered if it would be soft, or if it would abrade my palms pleasantly? I shook my head to dispel the thought.

He was a good deal taller than my height of five-foot-ten, his arms and chest corded with lithe muscles encased in more delectably bronzed skin. His clothes gave me pause though, all his rugged refinement was shoved into loosely fitted cargo pants, and a sleeveless shirt. The color of both a dingy green.

Even I had to admit that despite his abysmal choice in

clothing, he was absolutely stunning. And he definitely knew it.

EVERYTHING *about him makes me want to punch him in his smug face.*

"*God?* I haven't heard that term in a long time." His golden eyes danced with mirth. "A human?"

I clenched my jaw so tight I was lucky my teeth didn't crack. *At least he didn't call me a hu-mutt. That's a step in the right direction.* "Go away. I'm busy." I turned my attention back to my bounty—the would-be fire-starter—who was no longer there.

Squeezing my eyes shut for a brief moment, I swore under my breath. Then with nostrils flaring, and anger thrumming through my veins, I slowly turned back around to face Mr. Sexy ... and Annoying. "He got away thanks to you."

"I saved your life, you mean. He would have burnt you to a crisp."

Marching the few feet of distance between us, I poked him roughly in the chest with the end of my laser gun. "I should shoot you. You just cost me a lot of money. Maybe I could sell your parts for a decent chunk of change."

"He would have—"

"Look, asshat, fire I can handle. He would have been some seriously easy money."

His full lips curled up into a sneer. "You may think you can handle fire, but—"

I dug my gun harder into his chest. "I said I could have handled it! I—"

My next breath lodged in my lungs when his large hand came up to wrap around my wrist. Warmth suffused my system with sudden intensity, and I gazed up into his golden eyes, which seemed to flicker with flames. The urge to lean into him, to press my mouth to his, to rub my body against his ... to throw him to the ground and—

"What the hell?" I grated, yanking away from him.

But Mr. Sexy and Annoying appeared to be as stunned as I was.

It was undoubtedly a ploy.

He pursed his lips, and opened his mouth to speak, but nothing came out. A white-hot fury boiled my blood. He was obviously packing some kind of pheromone or seduction power, one that he was currently trying to use on me.

Oh, hell, no. I'm not having any of that shit.

I tapped my finger on the trigger of my gun menacingly, getting his attention. "You stay the hell away from me or I swear to *God*, I'll kill you."

Backing away from him slowly, I kept my gaze locked with his. "I mean it, I *will* kill you." I spun on my heels, and dashed off to where my ship was docked.

And my day started with such promise.

IN A BAD MOOD TO rival all bad moods, a colorful array of obscenities spewed from my mouth, slamming into anyone within earshot. There was just something about Mr. Sexy and Annoying that had gotten under my skin. It was probably because he'd managed to cost me my bounty, insult me, and I'd still been attracted to him. *He must have been packing some serious magic mojo to pull that one off.*

I'd been emotionally and mentally violated … and was strangely turned on. My skin was too hot, and sweat dribbled down my spine, my body humming with need. His piercing gaze hovered in the forefront of my mind, taunting and sexy. *Aaaah!* "I should have shot him," I grumbled, stomping my way towards my living quarters. And to make matters worse, I'd let my crew down. There was no way I could face any of them right now. We needed the money and—

"Jane!" Masha, our ship's engineer, called out to me as I passed the engine room.

Grimacing, I sped up my pace, trying to ignore her. Unfortunately for me, she excelled at getting underfoot, mine in particular. Her tiny five-foot-one frame maneuvered with lightning-speed to stop in front of me, her solid black eyes snagging mine. "We need to talk." She anxiously twirled one of her dark curls around her finger, her normally silver-toned skin so pale it appeared almost grey.

Sagging with sudden exhaustion, I leaned one arm against the wall for support. I knew exactly what Masha wanted to talk about. "We'll get the maintenance done as soon as we can. I can't get blood out of a stone, Masha."

Her bottom lip quivered. "What happened with the bounty you were supposed to pick up? I thought you said it was going to be eas—"

"Easy money?" I finished for her. "Yeah, I ran into a little ... trouble. And now that he knows I'm after him he's probably halfway across the galaxy. I'll just have to find someone else. There are plenty of bounties in the database."

A single tear crept down Masha's face. "But you know I—"

"I know, I know." I flicked my gaze away. If I didn't *see* the tears then I couldn't fall under their thrall. "You get all emotional when things aren't working right in your engine. Which—let me remind you—is technically *my* engine since I own this damn ship." I slid past Masha, continuing on my way up the corridor. "Don't worry, I'll go pick someone new now." And get to hear an earful from Zula while I was at it, I was sure.

Masha had a way of guilting me like no one else could. I blamed her resemblance to a human child for my weakness. She was a Guaviva, a species who 'spoke' to anything electronic or mechanical. I didn't understand it exactly, but I did know that Masha had a breakdown every time the ship wasn't running perfectly, as if it was in pain somehow, and affecting her. She'd come at me with her cherub face twisted up with anxiety, and I'd crack. Every. Single. Time. It was shameful, really. *If only she was all scaly or had boils, then maybe I wouldn't be so vulnerable to her tears.*

"Well, at least you weren't thrown into a coma." Zula's sarcastic remark met my ears before I could even make eye contact. "So what happened?"

"I'll tell you what happened," I huffed. "Some arrogant asshat got in the way, and my bounty flew the coop." Leaning against the control panel, I crossed my arms over my chest. "I don't think it needs to be said, but I'll say it anyways ... we need to find someone else ASAP. Masha is in another one of her states about ship maintenance."

"She manipulates your human side. Her kind doesn't have the need to cry when upset. She—"

"Does an amazing job tugging on my human heartstrings, I know. I don't want to talk about it anymore. What I do want to talk about is who my next victim is going to be." I turned my attention to the computer screen as Zula pulled up the current database. She scrolled through silently, waiting for me to tell her to—

"Stop!" I exclaimed, practically falling over. I slapped the screen as if it was his actual smug face staring back at me, not just an image. "That's him." I narrowed my eyes, skimming the information. *Ash? His name is Ash? What kind of stupid name is Ash? No second name, surname—no aliases? And—* "You have to be fucking kidding me!" I ground my teeth together. *He's a friggin' Species Class 4.*

"What's with the dramatics?" Zula asked, skimming the information herself. "Where do you know him from?"

"He's the asshat who got in the way of me collecting the—"

"Other Class 4. Coincidence? Probably not. They were most likely there together. It would make sense that he would distract you from getting his friend so they could both get away."

"I don't care. I'm going back out there to track him. Ash's ass is mine." *Yep, that has a nice ring to it.*

Zula sighed, something she did a lot around me. *Go figure.* "Not this again. Just pick—"

"Nope. He's the one I'm going after. I'm going to take a quick shower to regroup, and then little 'just Ash' isn't going to know what hit him."

"You are in rare form, even for you. Are you getting your menstrual cycle? Your human side gets so emotional when—"

"Oh, my God! Shut up, Zula! That's an order from your captain!"

I stomped out of the control room, vibrating with annoyance. With that big brain of hers, Zula thought she had everything all figured out, including my hormones. The truth was ... my human side was confusing, but so was the rest of me. I was the sum of several parts that equaled indecipherable. Even I didn't know what the hell was happening to me most of the time.

But at least I'm never boring.

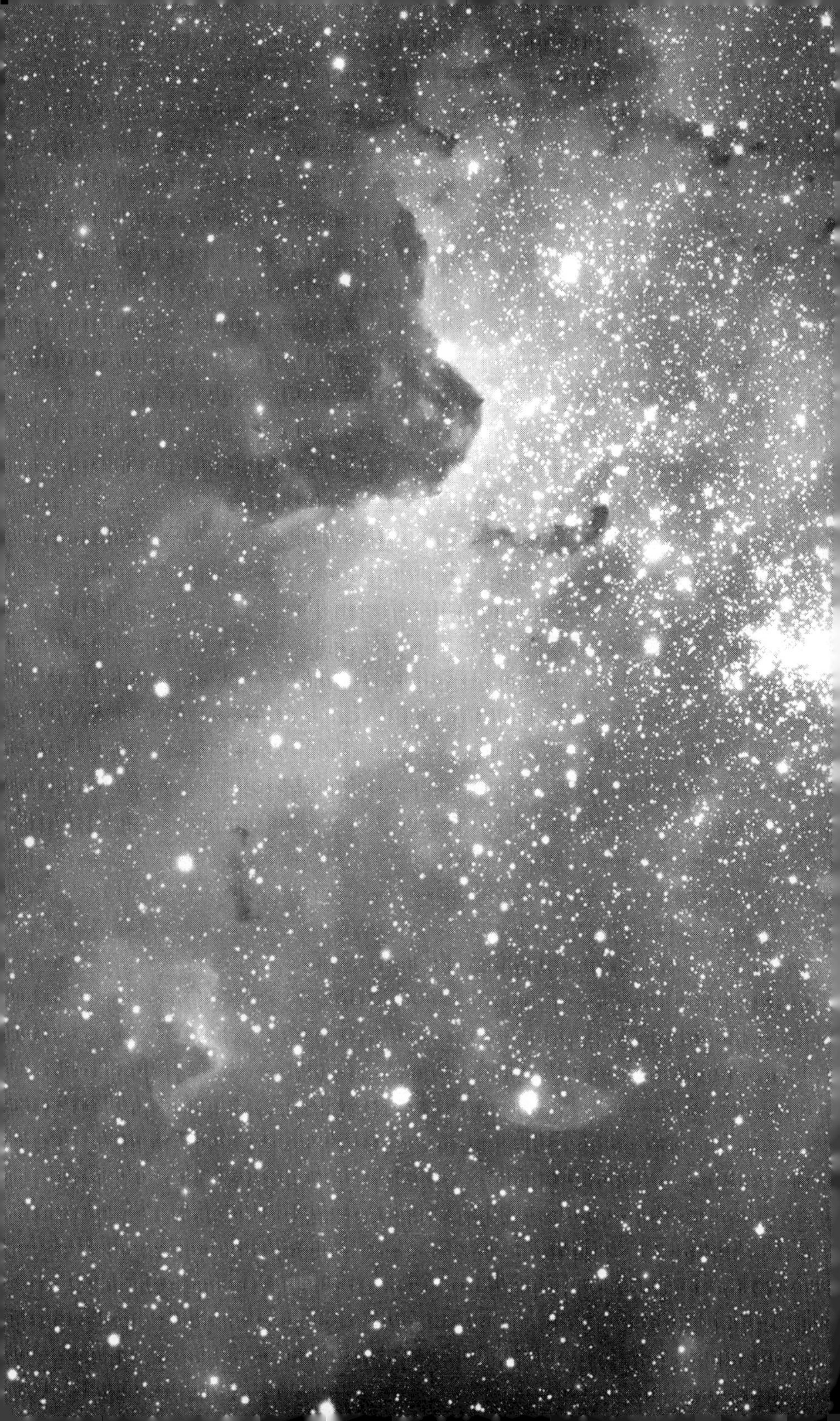

Chapter 3

After my not so refreshing enzyme powdered shower—since our water filtration system was down again—I stood naked in front of the full-length mirror in my living quarters, holding up different outfits in front of me. It was taking me longer than normal to pick out an ensemble. I blamed *the asshat* for that one.

I knew I didn't wear the most popular fashions in the Universe. Hell, even in our current galaxy, the Milky Way. But I was trying to not only make a statement about my status as a successful bounty hunter but to pay homage to my human genetics. I was mixed, or a hu-mutt, as I was so often referred to, but since I didn't know what else I was, I identified with my human heritage. I did waste more money than I should on Earth relics, books, and clothes ... hell, I'd even named my ship The Pittsburgh after an Earth city I'd read about in one of my history books. I simply liked imagining what it would be like to have a planet I could call home.

I was conceived and altered on New Earth, where what was left of humanity pretended to thrive. What I'd experienced there was nothing like in the history books. New Earth was cold and empty—children seen only as what they could provide for the future. I was never permitted to wear anything but a uniform. And when I was old enough to have my aptitude tested ... I'd been labeled useless. Even my own parents turned their backs on me.

I discarded the dress in my hands, shaking my head harshly. *You will not think of those dark times when your survival was questionable. They're long gone and never coming back.*

Although unconventional, I'd found a place and a family of sorts. I was happy. And a part of that happiness was the connection I felt to Earth.

Decision made, I picked up a variation of the outfit I'd had on earlier—more Steampunk clothing—only this one included a short skirt instead of pants, and showed off more of my golden-hued skin. *Maybe I can use it to my advantage with asshat.* Men of most species loved my long, toned legs. They were my best feature, or so I'd been told more times than I could count. I was tall, on the thin side, and yet athletic. I thought I was pretty, but some species preferred more meat on their females. Who was I to judge? Some female somewhere probably thought Lizard-man was sexy. I shuddered at the memory of his ugly reptilian face.

Pulling my long, golden-brown hair up into a ponytail, I met my amber gaze in the mirror. My lips twisted into a feral grin. *Well, hello there, Ash. Ready to be thrown into the prison quarters on my ship? I certainly hope so.* That would teach him to laugh at my clothes and to doubt my prowess as a bounty hunter.

"HEY THERE, SWEETS. LOOKING FOR SOMEONE?"

Stifling a groan, I was unable to keep from rolling my eyes. I knew that voice. *Fuuuuuck. Not today. If I have to deal with stupid, arrogant, egotistical, pain in my ass, Jassen, I might just snap.*

Jassen was a Talsen, a species of warrior-like men who were big as hell, as in not only tall but wide with muscles. His dusky skin was luminescent and flawless, the man undeniably sexy, much to my chagrin. But he was also my biggest competitor for bounties.

If he's here, then he's probably after the same thing I am. Damnit.

"You stalking me again?" Shifting from foot to foot, I suppressed the urge to bolt, knowing it would only encourage him to follow me. Jassen and I kind of flirted, or bantered really, but in actuality, we hated each other … at least I hated him. If I could get away with shooting him right between the eyes, I would. Unfortunately, he knew some people in high places so I'd probably end up on a prison planet for my troubles, in the best-case scenario.

"Whatever answer you want to hear to get me back in between those lush thighs of yours." Jassen's white teeth flashed, a lecherous grin spreading across his face. "We could team up. We'd make the best bounty-hunting pair in the galaxy."

I snorted. "Please. I was drunk and you were ... there. Everyone is permitted to have one big mistake in their sexual history. Besides, I don't need a partner to be the best in the galaxy."

Crossing my arms over my chest, I covertly flicked my gaze over my surroundings. I hadn't made it more than fifteen feet from my ship. I was inside the supply space station, but barely. I'd been joking, but maybe he really was stalking me. *Ugh. I don't have time for this.* I wanted to retrace my steps to the bar I'd been at before, using it as a starting point for tracking Ash. I didn't need or want Jassen tagging along.

"You're slipping, Jane. I heard you let a bounty walk away earlier today. Don't come crawling to me when you—"

"I'll never come crawling to anyone. I'm always on top." I internally groaned, knowing I'd set myself up for what was about to come. *I really need to think about my word choices before I say them sometimes.*

"Yeah, if I remember correctly, you really enjoy being on top. And I liked you being there."

"Look, I don't have time for whatever this is." I waved

my hand between us, inching away from him. "Will you please just hop on your ship and light slide right over to another galaxy? This one isn't big enough for the both of us." I spun on my heels, not caring if he replied.

"Jane," Jassen snapped. His fingers dug into my arm, forcing me to halt.

I lifted my leg, not bothering to turn around, and jammed the back of my boot right into his crotch. For good measure, I elbowed him in the nose as he bent down to clutch himself.

Glancing over my shoulder, I grinned as he crumpled to the ground, moaning in agony. "Real nice seeing you again, Jassen."

I sprinted towards the bar, hoping to already have Ash in my custody before Jassen could find me again. I was due an easy bounty. The Universe owed me some good karma.

"Hey, watch it." I shoved at a humanoid-looking guy. He tripped, narrowly missing a faceplant into the nearest wall, and turned to flip me off. I returned the gesture without slowing my pace. Several other humanoids, and a small furry creature with red eyes, jumped out of my way having just witnessed the exchange.

I skidded to a stop at the front of the bar. It was tucked away in the far side of the supply space station. It was open, as in the space it inhabited wasn't closed off. It didn't have a door or a name, but that didn't mean it wasn't crowded. Libations that appealed to all species were common fare at supply space station bars, along with their unsavory patrons. Most upstanding citizens refueled, traded, or did whatever they had to, and avoided that part of the station. Not me, though. I frequented them because they were a wealth of information for my line of work.

Like right now. It wasn't Ash, but I recognized the bright blue shirt, and the back of his buddy's large, smooth, red head. It was the bounty that had simply walked away from me earlier. I rubbed my hands together in anticipation. Maybe I could bag him, and then get him to rat on Ash so I could come back for him later. *Finally! A hand in my favor.*

I slid up to the bar, and leaned forward, keeping my eyes straight ahead. "I have to say, I'm kind of shocked you're not halfway across the galaxy by now. Why did you come back here?" I lifted my hand, signaling the bar droid for service.

"Shit," Tall and Bald muttered. His muscles coiled, letting me know he was about to bolt. I dug my laser gun into his ribs before he could move another inch.

"Let's talk business, shall we?" The bar droid stopped in front of me. "Firejuice," I ordered, before turning my attention back to Tall and Bald. "As I was saying ... how about you tell me where your little friend Ash is, and I'll let you go."

The droid set a glass of bright red and orange liquid in front of me. I presented my left arm, letting the droid scan my money cuff to pay for the drink. A moment later, it floated away, the hum of its hover components buzzing softly. "Well, you're awfully quiet. You or him. Decide before I'm done with my drink."

Tall and Bald shifted, tugging on his shirt, but remained silent. I shrugged, pressing my gun into his side more firmly while lifting the drink to my lips. The sweet and spicy flavor burned and soothed my taste buds as I slammed the whole thing in one go. "Ah. Time's up. Loyalty gets you in my prison and nowhere else." *Damn, I was really hoping he'd give up Ash.* But at least I'd get the money for maintenance to make Masha happy.

I slapped a pair of laser cuffs on Tall and Bald, and shoved him off his stool. He seemed resigned to his position, which honestly surprised me. I wasn't going to question it though.

A satisfied grin spread across my face as Jassen limped into the bar, glaring at me. *I win again.* "Ice might help." I chuckled.

Jassen was smart enough to keep his mouth shut for the time being. He'd lick his wounds, and go right back to being the pain in my ass he always was. It wasn't the first time I'd roughed him up. I was beginning to wonder if he was a masochist. Why else would he pursue me so relentlessly? I'd seen tons of other females throw themselves at his feet. *I'm pretty, but definitely not stalker worthy. It has to be my winning personality ... and willingness to beat the shit out of him.*

"Were you looking for me?"

All the fine hairs on my body stood straight up. There was something about his deep voice that affected me. It seemed to caress things on my insides, and I embarrassingly had to stifle a visible shiver as it ran up my spine.

My gaze met Ash's humor-filled golden eyes. He had an arrogance about him, the kind that made it seem like he was laughing at me and not with me. And it triggered an urge to beat the shit out of him.

I plastered a fake, and hopefully believable, smile on my face. "You bet. I was hoping you hadn't gotten too far. As soon as I get your friend to my ship then I'll be back for you." Biting my lower lip, I batted my eyelashes. I was also hoping he'd stay put under the mistaken impression that I wanted him for a more carnal reason. I was glad I'd gone with my instinct to dress skimpy.

Ash smirked, his heated gaze blatantly roaming my exposed flesh. "He's no of friend of mine. Buuut ... I may be willing to wait for you here, if you're offering what I think you are." He moved forward, his large frame crowding into my space. His full lips skimmed my earlobe as his hot breath blew along my cheek. "My ship is docked off of port two. Come find me when you're done with him."

My nostrils flared with his spicy scent, the not quite cinnamon aroma filling my head completely. Something about it was familiar and enticing, and as I continued to inhale, I was launched into thoughts of us naked and entangled, his hard body covering mine while he pounded into me. *Maybe I'll take him for a spin before I lock him up. It's been a while since I've had any kind of sex. Besides, hate sex is always the hottest.*

"Yeah, okay," I rasped. My insides warmed, pulsing with desire, and suddenly it wasn't such a bad idea. In fact, it was the best one I'd had all day. I would take my release from him, and then collect his bounty. A complete win-win situation for me. "What's—" I cleared my throat, trying again, "What's the name of your ship?"

"The Phoenix." He strode away from me, and my eyes dropped to watch the sway of his muscular ass until he was out of view.

Damn. Why are all the hot ones such assholes?

"So the rumors are true," Tall and Bald said. "Why not me?"

"Shut up." I lightly tapped the back of his knee with my boot to get him moving again. "I wouldn't touch you if you were the last creature in the Universe."

I didn't feel like denying the rumors that so many male bounty hunters seemed to enjoy spreading about me. They weren't true, so I didn't really give a shit. You had to have tough skin to be at the top of a mostly male business. There was always talk of how I had to use sex to be so successful at my job. Men on the whole, no matter the species, had a hard time wrapping their testosterone-addled brains around the fact that sometimes women just did it better. The fact is, women have a kind of power that men can never duplicate, and it drives a certain type of male crazy. Women could rule the Universe if they stopped caring about their reputations.

I'd never cared, which was why I was at the top of the bounty-hunting game. *Say what you want about me, but you'll be saying it while tasting the bitterness of defeat.*

Tall and Bald was silent as I forced my laser gun into his shoulder. We made our way unharassed all the way back to The Pittsburgh. Once I loaded him into one of the ship's cells and made sure the security system was online and fully powered up, I hurried to get off the ship again. I passed Masha on my way out. "I bagged the guy from this morning. Let Zula know so we can collect. Go ahead and make an appointment for maintenance. I'll be back soon … I'm about to get us enough for that new part you've been wanting."

I was already down the ramp and in the station when Masha's excited shrieks met my ears. I just shook my head, continuing to port two. *She is absolutely ridiculous about that engine.* But it did make her the best mechanic I'd ever come across.

As the large starship with the name The Phoenix painted on the side loomed in front of me, I couldn't help but think: *My day just took a turn towards interesting.*

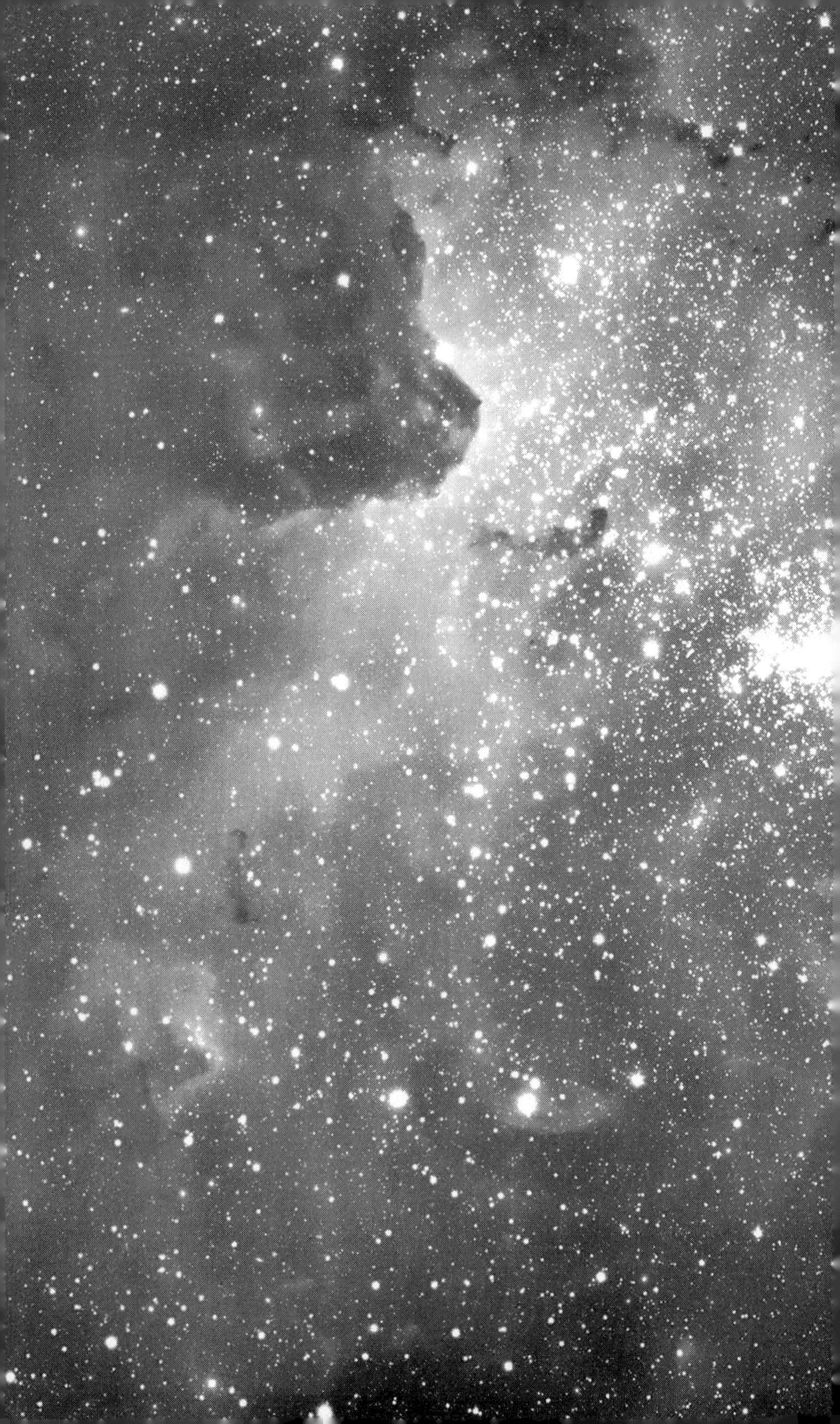

Chapter 4

Life as a bounty hunter, constantly moving from one place to the next, didn't allow for much dating or the cultivation of meaningful, lasting romantic relationships. I felt lucky to have my crew and never expected much else.

Unfortunately, my body still had needs, and occasionally I felt compelled to seek relief from something other than my battery-operated boyfriend. Ash intrigued me despite my dislike of his character. I didn't need to like someone to have chemistry with them sexually. In fact, some of the best sex I'd ever had was with men I couldn't stand.

I didn't hesitate before marching up the ramp that led into The Phoenix. I paused once I was inside to inspect things. Ash's ship was newer than mine—sleeker, too—on the inside and outside. I ran my fingers along the wall as I walked. Everything was smooth. *Yeah, definitely a better-*

grade ship than a Chimay. His ship felt sterile, though; too pristine, too perfect. Maybe I was biased, but I'd take my slightly older, beaten-up ship over his any day. The imperfections of The Pittsburgh gave it character and made it my home.

"Does The Phoenix pass your inspection?" Ash seemed to appear out of nowhere directly in front of me. He stood with his legs spread apart, and his arms hanging loosely at his sides. He wanted me to think he was relaxed, but the tension in his muscles belied his true feelings.

Is he anticipating his interaction with me as much as I am with him?

"Do you really care what I think about your ship? Oooor," I drawled out as I approached him slowly, sashaying my hips seductively, "would you rather know what I think about you?"

I reached out my hand to touch him, but he snagged my wrist, holding it away from his body. I squirmed, wanting to yank away, but allowed him to control our interaction. *For now.*

"I wondered if you'd show up. I had my doubts."

As I licked my lips, his gaze followed the movement. "Well, here I am. What are you going to do about it?"

He shook his head while studying me. "I know what I should do."

I quirked an eyebrow. "Oh? What's that?"

"Toss you and that sexy little ass right off this ship. I know you're after the bounty on my head." Despite his words, he pulled me abruptly into his chest. My hands curled into his shirt on instinct and my body hummed with anticipation. He was so warm, and something about that warmth called to me, just like it had the first time I'd run into him.

"Then why would you keep your seduction mojo going? Why invite me here in the first place? You want me as much as I want you. We can sort the rest out ... after." I hooked my leg around his hip, pressing myself against him.

"No mojo." His voice dipped low, rough with desire. "What are you? Besides human? What I think you are ... is wishful thinking on my part and that's all."

I swiveled my pelvis, and he hissed in response. "I don't know and don't care. What are you?" Gripping his shoulders, I pulled myself tightly into him and dipped my face to the exposed skin of his neck. *God, he smells divine.* How could someone who dressed in such crappy clothes smell so damn good? Of its own volition, my tongue snaked out to taste him. *Mmm ... he's delicious, too.* His flavor was indefinable, and yet strangely familiar to some part of me. I wanted to lick every inch of him. Twice.

"It doesn't matter," he said, groaning.

"What?" I muttered. I'd forgotten what we were talking about. *Words are overrated anyways.* I sucked on the patch of skin I'd just licked. I was hot and achy. I needed ... I just needed Ash.

"Fuck it," Ash growled, and I found myself suddenly pressed against the smooth metal wall. His lips slanted over mine, his tongue plunging in to take control of my

35

mouth. The kiss only lasted a moment before his overheated lips blazed a trail down my body.

"Wha—Aaaah!" I tried to speak, tried to ask him what he was doing, or about to do ... I was surprised he wasn't just going to fuck me right there against the wall. But when my skirt was pushed above my hips, my underwear ripped from my body, and Ash's tongue delved inside of me ... well, my brain completely short-circuited.

"You taste so fucking good," he purred against my sensitive flesh, causing me to moan loudly. I clutched wildly at the wall, sliding down a bit when I couldn't find anything to dig my fingers into. Ash cupped my ass and lifted, settling my legs over his shoulders so he had better access.

As he worked me over with his mouth and tongue, I continued making nonsensical noises. I'd never felt anything like what he was doing to me. I didn't want him to stop, and yet it was almost too much. I tried to push him away, but my actions only made him redouble his efforts. My body heated, and Ash no longer felt warmer than me; we were the same temperature. My muscles coiled tight. I threw my head back, arching against the wall.

"Holy fuck!" I screamed, convulsing around his tongue. I was on fire. Every nerve ending in my body had gone up in flames.

Before I had time to collect myself, I was on my feet and spun around to face the wall. Ash's rough hands tipped my ass up, and he pushed into me from behind. I whimpered.

"Fuck," he growled into my ear, his teeth clamping over my lobe.

He moved roughly against me—no slow build for him. He started fast and moved into a brutal pace. He filled me up so perfectly. The friction between us dropped me over the edge into another mind-blowing orgasm. I clawed at the wall, bucking against him. As I quivered around him, he exploded inside of me, which rolled me right into orgasm number three. I was dumb with bliss. Spots of color danced in front of my eyes, and my entire existence seemed to narrow down to focus solely on Ash. *Ash. Ash. God, I want more. So much more of him.* I ground against him, trembling with need.

But there was something I needed to do ... something —*Shit. How did I forget?* I fumbled for the laser cuffs on my belt, somehow managing to get one cuff around Ash's wrist.

"Un-fucking-believable. My dick is still inside of you."

"I'm well aware." My chest heaved as I tried to catch my breath. "Please ... um, pull out." I winced. I was glad no one was around to witness what was going on between Ash and me. It definitely wouldn't help with the rumors. *Not that I care about anyone's opinions, except my crew's. I can almost hear Zula now ... she'd be beyond angry at my stupidity.*

While still holding the other end of the cuffs, I pushed myself off of the wall as Ash disengaged himself from me. Turning around to face him, I tried not to look at his cock, which was still semi-hard and hanging out of the front of his pants.

Ash grinned at me, his golden eyes erupting in flames. "Thanks for that. It was exactly what I needed. And now I have my answers about you." He leaned forward, smashing his lips against mine before his entire body morphed into flames only vaguely in the shape of a person. I swore, jumping back as I watched the flame version of Ash slip right through the laser cuff.

The flame, or Ash, then zoomed down the corridor while laughter echoed in his wake. I raced after him, giving chase right off the ship without a second thought. The flame rounded me, caressing my skin, and dissipated into thin air. A moment later the ramp on The Phoenix slid up, and the ship's engines blazed to life.

With my mouth hanging open, I stood at port two, as The Phoenix moved away from me, Ash safely inside. I didn't know what to do or how to react. One minute I had the upper hand, and the next I was standing back in the supply space station with no underwear, and a skirt that barely covered my ass.

I cursed Ash to high heaven and back while hurrying to The Pittsburgh. I had lost the battle, but I would win the war. Because clearly, Ash had just declared war.

I would track him down for free if I had to.

The bounty I'd collect from the price on his head … it'd just be the icing on the cake of my victory.

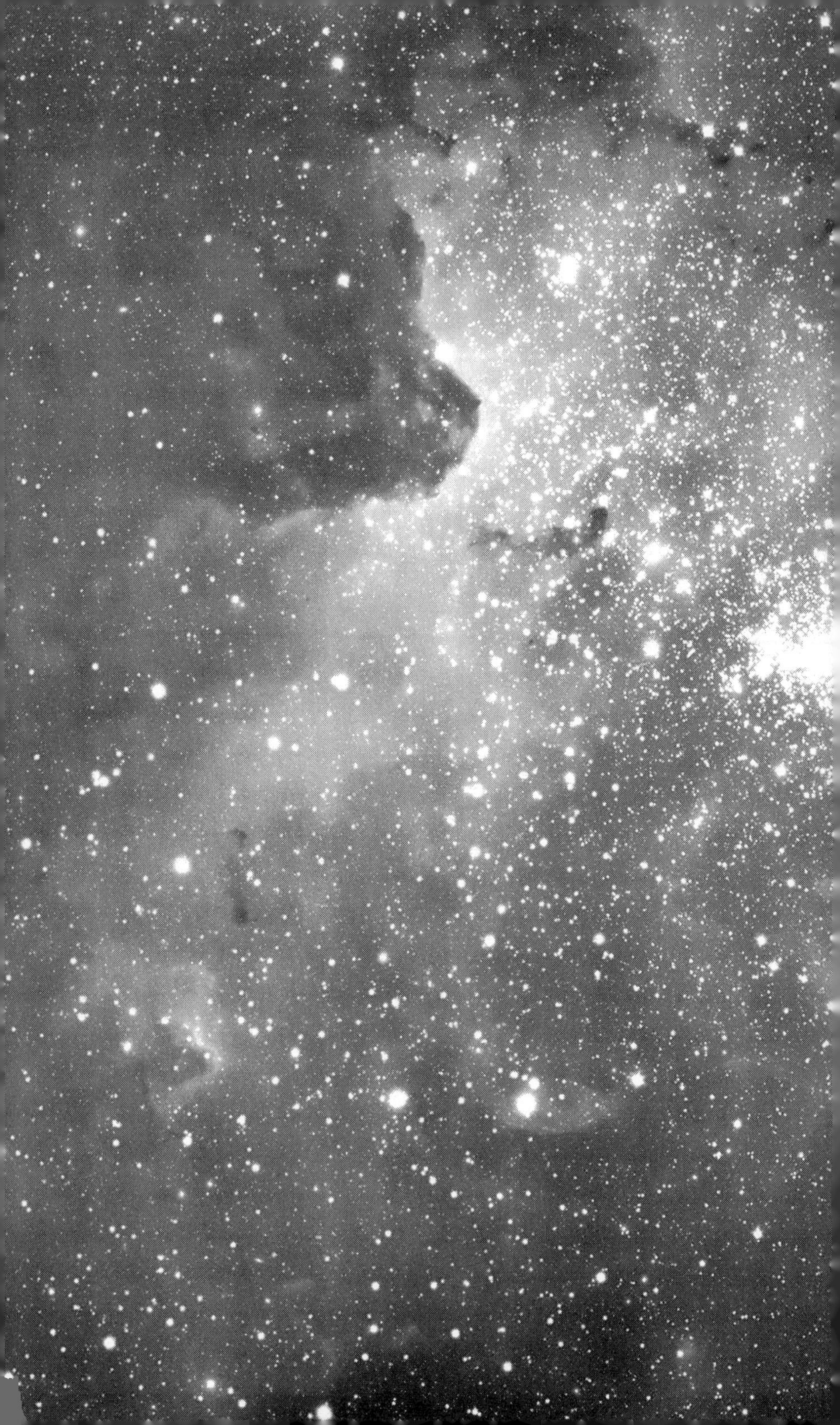

Chapter 5

"There is no way that man, or whatever the hell he is, doesn't have some kind of seduction mojo. No way," I hissed, stomping my way onto The Pittsburgh.

Masha was waiting expectantly for me, and when she saw me alone her face fell dramatically. "I thought you said you were going to get the money for my part."

"My ship, *my* part," I growled. Fury burned its way through my veins and boiled my blood, every molecule in my body approaching combustion. I had gone into the situation with Ash intending to use him for my own sexual gratification, and then to turn him over for the bounty on his head. But he'd turned the tables on me, and I'd totally gotten played. It was humiliating, and yet ...

I got off. And he got me there quickly. Quicker than I ever experienced before. And the way he touched me —

Goose bumps erupted in quick succession across my

skin, my thoughts falling into the visceral memory of what it felt like to have his body pressed up against mine. *God, he was so good. And he filled me up so completely ... so perfectly. If only—*

"I hate him. I fucking hate him." His mojo was undeniable, the force of it rivaling my anger. I wanted another taste of him—needed it.

"This ship wouldn't even run if it wasn't for me. Maybe if you got me the part I need, and some better equipment, I could do everything that's needed for maintenance myself. I'm skilled enough to do it, I just—"

I halted, keeping my back to Masha. At least she wasn't trying to manipulate me with tears this time. Nope, this time she was going for the petulant teenager routine. *Less effective and more annoying by a landslide.* "When I have the money, I'll get you everything you need. It would save me money and aggravation to have you be able to do everything yourself."

Heaving a huge sigh, I dropped my anger into a box deep within me, effectively compartmentalizing it. Masha shouldn't have to suffer just because she was the first one I saw after my interaction with Ash. "We can at least afford to pay for the maintenance, and hopefully next time we won't need to go to someone else. I know how much you hate other mechanics touching the engine."

Masha hummed under her breath, remaining otherwise silent, so I decided to continue on my way. My current top priority was to figure out how to block or control the pheromones Ash gave off. Tamzea was my best bet for finding the information I needed.

I headed straight to the med wing, finding Tamzea taking stock of her supplies. Her lavender eyes rounded with surprise when they alighted on me. "Uh-oh. What happened?" She hastily shut the metal locker she'd been in, and waved me over to the nearest bed. "Tell me what's wrong?" Her hands were already flittering around me trying to get a reading.

I waved her off. "Nothing's wrong physically. I just need some information." I grimaced. I was not ready to admit to anyone what happened between Ash and me. Normally, I had no problem owning up to my sexual needs, but this was different, I'd let him get the better of me, and the entire debacle was completely humiliating.

I sucked on my teeth and flicked my gaze away. "Medical information. I just need some medical information."

Tamzea's head tilted to the side, her gaze assessing. "What kind of medical information?"

I shifted uncomfortably, my gaze dancing around the room as I continued to avoid making eye contact with her. "Well, you see ..." I cleared my throat. "Is there anything I can do to stave off the effects of some kind of seduction slash attraction pheromones?"

Tamzea leaned forward, dipping uncomfortably close, her nostrils flaring demonstratively. "You had sex."

Jumping away from her, I scowled. "No ... I didn't."

Tamzea crossed her arms over her chest. "Don't lie to me, Jane. I can smell it."

"How? How the hell can you smell it?" I sniffed at myself, coming away with nothing unusual. I growled under my breath. Did Tamzea have hidden sex-sniffing abilities that I didn't know about?

"Ha! I couldn't, but you just told me!" A triumphant grin spread across her face.

"Oh! I can't believe you," I hissed. I suddenly didn't want to talk to Tamzea anymore. I'd figure everything out on my own. Whirling around, I started to march back the way I came.

"If you storm off then I won't tell you what I know."

Gritting my teeth, I turned slowly to face Tamzea, my fists balled at my sides. "Do you know something or are you going to try and trick more information out of me?"

Tamzea shrugged, another grin tugging at her lips. "A little of both."

"Fine," I grated. It would be easier to have her tell me what I needed to know instead of going on a wild goose chase.

"Hey," Zula's even tone came from behind me, "I thought you were out hunting the second bounty? Masha said you came back emptyhanded. What happened?"

"Well, I might as well tell everyone since I apparently can't have any secrets around here." I glanced over my shoulder to see Masha hovering behind Zula. I was being sarcastic, but it looked like everyone actually was there to hear my sordid tale.

Great. Just fucking great. "I made arrangements to ... meet up with Ash ... on his ship." My cheeks heated under the scrutiny of my crew. *I'm their captain, damnit. I have nothing to defend or prove.* I notched my chin up a few degrees. "I decided that I needed something other than my battery-operated toys. Ash ... he intrigued me. I thought it would be a win-win situation for me. I could have my way with him, and then collect the bounty on his head."

Zula raised her eyebrows and pressed her lips into a thin line. Masha ducked behind her, giggling.

Tamzea shook her head at me, smirking. "And then something went terribly wrong."

I ignored her tone. "Yeah, it did. I had my laser cuffs on him, and then he just *poof,* turned into flames."

Zula's eyes narrowed, and she leaned forward, her blonde hair swinging against her face. "No. All phoenixes were eradicated decades ago. The Denards destroyed their colony planets and tracked down every last one of them. They considered it a cleansing. The phoenix—"

"Whoa, hold on. Did I say anything about him being a phoenix?" But it made sense. After all, even his ship bore the name. "Are you sure? I mean, couldn't the Denards have missed a few?" The Denards weren't a species I was familiar with, but of course, Zula seemed to know everything about ... well, everything. It was beyond annoying.

"No, the Denards wouldn't simply miss a few. And in the very improbable case that they did, the survivor wouldn't be flaunting himself around like Ash does. No," she shook her head, "he's not a phoenix. He has to be some other fire being. Although I've never heard of such a creature, that doesn't mean they aren't out there."

Ah-ha! Is it possible that there is something Zula doesn't know? A smug smile curled my lips. "But what if he is a phoenix?" I pressed.

My mind had already dug its claws into the idea, the sum of it making complete sense. Only the tiniest little bit of me was pushing the issue to get under Zula's skin. Ash actually could be a phoenix. "Maybe he's hiding by flaunting it. It's something I would do." And it was. Hiding in plain sight worked more than most realized. Maybe Ash figured that out for himself. "Quite possibly the Denards are an arrogant species, and that would be the best strategy to get one over on them."

"No—" Zula started in again, but Tamzea had obviously had enough.

"What Ash is doesn't matter right now. What does is that Jane was about to tell us what happened between them." Her eyes glittered with curiosity. Even though Tamzea was zero percent human, her emotions ran the closest to mine. In fact, some days she acted more human than me. Case in point, she was currently trying to get all up in my business.

"I just told you guys what happened. I went to see him and he got away. End of story."

"No, it isn't. You came in here wanting to know how to ward off pheromones. Why is that, Jane?"

I glared pointedly at Tamzea. "Because," I growled, "I

just had the best sex of my entire life. We barely had any foreplay either, and even though he played me for a fool, I'm pretty sure I'll do him again the first chance I get. He's obviously working some kind of pheromone mojo on me to make me want him so much. Therefore, I need to know how to combat it so the next time I see him I'll be able to bring him in."

"Oh no," Zula interjected. "That creature, whatever he is, turns into a flame. How do you plan on containing him? Plus, if he has half a brain I'm sure he's already figured out you're the type that will be gunning for him. Let him go. He bested you. Sometimes you have the pride of a m—"

I crowded into Zula's face, my temper flaring. "No. I'm the *captain* of this ship, and we do what I say. I *will* find a way to contain him and combat his stupid pheromones. He will not win."

Zula stepped away from me, frowning. "I wasn't questioning your—"

"Yes, you were. You were questioning everything. If you're so smart, like you enjoy constantly reminding me, then you can figure out a way to contain him."

Turning towards Tamzea, I stabbed my index finger in her direction. "And you figure out the pheromone neutralizer."

I glanced down at Masha, who was staring at me with round eyes. "And you, you make sure we're on time for maintenance."

Pushing past my crew, I retreated, not wanting to deal

with them anymore at the moment. "I'll be in my quarters if anyone needs me. And it better be incredibly important if you do."

Silence hovered, thick and heavy, as I strode out of the med wing. *Sometimes I just need to remind them who's boss.* It was something I was looking forward to showing Ash as well.

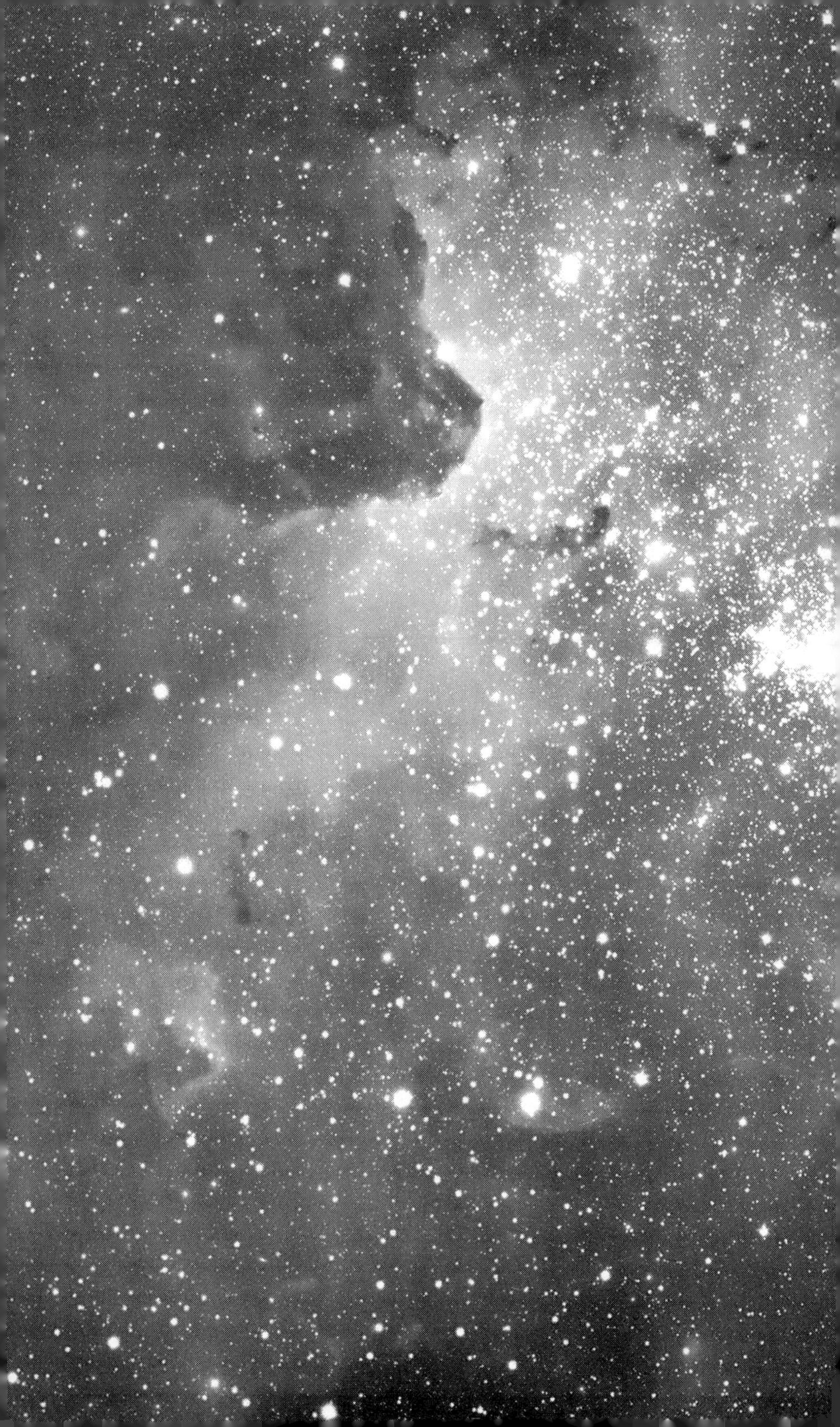

Chapter 6

"What do you mean we don't have enough?" I groaned into my pillow.

Is that drool? Smacking my lips, I rolled to my side and swiped at my mouth. *Yep, drool. Ugh.*

I'd been having a rather ... fulfilling dream, involving me and a certain man who was much more accommodating in my imagination than real life. Then I'd been unceremoniously ripped from my delightful slumber when my door slid open—despite the fact that it had been locked—and Masha appeared over me, blubbering about not having enough money to pay the mechanic who had done the maintenance on the ship.

"He said we're short. And it's not my fault, I swear. He quoted one price, and after he did the work he—"

"He's trying to work you over, and by default me." I punched my pillow, sitting up as rage sizzled through my veins, waking me fully. I quickly pulled my boots on and buckled my weapons' belt around my waist. "Point me in his direction and I'll take care of it."

"He's in the engine room. He's refusing to leave until he gets payment. He's threatening to take possession of the ship. He said—"

I placed my hand on top of Masha's soft black curls, smiling at her. At least I think it was a smile. "I'll take care of it. No one is taking *my* ship."

I stepped past her, beginning my march to the engine room. By the time I got there, I was ready to explode, my pulse banging against my eardrums like a countdown clock. *How dare someone come on my ship and try to take advantage of my crew! Especially Masha!*

A humanoid was leaning over the engine with his back to me. I jabbed my laser gun into his spine. "I heard you're trying to pull a fast one on me."

"Whoa, whoa, whoa! I'm just trying to get paid for my services."

"Turn around nice and slow. If you make one move I don't like, you're going to be dead before you get a chance to regret it." I stepped back a few paces, giving him room to maneuver.

He stood slowly, turning to face me, his beady little eyes darting around nervously. The man was thin, short, deathly pale, and greasy looking. I shuddered with revulsion. "Did you bathe in engine grease or something?" I crinkled my nose in disdain.

"First you threaten me, and then you insult me."

Pffft ... he actually has the nerve to act outraged. I'll do a lot more than insult and threaten him if he's not careful. "Look here, asshole. I have no patience for creatures like you who try to take advantage of sweet beings such as my engineer, Masha. What? Did you take one look at her adorable little face and think she'd be an easy target? Maybe she is since she communicates best with mechanical things." I bared my teeth. "But not me. You've fucked with the wrong captain."

"I-I simply want to be paid for my services." Grease-man's tone had morphed from outraged to sniveling.

I choked back a laugh at the predictability of it all.

"What Masha paid you, what you quoted, that's all you're getting. But I guess you'd like a bonus of a laser wound to your," I pulled the trigger, and Grease-man howled in pain, "foot?"

He clutched his foot, hopping around on the good one. "You're insane. I'm going to report you to the—"

I waved my gun in the air. "Look, buddy. You threaten me or my crew one more time and you won't be alive to report anything to anyone ever again. You got me?"

Finally, the truth of my words settled fear into his eyes. *Took him long enough.* "Yeah. I understand. I won't cause any more trouble."

I grinned. "Good. Now get the hell off my ship and don't tell anyone about this or I will be paying you another visit. The second time won't end as well for you."

As he hobbled past me, his beady eyes averted, I noticed a bank cuff stuffed in his back pocket. I snagged it. "Hey!" he exclaimed. "That's mine!"

"Not anymore. That's what happens when you get greedy. Now get off my damn ship. Now."

"It's encrypted, anyhow. You won't be able to—"

"I'll hack into it just fine," I said with saccharine sweetness. "Now, last warning." Cocking my gun, I aimed right between his eyes. "You're trying what little patience I have left. And you really don't want to see me when you've pushed me past my breaking point."

Grease-man squeaked, and with hands in the air, he scurried out of the engine room. I followed close behind, gun still at the ready, making sure he left without any more trouble.

"Huh," I muttered to myself. He was moving a lot faster than I would have thought possible with a gun wound in his foot, although because of the laser it was cauterized. For the first time since I'd started carrying a laser gun, instead of an antique Earth gun, I was appreciative. After all, if I'd shot Grease-man with a bullet then I would have had a bit of a mess on my hands. And blood is no fun to clean up.

Masha came ambling down the corridor from the direction of my quarters a moment later. She regarded me with hope in her black eyes as she sniffled. "Is he gone?" I tossed the bank cuff in her general direction, her nimble fingers closing around it deftly. "You got his bank cuff?"

"Yep. I'm guessing I don't have to tell you what to do with it."

"I'll have the funds in your account and the tracking codes erased within the hour." Masha grinned, her entire visage lighting up. "Maybe he'll have enough for the new part."

I tried, very unsuccessfully, not to roll my eyes. Masha was friggin' relentless when she wanted something. "Maybe." I holstered my gun. "Let's plan on hitting space, too. I'm tired of being stationary. Now that we've had maintenance, I'd like to put some distance between us and this supply station. We can pick up the part, if there's enough on that cuff, at our next stop. And don't worry, it won't be long, I'm in tracking mode."

Masha nodded. "Yes, Captain Jane."

Yep, she was happy. Masha only indulged me by calling me Captain Jane when she wanted to stroke my ego because she was pleased about something I'd done. I'm pretty sure she was trying to train me with positive reinforcement. Masha really knew how to manipulate me. *Why can't she be ugly with scales? It's next to impossible to not fall prey to someone who looks as angelic as she does.*

I sighed, heading back to my quarters.

Maybe I can pick back up where I left off in my dream.

"JANE, COME HERE," Ash commanded.

I shook my head in protest, even as my feet carried me towards him. Stopping scant inches away, I watched as he slowly trailed his index finger between my breasts. It was then I noticed that I was naked, not that I minded one bit at the moment. Ash's heated caress continued down the line of my body, his large hand settling between my legs. A moan erupted from my chest as I arched into him, my eyelids fluttering shut.

"You want more." Not a question but a statement.

The desire to deny it arose within me, even as I found myself wondering why he was still fully clothed and how exactly I could rectify that situation. My entire body quivered in anticipation of him moving inside of me again. I more than wanted it—I needed it.

I'm dreaming. I have to be.

I didn't remember the events that had led up to me being naked in front of Ash, and I didn't recognize the room we were in. The space was dominated by a large bed with black satin sheets, the rest of the surroundings fuzzy around the edges.

Yep, definitely a dream. Why not enjoy it? And since it is a dream—I want to be in control...

My eyes snapped open as I let my blazing desire take center stage. "Take off your clothes. I need you inside of me. Now."

Ash chuckled. "Needy? I think I like it."

"Of course you do, it's my dream."

He smirked. "Ah. Right. Of course it is." He tugged his shirt over his head and stepped out of his pants. "Better?" he asked, raising his arms to spin in a slow circle.

Being that in our real-life encounter Ash hadn't done anything but unzip his pants, I didn't get a chance to study his naked physique. Fortunately, the details I'd missed while awake were happily supplied by my dreaming imagination with spectacular clarity.

He was all hard lines of lithe muscle, wrapped in delectably bronzed skin, from his sculpted shoulders, to his six-pack abs, down to that masculine V which seemed to point to his impressive cock. *Mmm ... yes.* And that pleasure-inducing piece of him was just the right length and girth, the memory of the way it stretched me so perfectly enough to make my pussy weep at just the sight of it.

"You just going to stare? Or are you going to do something?"

My cheeks flushed. *I kind of want to punch him even in my dream.* "Lie down," I commanded. "On the bed."

Ash went to the bed without hesitation, sprawling his large frame across the middle. He propped his hands under his head, watching me approach with a lecherous grin.

"Good," I murmured. "Now just sit back and relax."

"I like you this way," Ash rasped, his eyes swirling with flames.

"Stop talking," I grated, "you'll ruin it."

I climbed up to straddle him. Meeting his gaze, I hovered my trembling body over his for several heartbeats before plunging down. His large hands flew up to cup my breasts as I began to ride him, hard. I closed my eyes and threw my head back as I ground my pelvis into his on every downward stroke. I was already on the edge, my entire body crackling like it was on fire.

"Look at me, Jane." Ash's voice held something within it that made me want to obey, so I did. After all, there was no point in fighting since it was just a dream.

A gasp lodged in my throat. White-hot flames surrounded us, burning brightly. "I should have believed you about your ability to handle fire," Ash growled.

It only took a moment for me to grow accustomed, the burning caress of the flames an extension of Ash, as they fondled and sucked all at once. I writhed in ecstasy, overwhelmed and yet needing more, more, more. I was utterly consumed, free-falling into a bliss I didn't know was possible.

"That's right, give yourself over to me."

The command delivered in that deep rumble of his triggered my orgasm, flames exploding around us as my thighs trembled. Squeezing my eyes shut again, I continued to ride him, wanting—needing more, more, more.

A moment later, with a painful-sounding groan, Ash pulsed his own release into me, the heat of it ripping another orgasm from me. I dug my fingers into his back, clawing frantically. *More, more, more.*

Slowly the frenzy receded, and we rocked against each other languidly. Ash smoothed my hair away from my sweaty face. "And to think, that was just the beginning. I've decided I'm going to keep you ... even though you get too friendly with laser cuffs."

"What?" I opened my eyes, staring down at him. "What do you mean?" I was not a fan of the sudden turn in my dream. I just wanted a quick, imaginary fuck, not talk of keeping anyone or any other relationship bullshit. Wasn't it supposed to be my fantasy?

Sitting up with me still impaled on him, Ash rested his forehead against mine, his hot breath washing across my face. "I said that I've decided to keep you." Amusement twinkled in his eyes when I frowned. "This isn't a dream, Jane. Just thought you should know. Oh, and maybe it's time you start questioning what kind of DNA you carry ... besides human that is. You might be pleasantly surprised. I know I was."

Jolting up in a puddle of my own sweat, my gaze swept over my dimly lit living quarters. Everything seemed to be in its proper place, and I, of course, was completely alone.

What the hell kind of messed up dream was that? It was hot, though, in more ways than one. A shiver ran up my spine despite my heated skin. *It was just a dream. Nothing more and nothing less. It just got a little weird at the end. Dreams do that sometimes.*

Cold shower. I need a cold shower. Hopefully, our water filtration system would be up and running since the ship had just gotten maintenance done. I really missed showers with real water.

In the meantime, I'd consider the next step in tracking down Ash ... and not think about the super sexy dream I'd just had about him. Nope, I wouldn't think about naked Ash or what I wanted him to do to me. I wouldn't think about it at all. *Cold shower. Cold shower. I need a cold shower.*

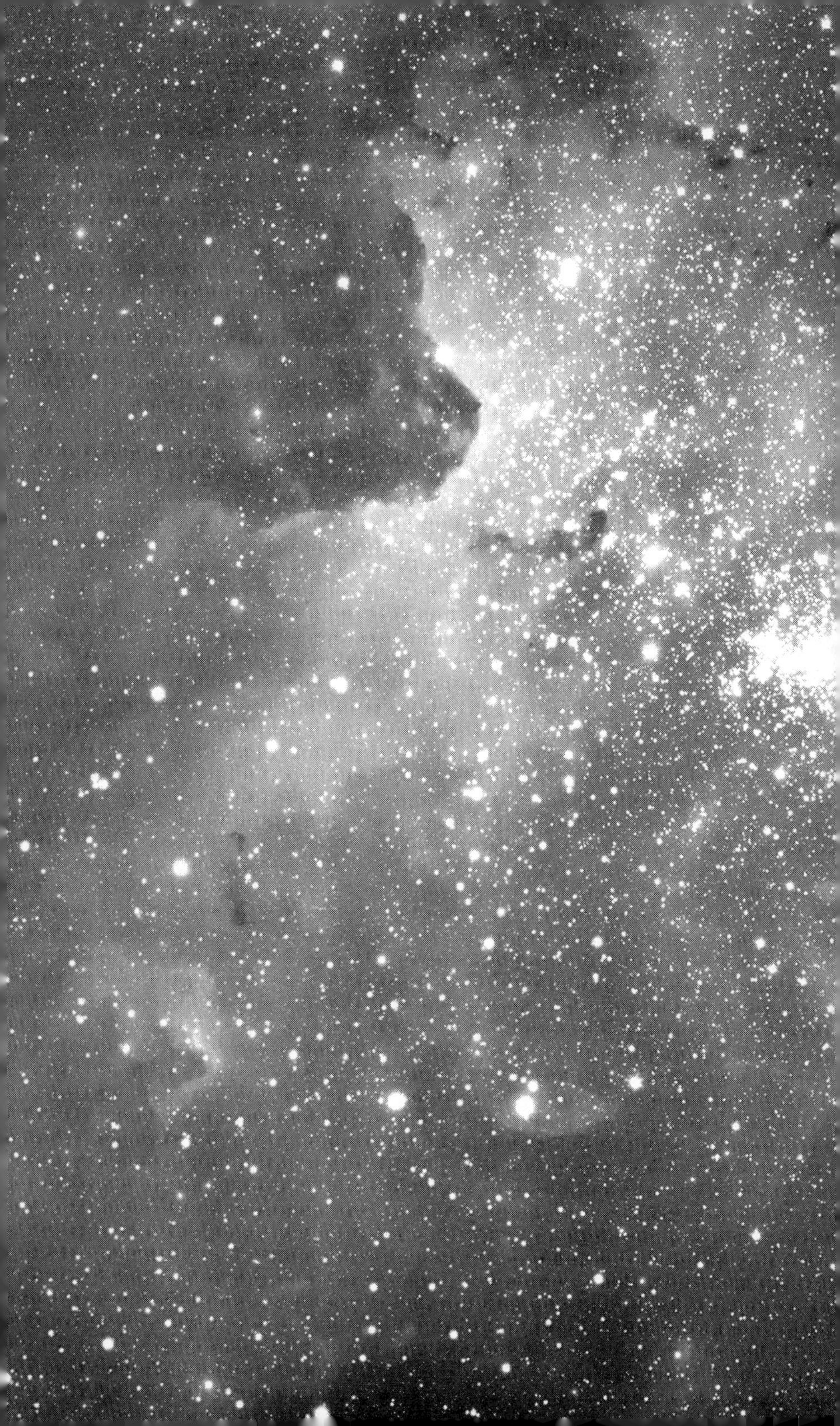

Chapter 7

Having the water filtration system up and running was not the blessing I'd hoped for. Even with the temperature set to ice cold, my body remained overheated from my slumbering nocturnal naughtiness with Ash. I ended up pleasuring myself several times while thinking about him. I left the bathroom physically cleaner but feeling mentally dirtier. *So much for not thinking about him.*

Ash was an anomaly when it came to the attraction I felt for him. Most of the men I'd been with were easily forgotten as soon as I took them for a ride. The only exception prior to Ash, was my boyfriend from when I'd lived on New Earth. Of course, that punk dropped me faster than a hot asteroid when I'd tested out as a 'normal human'. My response was to shoot him in the arm and high tail it off that oppressive planet immediately. There was definitely no love lost between us, even though I'd been attracted to him enough to stay with him. I think the entire relationship was mostly misguided teenager attachment. He'd been my first sexual partner, and therefore I thought I loved him. Or maybe I did love him, I just wasn't *in love* with him. Despite that, no one had ever come close to making me feel what he had physically ... until Ash. And the raw carnal need within me for that blasted man existed in its own stratosphere.

One quickie on his ship, and one ridiculously sexy dream and I am completely ready to let him—

I shook my head. *Nope. Nuh-uh. What the hell am I thinking? I will not have sex with that man again. I will track him down and exchange him for a large chunk of cash. End of story.* There would be no visitations from me when he was contained on my ship either. He was just another one and done, as far as I was concerned. My subconscious was going to have to cool it, too.

"What has you looking so pensive?" Zula asked, as she glided into our eating lounge.

"Just trying to come up with a plan to track Ash." *One that doesn't end with us naked and him inside of me.*

Picking up my spoon, I scraped the edge of my bowl and forced a bite of the beige sludge into my mouth. It was mushy and runny, without much flavor. I swallowed, pushing the rest of my meal away. I'd prepared it like I'd been instructed, but either oatmeal wasn't the Earth breakfast delicacy I'd been told, or I'd done something wrong.

"Have some of my rations. It may not be Earth food, which let me remind you—"

"I know!" I snapped. "I wasn't even born yet when Earth was destroyed. You don't have to keep reminding me."

Sitting down at the table across from me, Zula started munching on what looked like a blue sandwich while she eyed my oatmeal. "Apparently I do have to keep reminding you."

"Yeah, well, maybe I'm afraid eating blue food will turn me into a Smurfette like you."

"Do not call me that," Zula growled, blue crumbs falling from her mouth.

Every. Single. Time. It never failed. I loved having something that riled her up faultlessly. "It's a genuine concern." I picked up my bowl and took it over to the food waste disposal unit. After I'd vaporized the oatmeal, I began rummaging for something actually edible. "I think we need to stop somewhere to get better food. I—"

"Wasted all of your money on Earth food and Earth clothing," Zula finished for me.

Straightening my spine, I adjusted my Steampunk outfit. I was going to have to look into tracking down more clothing like the pieces I'd recently purchased. I was enjoying the mix of functionality with style that Steampunk Earth clothing offered. Plus, it was a part of my heritage. I met Zula's gaze, and cracked my neck, sighing. "It's never a waste. I told you that my clothes are part of the job. An incredibly important part."

"You're not on the job now."

"I will be soon. I'm just trying to come up with a good pl—"

"Jane," Tamzea's voice echoed through the ship's intercom, "we're being hailed by a UGFS diplomatic cruiser. They're requesting to speak with you personally."

"Ohh—ookay," I stammered. What reason would someone on a UGFS diplomatic cruiser have for wanting to talk to me? *I haven't done anything wrong ... lately. I don't think.* I bit the inside of my cheek. "I'll meet you in the control room."

Hurrying out of the eating lounge, I sprinted down the long corridor and climbed the ladder that took me to the upper level of The Pittsburgh. Just outside the entrance I paused to catch my breath, wiping sweat from my forehead, and smoothed my hands over my clothes to make sure I was presentable.

I inhaled deeply, and rounded the corner, hoping I didn't appear as flustered as I felt. "Hello, Captain Wexis here. How may I be of service?" I directed my question to the large communication screen on the wall.

An attractive male humanoid, who appeared to be in his early thirties, with dark hair, dark eyes, and light skin, smiled at me congenially. He was wearing the dual-toned blue uniform of all UGFS personnel. By the larger insignia on his chest and decorative pads on his shoulders, I knew immediately he was the ambassador on the cruiser. My apprehension racketed up another level, fresh sweat gathering along my hairline. "Yes. I am Ambassador

Aralias. There is a sensitive matter I wish to speak with you about. Are your lines secure?"

I shifted, locking my hands behind my back so my fidgeting fingers weren't visible, and bowed in deference before responding. I wasn't the best at etiquette, but if I appeared to be trying it would be good enough—or at least that strategy hadn't failed me yet. "Our lines are secure, Ambassador. What would you like to discuss?"

"I was recently informed that you expressed interest in the bounty on the creature simply known as Ash." The ambassador blinked at me expectantly.

I cleared my throat. "Yeah ... I mean, yes."

"We, of the UGFS, would like to make you aware that this Ash has stolen some highly sensitive material we must have returned to us. It's a data chip carrying the standard UGFS verifying code and seal. The information contained on it is top secret. We need the chip and Ash both in one piece. However, if you find yourself in a position where you may have to choose ... bring us the chip. If you can do it within a fortnight your fee will be doubled."

"Doubled?" I squeaked.

"Yes, Captain Wexis, doubled. I have been informed that you are one of the best at what you do, but I also need the issue of the chip to be kept secret. If the information on that chip is leaked, it could lead to ... many problems. If you are confident you can do these things for us, I will pull Ash from the database, and officially the job will be yours."

I was rendered speechless. Normally bounties were

listed in the database, and if you had the clearance to view them, then whoever got to the bounty first collected. I had higher clearance than most, but I'd never heard of an exclusive contract with the UGFS before. I was pretty sure if one had been out there, at any point, one of my competitors would have bragged about it. I cleared my throat again. "I won't let you and the UGFS down, sir. I'm honored that you have entrusted me with this job. Is there any other information I may need?"

"No. Thank you for your time, Captain Wexis. I look forward to the successful outcome of your mission within the fortnight." The ambassador smiled at me again, but it didn't reach his eyes. I could have sworn his gaze raked over me with disdain, but the emotion was gone so fast I was sure I'd imagined it because of my unease.

"Thank you again, sir." I tipped my lips up in what I hoped looked like a smile, remaining still until the screen went blank. It was followed by the beep signaling Tamzea turning everything off on our end as well. I blinked rapidly, unable to stop staring at the screen. "I'm not sure if I should be nervous or excited about this." My gut fluttered with anxiety in response. Something felt *off* about the entire situation. *Of course it could also be that oatmeal I just had.* The stuff was sitting like a rock in my stomach.

"Maybe … maybe we shouldn't take this job," I muttered.

"What?" Tamzea approached me, shock etched into the worry lines on her face. "Are you feeling okay? I mean, you were planning on bagging Ash anyways, but now the fee will be doubled. That money would not only pay for everything Masha has been pushing for, but it could keep us all very comfortable for some time. You would only have to take easy bounties for a while. No Class 4s—"

"How much money did we get from the guy who tried to rip us off? Did Masha tell you?"

"Not enough to get her everything, and definitely not enough to keep you and the rest of us happy. Especially with how quickly you blow through your funds on fashion." She tilted her head at me, her gaze raking over my outfit. "What's with the goggles? Were you helping Masha with something?"

I reached up, adjusting the Steampunk goggles perched on my head. "Nooo, they go with the outfit. But you know, I may need them … for something." My nostrils flared when Tamzea's lips twitched up into a smile. "Not another word about my clothes, got it?"

Attempting to appear innocent, even as a grin spread across her face, Tamzea flicked her gaze away. "So, the job?"

I gnawed on my lower lip, considering. I had no sane reason not to accept the job from the UGFS, and technically I already had. Plus, Tamzea was right. I was going after Ash regardless, so none of the rest should matter. And it didn't.

It was just … a sudden cloud of trepidation had settled over me, twisting my gut into knots.

Sighing, I said, "Yeah, I'm going to do it." My heart

sped up as that innocent-sounding sentence, those six little inconspicuous words, echoed in my head and clanged through my skull. *Why does it feel like this decision is about to alter my life irrevocably? And not for the better.*

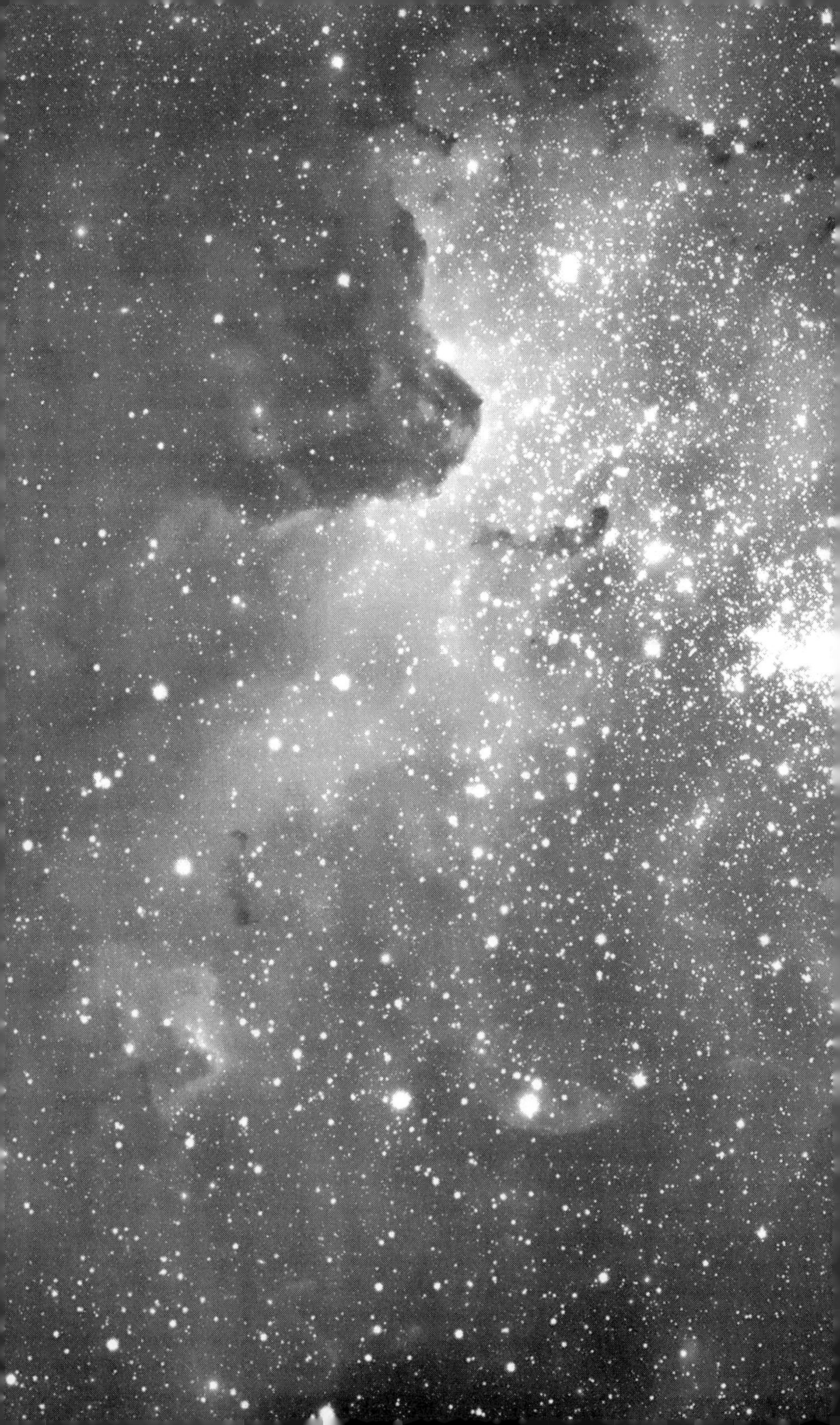

Chapter 8

"Anything yet?" I paced, while Zula fiddled around with some equipment, the sound of metal clanging against metal filling the air. We were in what she liked to call the science wing of The Pittsburgh. In reality, it was what would be more living quarters if we had a bigger crew. I was confident she'd find a way for me to safely contain a being such as Ash, who could turn into flame. That wasn't the problem, nope. My issue was that it was taking too damn long for my tastes.

"If you give me more than five minutes, I'll find the solution," Zula stated coolly. She was used to my impatience, even though she was not a fan.

"So much for being from a genius race. Maybe you didn't leave on your own accord, like you claim, maybe you were kicked off your planet for being the dumbest Galvraron ever." I grimaced at my own words. I was irritated and anxious, and sure I liked to get under Zula's skin in a good-natured way, but sometimes I came off cruel without meaning to.

The truth was, I didn't know why any of my crew had decided that serving under me was what they wanted. When I'd saved up enough money to purchase The Pittsburgh, which admittedly was a piece of junk when I got it, I'd put out word that I needed a crew. Masha had been the first to show up, unable to resist the call of a Chimay grade engine or some such crap as that. Tamzea took one look at me, and her Mazatimz maternal instincts had kicked in. But Zula, well, she was an enigma. That was the thing, though—we all had pasts, I was sure of it, but none of us cared. The present was all that mattered, and presently Zula was being too damn slow.

"Weeeell, anything yet?"

"You asking me over and over does not force me to produce the results you want," Zula hissed. She slammed down the tools she'd been working with. "I need more materials... materials we don't have."

I peered over her shoulder, not having the faintest clue what I was looking at. "So, we'll get them."

"It's not that easy."

"It can't be as difficult as you're making it seem either." I picked up a piece of sheet metal, studying the way it was bent and wavy in the middle. "What's going on with this?"

"That," Zula snatched the sheet from me, dropping it back onto her workbench, "is the problem. We need stronger metal. I wanted to make some kind of containment trap, one that you could suck Ash into while he was in flame form. I was testing out what could stand up to the heat ... and we need something stronger."

"So we'll get it. We—"

"We need Gartian grade alloy."

I blinked rapidly, the shock of what she'd just said taking time to penetrate my mind. "Gartian grade alloy," I muttered, before turning away to swear under my breath.

"Now you see the problem."

"And nothing else will work?"

"No."

I pinched the bridge of my nose, swearing again. "I knew it. I had a bad feeling about this one. This could ruin my reputation. I—" I bit the inside of my cheek, gnawing until I tasted blood. As the tang of copper filled my mouth, determination washed over me. I wanted the money, and I needed to prove to myself that I could best Ash.

"We're going to have to go into Gartian territory then." I was met with silence. I turned my gaze to take in the blank expression on Zula's blue face. She was shocked beyond words. *This is a first.* I snapped my fingers in front of her. "Ummm ... Hello? Anyone in there? Or did I just short-circuit that big brain of yours?"

"If you're serious about this, we're going to have to drop off the bounty we already have before going into Gartian territory—we already collected on him. With your reputation, it was no problem getting the money upfront for our maintenance. They were planning to come to us, as usual, but our unscheduled trip will change everything on our timeline. We'll also need to stop at another supply space station."

Bounty? Oh yeah, Tall and Bald. I'd almost forgotten about him. *Oops.* I hoped someone had been checking on him, and feeding him. I didn't need a dead bounty to deal with. Plus, that would be bad for business. Dealing with Ash was putting me off my game. Good thing I had Zula to remind me of such things. "Pffft ... Yes, of course. Tall and Bald, I remember." I flicked my gaze away from Zula, but I knew it was too late.

"Unbelievable. You completely forgot about him. Don't try to deny it. It's written all over your face." Zula slammed her fists down on the workbench, causing me to jump. "No. We can't do this. You're too distracted. Too personally involved since you had sex with Ash. You do a lot of stupid things, but this one— No. I'm not going to let you get killed because of an injured sense of pride."

"It's not my job to remember about the bounties. I bag them, and you and everyone else does the rest. If he's been left down there in his cell to rot that's on your head, not mine." I crossed my arms over my chest, staring Zula down. I didn't see anyone else risking their lives to make money for us. I was the talent, and my crew was the support I needed. Okay, so maybe I was rationalizing, but—

I'm the captain, damnit! I couldn't do everything myself, which was why I had my crew to begin with.

Zula glared back. "Fine, I will take care of it. But then

we're going to talk about the rest. You need to seriously take into consideration the fact that you're too close to the situation with Ash now that you've been intimate with him."

I snorted. "I had sex with him. Big difference between sex and intimacy."

Zula's face scrunched up. "Please. As a Galvraron I may think first, and feel second, but even I know that you're fooling yourself on this one. There's more between you and Ash than just sex."

Zula and Tamzea always thought they knew me better than I knew myself. Sometimes they made valid points, but Zula couldn't be further from the mark on this one. "You're worrying too much, as usual. Don't. Things will work out just like they always do." I turned away from Zula, heading for the door. "I'm going to go check on our guest, even though it's not my job. Let me know the ETA for his ride off this boat."

I PEERED through the small window on the door to the airlock. Two forms in space suits propelled towards us, their personal thrusters keeping them steady as they crossed the scant distance from their ship to ours. It was the way we received guests when not at port. It was also the exit/entry I preferred for myself at all times. I hated leaving the cargo doors open so anyone could traipse right on The Pittsburgh when we weren't in space. A security code was needed to get past the secondary door in the airlock, which was much safer in my opinion.

"Please, I'll pay you double whatever she's given you," Tall and Bald sniveled from behind me. "I-I can't go back. You don't understand."

"It's a little late to bargain," I said, not bothering to look at him. Zula had him trussed up in laser bands, the best on the market. "We already accepted payment for you."

"Please ... "

"Oh, come on. Stop being such a baby. If you don't want to pay for the crime, then don't ... umm ... " That wasn't how the saying went. Hmm ... "Just don't be a dumbass if you don't want to end up being someone's bitch."

Our visitors moved into the airlock, pressing the button to close the outer door behind them. As soon as it was secure, a red light flashed to signal that air was flooding the chamber. When it flashed to green, I entered the code to let them in. I shuffled back from the door, readying my weapons. It was the biggest reason I preferred non-UGFS bounties to collect on The Pittsburgh ... home ship advantage.

The visitor closest to me unlocked the helmet on their space suit. A woman's face was revealed. She looked like a feminine version of Tall and Bald, down to the bald part. She smiled at me. "Hello, my name is Zeatha. I have come to collect my brother."

I swung my gaze back to Tall and Bald, who was

leaking red-tinted tears. I scrunched my face up in disgust. "Are you sure you want him?"

Zeatha sucked on her teeth. "I don't. His soon-to-be wife does."

It all became clear. Tall and Bald wasn't a criminal at all. He was just an asshat who was on the run from his future wife for some reason. "Alrighty then. He's all yours." Holstering my gun, I stepped aside as Zula shoved Tall and Bald forward.

"Please, Zeatha. Don't make me go back. I don't want—"

She grabbed Tall and Bald by his ear, twisting it sharply. "Then you should have thought of that before you defied our laws and impregnated one of the pure ones. You will marry her. You've done just about enough to disgrace our family for one millennium."

I watched with morbid curiosity as Tall and Bald was unlocked, and fitted with a space suit by Zeatha and her unknown companion. When they were finished she turned to regard me. "Thank you. You have saved my family's face."

"Just doing my job." Thank God Tall and Bald hadn't wasted away in his prison cell. Apparently, his species was pretty resilient. She nodded and forced Tall and Bald back into the airlock chamber. I watched until they were back on their ship. "Well, that's taken care of. Time to bring down Ash."

Zula groaned. "I urge you again to reconsider."

"Nope. Ash is mine." I rubbed my hands together,

smiling eagerly. I couldn't wait to see the expression on his face when I had him trapped in the containment system Zula was building for me. Hopefully, we wouldn't run into any more obstacles. The Universe still owed me some good karma so I was thinking it was time to collect.

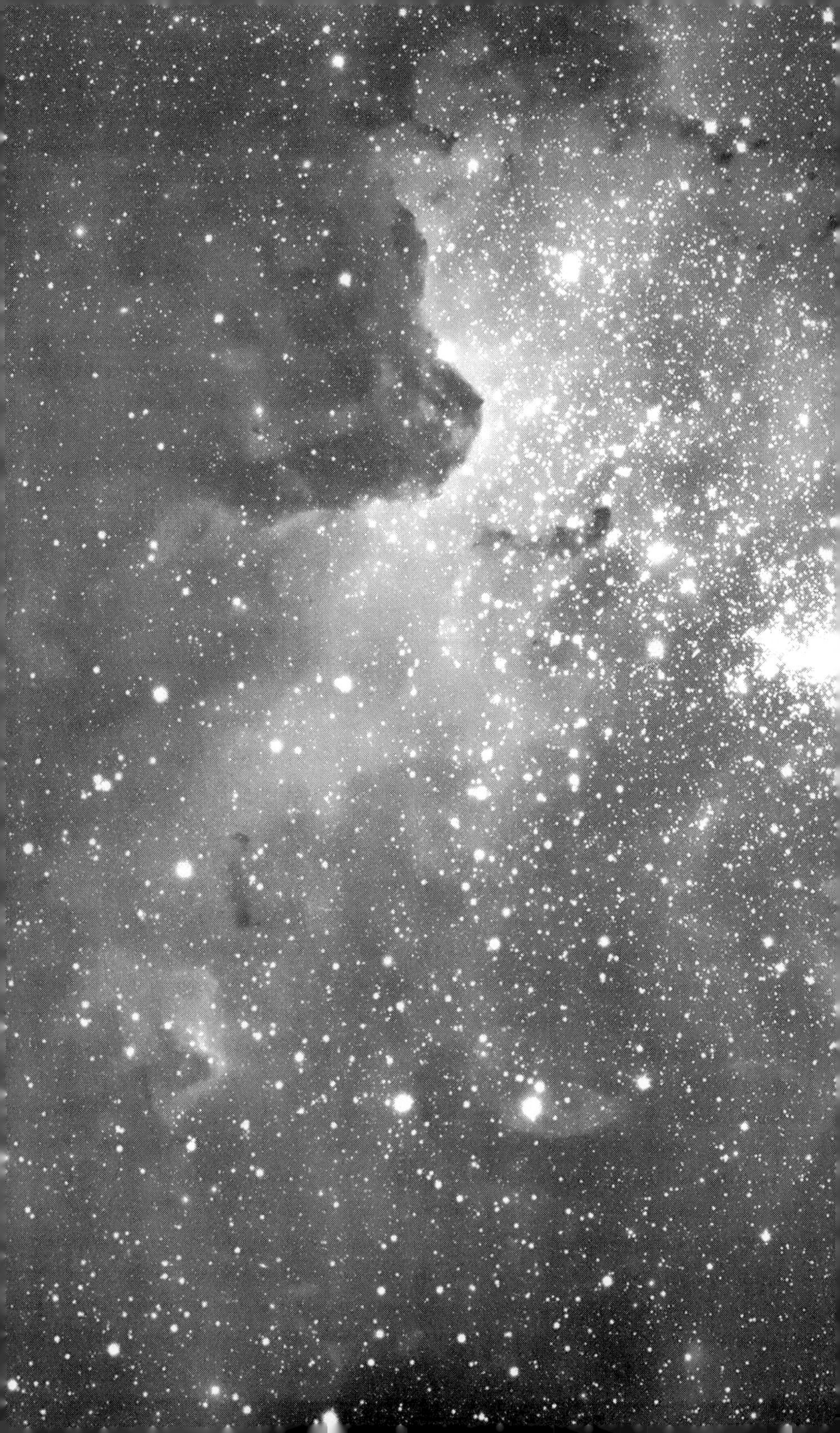

Chapter 9

Gartian territory was avoided by most species, even the fiercest. I didn't know if the rumors were true, but I'd been told that Gartians were once peaceful humanoids with a special kind of knack for working with metals. They'd perfected their own grade of alloy that was surpassed by none.

That was before the sickness.

Their kind had been ravaged by a plague that had come to be known as the G-Pox. There was no known cure. It rotted limbs and pieces of flesh away. It was also unknown what caused G-Pox or why only certain parts would rot. G-Pox killed most Gartians who were infected, but the ones who survived ... did so by replacing their missing pieces with their alloy. Eventually, the Gartians became cold and hard, like the alloy that held them together, their minds addled—they were said to be completely insane.

Personally, I'd never seen a Gartian, but the stories were enough to keep me away. An unstable species with nearly unbreakable ships ... it was a terrifying combination. And I was currently on my way into the belly of the beast. Or rather The Pittsburgh was headed straight for the main planet that housed what was left of the Gartians. It had no name and was only whispered about as if its existence alone was a cautionary tale. Of what it warned, I had no clue, and I hoped I wouldn't find out.

Zula, Tamzea, and I were all on the flight deck watching in morbid fascination as the Gartian planet slowly came into view. It was shiny, just like metal, and I wondered if maybe it actually was. *Perhaps they replaced things on it just like on their bodies.* I shuddered at the thought. Or quite possibly it was a space station. That seemed like the most plausible explanation.

I shifted my mind to the task at hand. So far no one had responded to our hails. Nibbling on my thumb, I said, "So ... um ... what should we do?" My voice was calm and steady, belying the nerves I was trying to hide.

"Turn around?" Tamzea's voice wavered.

"They do still trade. Selling their alloy is what keeps them fed," Zula offered in a blasé tone. Her white-ish knuckles on the console in front of her told me she wasn't as calm internally.

"Okaay ... " I drawled. "So this shouldn't be a big deal then."

"They only trade with a few trusted people who then

sell their goods on the open market. Unfortunately, the cost of Gartian Alloy is beyond our means at the price markup. Not to mention it sells out quicker than it can be supplied. There's a wait list years long," Zula stated.

"Still, I'm sure just flying up to their planet shouldn't be that much of a problem. They won't be worried about a teeny, tiny ship like The Pittsburgh when they have what they've got." Who was I trying to convince? "Try to hail them again. Maybe you need to reconfigure the code or something."

Zula punched the keys roughly. "My codes are always correct, but I will try to contact them again."

A startled gasp lodged in my esophagus as I staggered back. As if it appeared out of thin air, a giant starship arose directly above us. It had to have—"Holy shit! They were under some kind of cloaking shield!" *Fuuuuck! I thought those were rumors, too.* "Is that a Gartian ship?"

"I'm guessing ye—" Zula's attention was diverted to her earpiece. "We tried to contact you. We wish to speak with … We only wish to purchase … Yes. Yes, I understand." She lifted her head, meeting my gaze. "They're coming aboard."

"What?" I squeaked. "Did they sound pissed?"

"No. They sounded in charge. Which they very much are of this situation." Zula stood, ripped her earpiece out, and tossed it angrily on the console. "Why don't you ever listen to me? If we make it out of this situation alive things are going to change around here."

Excuse me? "I'm the captain, remember? Nothing

changes unless I say so." I crossed my arms over my chest and met Zula's dark eyes steadily. If she wanted a battle of wills, she'd find out no one was more stubborn than me. It was one of my best and worst personality traits.

Tamzea stepped in between us. "There's no time for this now."

"Right," I said. "Let's get ready to receive our visitors." *As if we have a choice.*

The ship's internal lights flashed to red in warning, and the buzzer that signaled a breach rang out through the air, piercing my eardrums. "And here I just went and assumed they'd wait for us to let them in." Adrenaline surged through my system, my heart rate accelerating times fifty. I instinctively reached for my laser gun at my hip, running my palm over it. I wasn't about to draw it in case the threat would get me killed, but I craved the reassurance the cold metal offered me.

Just as suddenly as our ship's alert system had been triggered, it shut off, all systems back to normal. "What the hell?"

Zula was already at the computer. "On it."

I glanced over at Tamzea, who was wringing her hands and gnawing on her lower lip. She didn't have the temperament for these kinds of situations. Bring in a bloody patient to heal and she was at her best. I gave her a reassuring smile. "Everything is going to be fine, Tamzea." *I hope I'm not lying to her.*

"I have no idea what's going on," Zula muttered, still hunched over the computer. "I—"

"Jane." Masha appeared at the door, which was odd since she usually hid out in the engine room during any kind of intense situation. "We have visitors." She grinned at us before spinning around to dash off.

My eyes widened as I stared after her. "Again ... What. The. Hell?"

"It's a good sign that Masha seems pleased, right?" Tamzea clutched at my shoulder, her lavender eyes filled with uncertainty and fear.

"I'm thinking that's a yes." I placed my hand over hers. "If you want, you can stay here. I'll go meet our visitors. I got us into this situation, and hopefully I can get us out of it." *And with some of that Gartian Alloy, too.* Despite everything I still had my eyes on the prize.

"No. We're a team?"

I chuckled. "You don't sound so sure. Is that a statement or a question?"

"I—"

I stepped away from Tamzea, meeting Zula's gaze. "You both stay here. That's an order. Disobey your captain and ... I'll think of something you won't like." I hurried to the metal ladder leading down to the control room without a backwards glance.

Fingers crossed that there will be a later for me ... or any of us. Masha wouldn't be happy about our visitors if they meant us harm, right? Unless she thought they could help with the engine, then maybe. *I swear she loves that damn engine more than anyone or anything. It's just not normal, even if she is a Guaviva.*

My heart pounded in my ears, making it difficult to hear anything else. I forced my body to yield to the command to move. It protested with each step I took, sweat dripping down my spine, and also gathering on my face. Somehow I managed to get to the lower level of the ship without passing out.

What the— My mind blanked as it tried to process the scene before me.

Three tall, warrior-like men stood around Masha in a semi-circle. They looked mostly humanoid except for their size ... and the fact that parts of them were made up of metal. But they were all smiling ... at Masha. She was talking animatedly with her hands as she gazed up at them with adoration. I shook my head, blinking rapidly. I didn't know what I'd been expecting, but certainly not what I got.

I cleared my throat. "Umm ... Hey, Masha ... You care to introduce me to your new friends?" *The ones that just boarded my ship without permission,* I added silently.

"Oh, Jane— I mean Captain Jane. This is Zar, Tar, and Dar. They're Gartians." She grinned at me, motioning to each of the three ... men.

All three of them had long black hair. The more I looked at them the more— "Are they triplets?"

"Yes," one of them, Zar maybe, responded. It at least would explain their names. As it turned out, all mothers of triplets, no matter the species, seemed to get weird about multiple births.

"Oh, right." I had no idea how I was supposed to react

to the whole situation. I was slightly more relaxed seeing how happy Masha was, but not completely at ease. After all, Zar, Tar, and Dar had just helped themselves onto my ship, and I still wasn't sure how or why.

"They promised to get me my part, but in Gartian grade alloy!" Masha exclaimed, jumping up and down with pure joy.

I scanned the three warriors from head to toe. Except for the slightly jarring effect of the metal fused onto their bodies—which looked almost natural, as if it had melded with them or maybe like they were some kind of cyborgs—they were actually kind of attractive.

What if that's why they were being so accommodating to Masha? What if they weren't insane freaks after all? What if they'd simply made themselves into some kind of cyborgs with their alloy? It wasn't like I could just come right out and ask, though. "That's great, Masha," I said, while still eyeing the triplets.

"You have no reason to fear us," Dar, maybe, stated in a deep rumble. "Masha has explained everything to us. You will be guests on our planet until the work has been done."

I nodded, at least I think I did—the whole situation was beyond surreal. "Okay. Great. Thanks. I'm glad that us coming here wasn't taken as some kind of insult or threat. I mean—"

"As I've said, Masha has explained it all. She told us that you are brash and rude with no sense of protocol, but your heart is in the right place."

Frowning, I managed to keep my mouth shut. *Masha*

and I are going to have some words later, that's for sure.

"Okay." I was beginning to sound like an audio file stuck on repeat. I just didn't know what else to say.

He then turned to Masha, addressing her. "You know what to do. We look forward to showing you the wonders of our planet." With that, all three of them vanished right before my eyes. The ship's alert system buzzed for a few moments before going silent, like when they'd entered.

"Masha," I growled. "What the hell was that?"

She blinked her big black eyes at me as if confused. "They're going to help me overhaul my engine and the ship." I didn't miss the fact that she'd referred to it as her engine again.

"We're kind of on a time crunch if we want to get the payment on Ash doubled."

"No problem. They said it would take no more than twenty-four hours. They promised they'd make it their top priority. And they're going to do it for a fraction of the money we have left."

I narrowed my eyes at Masha, zeroing in on her flushed face. I'd always thought of her as childlike, but I knew for her species she was fully-grown, and as icky as it was, sexually mature. Did she like one of the Gartians that had just been on the ship? Maybe one of them would be the perfect match for her since they seemed to be part machine. "Umm ... so they're like cyborgs, huh?"

Masha nodded with excitement. "Yes. They're so amazing! I can't wait to see how smoothly my engine runs when it's fitted with Gartian grade alloy!" She jumped up and down, clapping her hands.

So okay, maybe I was a bit of a pervert who translated almost everything into something sexual. It seemed like Masha was just enthused about the engine ... as usual.

"And you trust them?"

"Yes. I can read them perfectly."

"Alrighty then. I'm going to go let Tamzea and Zula know what's going on before they freak out up there." I motioned towards the ladder leading up to the second floor of The Pittsburgh.

Things just kept getting more and more interesting.

The life of a bounty hunter is never dull.

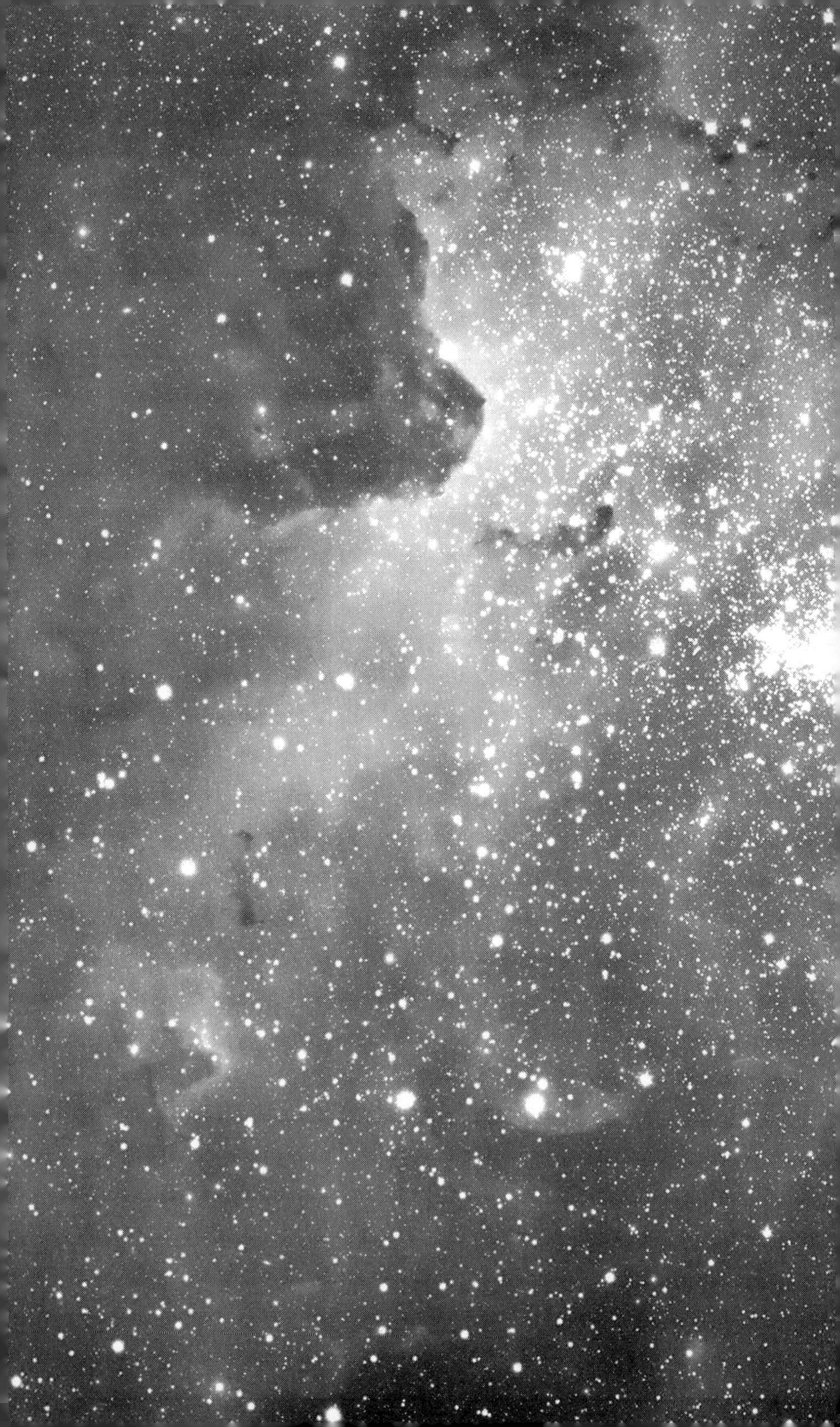

Chapter 10

What I found on the Gartian world was nothing like I'd expected. Even after meeting Zar, Tar, and Dar briefly on The Pittsburgh, my preconceived ideas wouldn't let go. All the rumors that I'd been told over the years ricocheted around in my mind, heightening my anxiety. But what I found in reality ... was family. A sense of unity. The Gartians, despite their horrible reputation, led an enviable life as a whole. I saw community and warmth. Not the cold insanity I'd been expecting. Some of them were more machine than anything else, and yet they exuded more of what I thought of as humanity than I'd ever felt on New Earth. It was the sense of home that I'd always craved.

But, as usual, I was on the outside looking in.

My crew and I had been welcomed with open arms, Masha being the guest of honor, of course. I suspected any Guaviva with their ability to communicate with machines would have been in the spotlight. Masha was happier than I'd ever seen her ... again, of course. The Gartian world was a marvel to me, not just the Gartians themselves, but the planet. It also was mostly machine, like its creators. But it was bright and clean ... there was no industrial feel to it like a space station. It was stunning—absolutely beautiful in every way imaginable—and it made me curl into myself just a bit more.

All of it conjured insecurities born from my time on New Earth. Why hadn't my parents wanted me? Sure, I'd tested out as a normal human, Species Class 1, when most spliced humans were expected to be Class 2 or 3 at the very least. Wasn't I worth unconditional love, though? They'd just turned their backs on me like I was nothing.

"Jane?" Zula's voice cut into my interlude of self-pity. "Dar was just explaining to us how their air filtration system works. He said they're installing a similar type of technology on The Pittsburgh."

I cleared my throat, focusing on the large male standing in front of us. "Right. Yes, I was listening." Except I hadn't been at all. Everything had been a blur since I'd seen what the Gartians were really like. I couldn't decide if I was jealous or if I hated them. Maybe the two went hand in hand? How screwed up emotionally was I that I envied a species that had been ravaged by a plague? And yet they still thrived. The rumors of their failing mental states had no basis in reality. I wondered why they let the lies persist. I had my theories, but I was too chicken shit to woman up and ask.

"When a phoenix finds its twin flame, they love unconditionally." A voice that sounded suspiciously like Ash's slithered through my mind. Goose bumps erupted across my skin, and my vision faltered. *I'm having some kind of auditory hallucination. Yep, that's it.* I forced my body into submission, demanding for it to be calm. I waited, and no other phantom words from the very man I was tracking were heard. I heaved a sigh of relief. *I haven't been getting enough sleep lately. Yep, that's the problem.*

I blinked repeatedly, trying to focus on Zula, who was saying something to me, but I had absolutely no idea about what. I leaned forward, narrowing my eyes in an attempt to read her lips. Tamzea stepped in front of Zula, her features scrunched up with concern. Swaying, dark spots danced in my field of vision. My knees buckled, and the ground came up to meet me.

SCREAMING, I threw my head back as pleasure assaulted my system. Heat suffused me down to a subatomic level. Colors exploded behind my eyelids while my body quivered, sweat coating my skin. "Wh-what's … " I couldn't even form a coherent sentence. The last thing I remembered was being on the Gartian planet with my crew and the next …

"I've said it before and I'll say it again … You taste so fucking good."

Well, and then the next moment … I was being eaten

alive, but in a good way. I didn't have to raise my head to know who was languorously torturing me with his tongue between my thighs. I must have passed out, and I was again having an erotic dream about Ash. No one else had ever so completely taken over my psyche. "Stop! Just — Aaaahhh!" My legs trembled when Ash sucked on my clit.

"I don't think you want me to." A whimper escaped my chest as his words vibrated against my slick flesh. I could hear the smirk in his voice. I hated him for it, especially because he was right.

Lurching to the side with my eyes squeezed tight, I tried to roll away from him. "Wake up, wake up … just wake up, damnit."

"I don't think you want that either." Ash's lips brushed my ear as his body pinned me down. "Now open up those beautiful eyes, and look at me," he rumbled low.

I immediately complied. I couldn't seem to help myself. His sculpted face, high cheekbones, and full, supple lips filled my vision. And there in his eyes danced those now familiar flames, their presence enthralling me.

He stared at me intently. "I need to see you again in the flesh, so to speak. And it needs to be soon. We started something that can only be finished in the physical plane."

I blinked rapidly, trying to process what he was saying. Shouldn't I have more control of my own dream like I had before? Ash was getting awfully pushy for a figment of my imagination. "Get off of me." I shoved at his chest.

The muscles in Ash's jaw jumped as his gaze ran over

the contours of my face. "So stubborn. You don't even know what's happening between us."

"Nothing's happening. You're a figment of my sex-deprived imagination."

His hands slid up to capture my wrists, and I lurched up to bite him. He shifted just out of reach with barely any effort.

And much to my consternation, my aggression merely made him chuckle, the sound causing goose bumps to skitter across my skin. Ash leaned in to whisper in my ear, "I thought you wanted to feel connected. I can give you everything you've ever wanted, and things you didn't even realize you needed."

"I don't want anything from you," I spat. It was a bald-faced lie, and I had a feeling he knew it.

He moved his face away from me, his lips curling up. "I guess it's true what they say."

"What?"

"Nothing good comes easy." Ash released me, fading away right before my eyes, even as I took a swing at him.

JOLTING AWAKE, I sat straight up to take in my surroundings. I sighed with relief when I was met with the familiar sight of my quarters on The Pittsburgh. My gaze flittered along the array of Earth things cluttering every available surface, the objects normally making me feel safe—which was probably why they'd been brought back on the ship in the first place—but something had shifted in me.

Instead of comfort, the prized pieces from a planet I would never know taunted me with a history I would never actually be able to connect with. I was alone. Utterly and completely alone. I had no real family and no ties that truly bonded. It was something I'd always wanted, and yet never shared with anyone. It was my weakness, and suddenly something about Ash was causing me to think more deeply about my issues. *No. It's only a weakness if I let it be. I've turned it into my strength.*

I collected Earth items, dressing in days-gone-by clothing because I wanted to define my own past ... and therefore my own future. The rejections I'd suffered being raised on New Earth were just distant memories. They would never be allowed to affect any decisions in my new life.

If some misguided part of me felt a connection with Ash after being with him sexually, then I had to focus on capturing him even more. I needed to turn him over for the bounty on his head, not just for my pride, but because if he was someone that I could develop a relationship with —as twisted as that thought was—then I had to remove any possibility of him being in my life ... permanently. I would never again let myself be vulnerable to a romantic-type relationship. I'd learned my lessons from New Earth very well.

Standing, I marched for my door just as it slid open,

Tamzea stepping through to narrowly avoid colliding with me. "Hey! Again with the not knocking?" I snapped.

Tamzea met my gaze, smiling demurely. "I'm glad to see you're up. How are you feeling?" Her hands flitted around me, checking and assessing.

I slapped at them with my own hands. "I'm fine. Care to fill me in on what you know … about what happened and everything else that I missed while I took my unscheduled nap?"

Tamzea pushed past me to move into my room. "Have a seat, Jane. We need to talk."

I grimaced. Was there something actually wrong with me? I hadn't considered the possibility. Looking at Tamzea's suddenly serious face caused a lump to form in my throat. "Okay," I squeaked. Maybe I had some kind of incurable disease or— "Oh my God! I have G-Pox, don't I?"

"What? Jane, calm down."

But it was too late. I was already working myself into a panic. It wasn't completely unrealistic to think that maybe I had some Gartian DNA. And if I had even a smidgen of it in my system then I could be infected. "Am I going to rot away?" I clutched at the wall and stumbled face-first onto my bed. I sucked in ragged breaths as my mind conjured up images of me with half of my face replaced by metal. I gasped. "What if I don't survive?"

An abrupt burst of laughter met my ears, surrounding me in its mocking tone. Lifting my head from my comforter, I found Tamzea sprawled on the floor doubled over, her arms wrapped around her middle, as the offending hysterical laughter erupted from her. The unprofessional response to my dilemma was disconcerting, to say the least. My face heated as anger raced through my system. "How dare you laugh at my condition!" I hissed.

"Jane, how ... just— Wh-why would you think that?" she sputtered.

I raised my arms, and then let them fall in exasperation before flopping back on my bed. "Then tell me what's wrong with me!"

I was beginning to feel like an idiot, and I didn't much appreciate Tamzea at that moment for encouraging those feelings. A good healer would never laugh at a panicked patient, ill-informed or not.

I glowered at her. *Maybe I need to trade her in for someone with more compassion. After she tells me what is wrong with me, I am seriously going to consider it.*

Tamzea straightened herself out, her lips pressing together to form a thin line. She wasn't fooling me, though, I could still see the humor dancing in her lavender eyes. "What I wanted to talk to you about is this obsession you've developed with capturing Ash."

My nostrils flared, and I dug my fingers into my pillow. "It has nothing to do with him. It has to do with the mone—"

"Save it." All mirth drained from Tamzea's face as she raised her hand to shut me up. "You were muttering his name while you were unconscious. You also insisted on going after him while you were in some kind of feverish state. I've never seen anything like it."

My mouth fell open, any retort dying in my throat. "Whaaat?" I finally managed. "What exactly do you mean I tried going after him in a feverish state?"

"It's like you weren't there, almost as if you were sleepwalking. Your eyes were open and you responded somewhat to external stimuli such as light and touch, but it was as if your subconscious was elsewhere. I had to sedate you to keep you from leaving. Not to mention that you were burning up with a fever at the time."

Ash's comment about our encounters not being dreams niggled at the back of my mind, but I stubbornly pushed it aside. "Obviously I had some kind of illness that caused the fever and I'm just really ... really focused on getting Ash— I mean the money. Ash equals that gigantic bounty from the UGFS as you well know." Yeah, it sounded pretty lame to me, too. I studied my nails in hopes of avoiding Tamzea's gaze.

"Normally I don't mind letting you hang on to some of your more harmless delusions, Jane. But this time ... we both know something more is going on." She slid onto the bed next to me, taking my hands within hers. "Please, Jane. I'm not just this ship's healer. I'm your friend. Talk to me."

"Fine," I grated. Maybe a part of the reason why I felt so disconnected from even the people I considered my friends and chosen family was because I refused to let them in. I was guarded, and I found it exceedingly difficult to talk about my feelings even when I wanted to. *I need to bite the bullet and come clean about Ash.*

I swallowed and then cleared my throat. "I've been having these very realistic dreams about me and Ash ... er —" I tugged my hands away from Tamzea, flicking my gaze to a poster depicting an Earth landscape, wishing I could actually be there. "Having sex. I'm having dreams about having sex with Ash. And earlier on the Gartian planet, I swore I heard his voice in my head. So go ahead and say it, I've finally gone and completely lost it."

"Hmmm ... " Tamzea leaned forward, placing her fingertips on my temples. "I wonder ... " She peered intently at me like I was a puzzle to be solved. And maybe I was.

"Can you heal mental disorders?"

"Shhh."

I scowled, hating that she'd shushed me like a small child, but who was I to argue? After all, I was the insane one apparently. "Weeell?" Patience was not one of my best attributes. In fact, I was pretty sure I didn't possess any at all.

Tamzea stood abruptly, heading for the door with jerky motions. "I need to consult with Zula. Stay put. And don't mind the noise, the Gartians are working on the ship. They know you're in here and have assured us that they can work around you until you're well enough to go back to their planet."

"Wait!" I shot to my feet, grabbing her arm roughly. "Why did you bring me back to The Pittsburgh if they're working on it? I thought it was for my comfort, but then again—"

"It was," she interrupted, "You were calmer here. Just like you always are. And now I'm wor—" Tamzea's expression closed off abruptly. "I shouldn't be long. Stay put until I can talk to Zula. And that's an order from a healer to a patient."

My arm dropped to my side, and I let her go without any more protest. My stomach fell into my feet, and I flung myself onto my bed, preparing for my imminent demise. I'd seen it in Tamzea's eyes, I knew the truth despite what she'd claimed. I had the G-Pox and it was rotting my brain away.

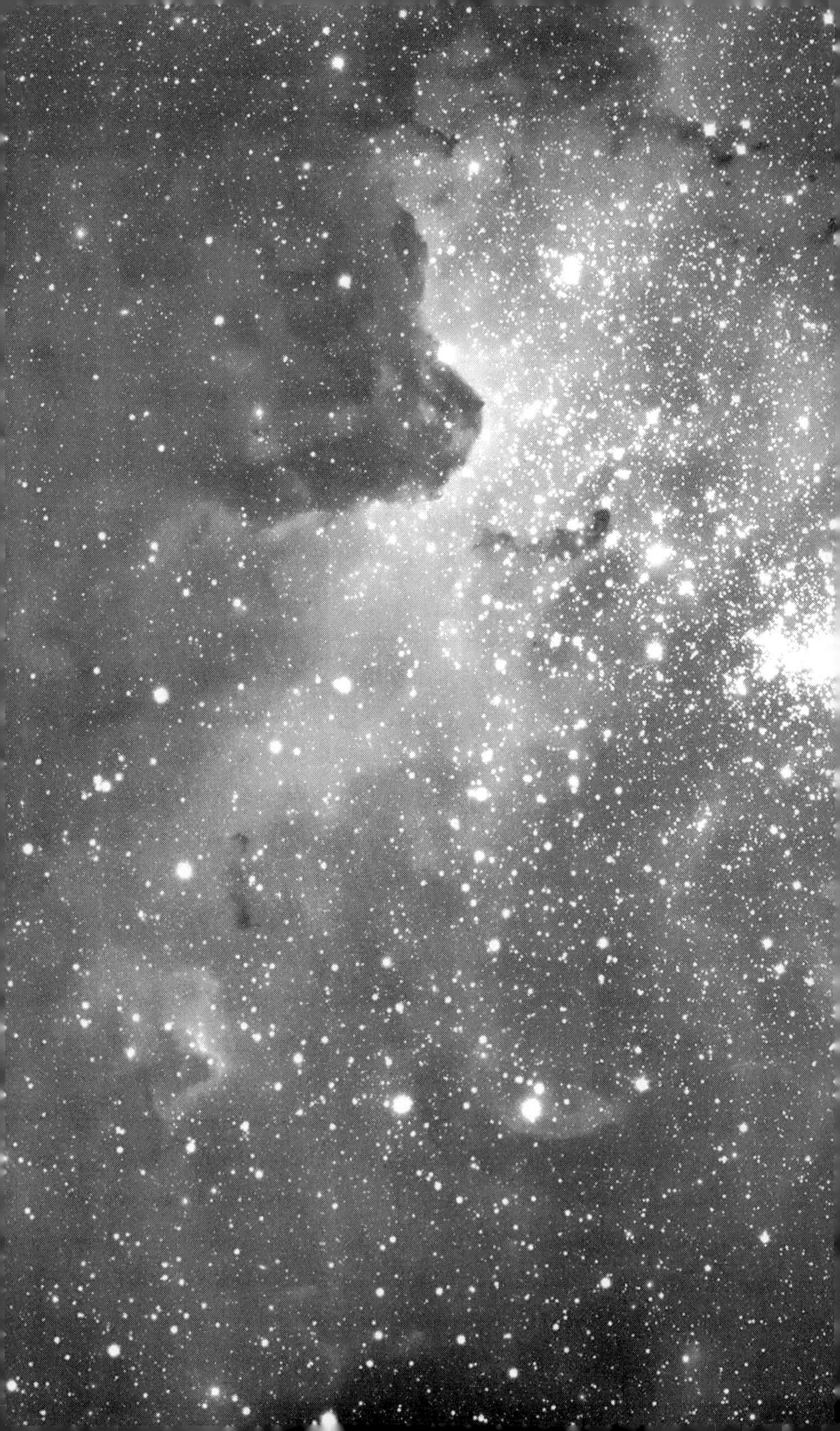

Chapter 11

I was burning up. My skin was blazing with desire—begging to be touched. "Ash," I moaned, his name rolling off my tongue as both a demand and plea in one. I knew he was what my body craved. He was the only thing that could satisfy the vast need building inside of me, which was like a small fire kindling into a raging inferno.

"I'm here." The rough words were whispered directly into my mind. My eyes flew open just in time to witness a mass of pure flame settle into Ash's human form. He pressed down on top of me, pushing my arms over my head.

I didn't stop to question if his presence was real or just another dream. The truth was, I was beginning to not be able to tell the difference anymore. I arched my body up and crashed my lips into his. The flavor of him was more potent than I'd remembered, and just like finely aged liquor, it went straight to my head. My senses reeled and my brain went on temporary vacation. The only thought that remained was centered on getting Ash inside of me again. Thankfully, he seemed to be on the same page as me.

"Fuck. I need you so damn much."

With one touch from Ash, my clothes incinerated. He was already naked, much to my delight. Without any preamble, he ensnared my lips, and plunged into me. The snap and crackle of things burning around us didn't even give me pause, nor did the smoky scent of it either. I wanted what Ash was doing to me—needed it on some primal level that I couldn't quite grasp, but was more than happy to give myself over to.

He pounded into me brutally, and I scaled my nails down his back, his blood burning my fingertips. No, that wasn't right ... he was burning me— No, we were on fire, just like in my dream. As pleasure like I'd never imagined ripped through my system, I threw my head back, screaming. It was as if every molecule in my body had combusted all at once. There was no more Jane, only the bliss of afterglow. Ash roared his own release a moment later, scalding me from the inside. I made nonsensical noises in approval.

And then my brain came back online like someone had flipped the power switch on. I instinctively knew what had just transpired between Ash and me was most definitely not a dream. I stared up at him as the flames in his eyes faded to their normal shade of gold.

His heavy-lidded gaze roamed my features with appreciation … and something I couldn't decipher. "I never thought—" Shock played across his features as one end of the laser cuffs clicked into place on his left wrist.

I grinned. "Thanks for that. It was exactly what I needed, and now—"

"Oh, Janey, really? Not this again." His full lips curled up into an already familiar smirk. "Give it up. Besides—" He dipped his head to deliver me a scorching kiss, which I couldn't seem to help but respond to. Of course, I hated myself for it. "You'd never be able to turn me in. Every man will leave you … cold after being with me." His laugh exploded around me, his human form bursting into flames just before he disappeared.

I cursed him to high heaven and back, as the laser cuffs fell to the ground of my incinerated quarters. What did I expect? I already knew how easily he could escape them.

My focus was then averted to what was left of my room. My comforter, mattress, posters … and everything in the immediate area of my bed had been completely charred. In other words … ruined. Not many things could make me cry, but I fought back the tears that pricked the corners of my eyes as I took in some of my most prized possessions in their new crispy state. "Damn him," I growled. "He's going to fucking pay for this."

Searing heat, emanating from the center of my naked back, snagged my attention. The intense sensation spread along my skin as if someone was carving into my flesh with a red-hot poker. I gritted my teeth, the pain crossing into a level of too-much-to-bear, even as I fought the darkness that pushed at me.

Until I couldn't anymore.

All went black, my scream echoing in my ears.

"I'M sure that's what it is," Zula stated calmly.

"But I thought you said—"

"I may be a genius but I'm not omniscient. By all accounts, it shouldn't be a possibility that Ash is a phoenix. Nevertheless, the evidence that he exists is right there on Jane's back. It also points to her human DNA being spliced with phoenix DNA, which would also explain her resistance to being injured by fire."

A thrill raced through my system at Zula's words. If what she was saying was true, then for the first time in my entire life I knew what the other part of me was. Of course, that would also mean—

I groaned loudly. "Is that twisted phoenix trying to make me his mate or something?" Everything he'd said to me was starting to make sense—the part about the twin flame and keeping me. Everything.

"Not trying," Zula stated dryly. "Already has."

"What?" I rolled off my bed, inhaling the lingering smell of smoke ... and Ash. His spicy, not quite cinnamon scent was somehow detectable above the burnt aroma of my things. I fought the urge to press my nose into the sheets to get a better whiff. "How is that even possible and how do you know?"

"Oh, honey, be careful." Tamzea came to my aid, helping me to my feet. That's when I realized I was still naked. I snatched what was left of my top sheet, wrapping it around my middle, my skin flushing with embarrassment.

Ignoring Tamzea's mother-hen attitude, I stepped towards Zula. "Okay, Smurfette, spill what you know. What the hell is going on?"

Scowling at me, Zula crossed her arms over her chest. "You are now bonded to Ash as his mate. The complicated mate pattern branded into your back is what tells me that what I say is a fact. For you to bear such a mark means that you have phoenix DNA. It's not complicated or it shouldn't be," she delivered me a scathing look, "even for you."

Panic swelled up within me, my heart thrashing against my ribcage. "What does it mean, that I'm his mate?"

"Exactly what it sounds like." Tamzea patted my shoulder gently.

"I told you that you needed to be more discerning about the men you let into your bed. I guess it's a little late for another warning, so I'll settle with an I told you so." Zula smirked smugly at me.

Had my first in command just implied that I was promiscuous? Was she attempting to slut-shame me? *Bitch!* I chose to ignore her smartass remarks, for the moment anyways. There would be retribution later. *Smurfette is going down.* "But what does it mean for me?" I nibbled on my bottom lip, mentally sorting through what I knew about other species that bonded as mates.

No mate bond I'd ever heard of could be broken without death. It wasn't like a simple bonding ceremony or a pledge like marriage. Mates were somehow connected … something I never thought I'd have to worry about, but maybe I should have being that I wasn't one hundred percent human. The most important questions were: how closely was I now connected to Ash? And what kind of power did he now hold over me?

Shivering with delight, an unbidden image of Ash moving inside of me flashed across my mind, his muscles flexing with each thrust. *Okay, so what kind of power besides making me a needy, hormone-addled, sex slave?* "Is there a way to break it?" I twisted the remnants of my sheet, unable to stop thinking about a naked Ash doing deliciously naughty things to me. My body heated despite my best efforts. *I am so screwed.*

"Not unless you kill him," Zula offered, her smug expression still in place.

"That can be arranged." Suddenly deflated, I flopped down on my bed. How did things go so wrong so quickly? Zula was right, I should have just kept my damn legs shut. Ash was like an incurable STD that I'd have to murder to shed myself of. My chest constricted. Sure, I'd killed before, but never in cold blood.

"So what does the thing on my back look like? Or

really, how bad is it?" I should have been happy to find out that I wasn't infected with G-Pox, but apparently it was my destiny to be physically altered against my will in some way. *At least my body isn't going to be half metal.*

"It's quite beautiful." Tamzea sat down beside me and stroked my arm reassuringly. "It's an intricate tribal-type design with what resembles a phoenix bird in the center. You have to look hard to see the bird, though. The pattern takes up your entire back from the nape of your neck to your tailbone. Some people would pay a lot for such a design. Not to mention, it's iridescent. The color moves and changes like a real flame. I've never seen anything quite like it."

"Great." The bright side was that at least it didn't sound hideous.

Zula tapped at her right ear, frowning. "If it wasn't for our ridiculous, mandatory translator implants then I could tell you what the mate brand is called, and I could also use the phoenix name for mate. But unfortunately whenever I say it you're just going to hear the word mate and so on."

"Yeah, yeah." I'd heard Zula complain about the UGFS regulated implants so many times that it was expected at this point. I had to admit that probably a lot of things were lost in translation, literally, with the implants. But with so many species and so many different languages, let alone dialects, it was better than the alternative. Being able to go anywhere I chose, and always being able to understand what every creature said, was an invaluable asset to a bounty hunter such as myself. Plus, humans didn't have the aptitude to pick up languages as quickly as some of the other species ... like Galvrarons.

I sighed. "But what does it all mean for me?"

"It means that you might have to rethink turning him over for the bounty."

"Like hell it does. Maybe we need to look into the whole dead or alive part of the requirements." I was only partly joking. How did I know that Ash hadn't mated me because he knew I was the only bounty hunter skilled enough to nab him? Maybe he didn't have a taste for cold-blooded murder either and he saw mating me as a win-win situation. I mean, he was clearly attracted to me. Turning me into his mate, who was at his sexual beck and call for the rest of our lives, probably only sweetened the deal. Zula hadn't mentioned anything about the whole sex slave thing, but if my already escalating need for Ash was any indication ... *Yep, I'm definitely in some deep shit.*

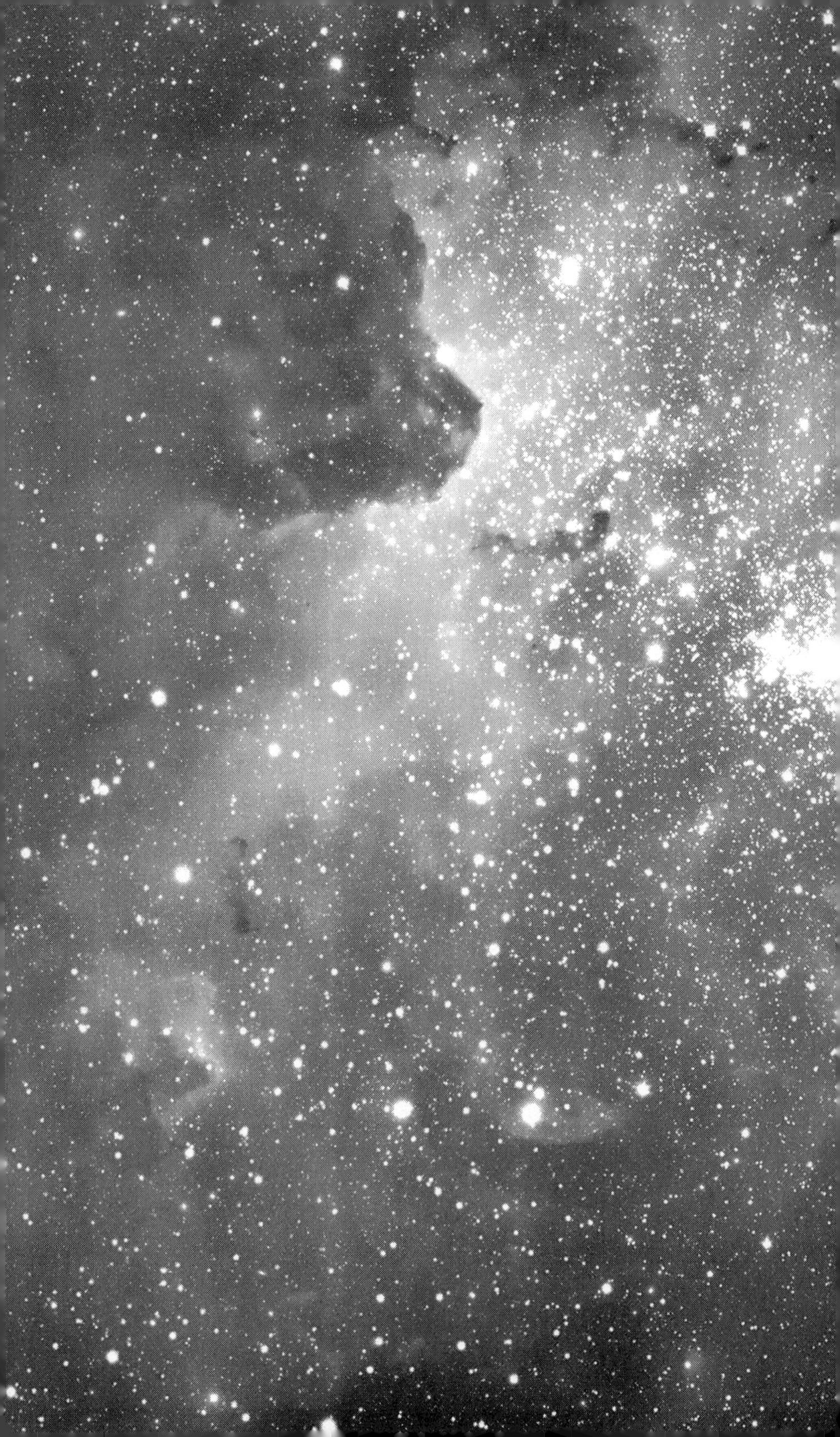

Chapter 12

I'd spent the better part of the last twenty-four hours twisted in a tumult of emotions, and swinging back and forth on the pendulum of reactions. I hated Ash. I needed to kill Ash. I wanted Ash. I craved Ash. I needed to have sex with Ash again immediately. I wanted to pummel Ash's face in. Throughout it all, I remained stubborn. Despite everything, I was determined to catch and turn Ash over to the UGFS. With any luck, he'd be executed for his crimes, and that outcome would ultimately solve the mate problem for me.

I stared at the Earth *Pittsburgh Steelers* football jersey in my hands. It was nothing more than a blackened rag now, no longer a prized possession to be displayed on my wall. I reluctantly tossed it down the trash chute, my gut roiling at the loss of so many beloved items. I knew they were just things, but they all served as a security blanket—one that Ash had ripped away from me in one fell swoop ... or in one deep thrust technically.

Anger flooded my system once more. My life had been uncomplicated before Ash had pushed his way into it, again, literally. It seemed as if my good karma wasn't as good as I had thought. Or maybe Ash fell into the 'careful what you wish for' category. I was always yearning for a deeper connection, a sense of belonging, and unconditional love. Suddenly I found myself strapped with a mate. I couldn't get more connected to someone if I actually went out and tried.

I pressed the small white intercom button on the wall, smearing soot on it. "Tamzea?"

"Yes, Captain?" The use of my title let me know she wasn't alone.

"How much longer did the Gartians say it would be?"

There was only a moment's pause before she responded, "About another hour."

"Thank you, Tamzea."

Just another hour, give or take, until we could get back out into space, and back on track with our mission. I didn't care who Ash was technically to me now. It changed nothing. I'd made no conscious decision to mate with him. I had no feelings for him beyond the yearning I felt for him physically. I would just have to learn to become celibate if that's what it meant. And maybe I needed to learn how to not be so attached to material things as well. Perhaps Tamzea and Zula had been right all along. Maybe—

Muttering a string of obscenities, I whirled around my room, grabbing everything I could, sending it all down the trash chute. My ridiculous attachment was a weakness. I wasn't human, and I'd never see Earth no matter how many things I collected from its history.

I paused when I came to my closet, my chest heaving. Slowly, I ran my fingertips over the most recent Earth pieces I'd acquired, the material soft, comforting. *No, I can't get rid of these. After all, I need them for my job. The rest, though ... all the rest can go.*

"IT'S a shame you didn't get to spend as much time with the Gartians as we did," Zula said, her fingers dancing along the buttons to set the navigation and pilot system. "They are quite technologically advanced. More so than I'd originally believed. Metal may be their specialty, but some of their other inventions are enviable even to me. I would have liked to spend more time studying them and picking their brains, so to speak."

"Yes, I missed out, I know." I fought the urge to roll my eyes. I didn't find new cultures and worlds as interesting as Zula, at least not in the same way. I'd been impressed with what I'd seen on the Gartian planet, and even more so by what they'd been able to do to The Pittsburgh in such a short amount of time. My ship had gotten a major overhaul that left it with the same 'homey' feeling it always had, but now it was fitted with top-of-the-line Gartian Alloy, which was practically indestructible. Oh, and it was a lot shinier and prettier now, too. The Pittsburgh would be the envy of ... well, anyone who saw it. *Note to self: Talk to Masha to see if the Gartians also installed a suped-up security system. I don't want anyone else getting their hands on my baby.*

"Sooo ..." I tapped my foot in a steady rhythm. "How long until you build the nifty contraption that was the whole point of coming into Gartian territory for?"

"First Masha has something she wants to talk to you about." Zula's lips tipped up slightly and she very carefully avoided my gaze.

"What about?"

She snickered. *Not good. Not good at all.* Instead of playing the little game any longer with Zula, who I was now seriously considering replacing as well, I went off in search of Masha. Okay, so it wouldn't be much of a search since I knew exactly where she'd be ... where she almost always was: the engine room.

Only she wasn't alone when I got there.

I nearly choked on my own spit when I laid eyes on Masha. She was sitting cross-legged on top of one of the machines. One of the Gartian triplets—Zar, Tar, or Dar— was leaning into her while stroking her face affectionately. I may, although I'll never admit it, have screamed like I was witnessing a grown man touch a child inappropriately. Okay, so that's how it felt to me, although

I knew Masha was technically older than me, and her body was just tiny, not actually childlike.

She just uses her cute little face to manipulate me.

She's not a child.

I so can't handle this.

"Captain J-Jane," Masha sputtered, which was a first for her. Usually, she was calm and collected while she managed to get me to do exactly what she wanted. Even her tears and lip quivers were perfectly masterminded for maximum effect. "I ... ah, this is Dar. You remember him? He's going to stay on with us for a while. To help out and—"

"Why?" I blurted out, not letting her finish. "And usually it's standard protocol to, at the very least, inform the captain and owner of a ship, if there's suddenly about to be a change in the number of crew members. It's my damn ship! You need to consult with me!" Not wanting or being able to handle Masha and her guest at the moment, I marched right back out the way I came without another word.

"Jane." Zula's voice echoed through the ship from the intercom. "We're being detained by a UGFS vessel and it looks like we're about to be boarded."

I clutched at the nearby wall for balance. "What the fuck is happening lately?" I threw my head back and glared. "Universe, you know you owe me better than all the shit you've been throwing my way. Why the hell are you fucking with me?"

Just then Dar and Masha scurried out of the engine

room. Masha's face held an edge of panic. "I need to hide him. The UGFS can't find him here."

I gritted my teeth. "And why is that exactly?"

Masha's eyes darted to Dar and then back to mine. "It would be bad."

My eyes slid shut for a moment, and I took a few deep breaths to try and calm myself. "Okay ... hide him in the smuggling compartment under the cargo deck. But if for whatever reason they find him, I'll do and say whatever I need to in order to protect me and mine. Got that, big guy?"

Dar inclined his head towards me. "Thank you."

Just as he and Masha turned to leave, I snagged her arm and stooped over to get right in her face. "After this is over, you are going to tell me everything. Understood?"

She bit her lower lip, nodding rapidly. I let her go, and the two of them dashed off. I pressed my cheek against the cool metal of the wall. It felt good against my flushed skin. After a few moments of allowing myself to panic, I straightened up and ran my hands over my clothes. I had nothing to hide ... well, nothing much anyways. Whatever the UGFS wanted probably had to do with the Ash case. Or at least I hoped.

"Jane?" Zula's voice blared at me, worry in her tone. "Where are you?"

"Coming," I muttered, heading in the direction of the airlock. I'd question why Dar felt he needed to hide from the UGFS later. Or rather, I'd drag all the answers out of him and Masha the first chance I got. I had a niggling feeling it was for the same reason the Gartians didn't seem to mind their reputation as an insane species. Their crazy status kept most visitors at bay, and involvement with the UGFS to a minimum. I also had a feeling what I would learn was going to fall under the category of things I would later wish I never knew.

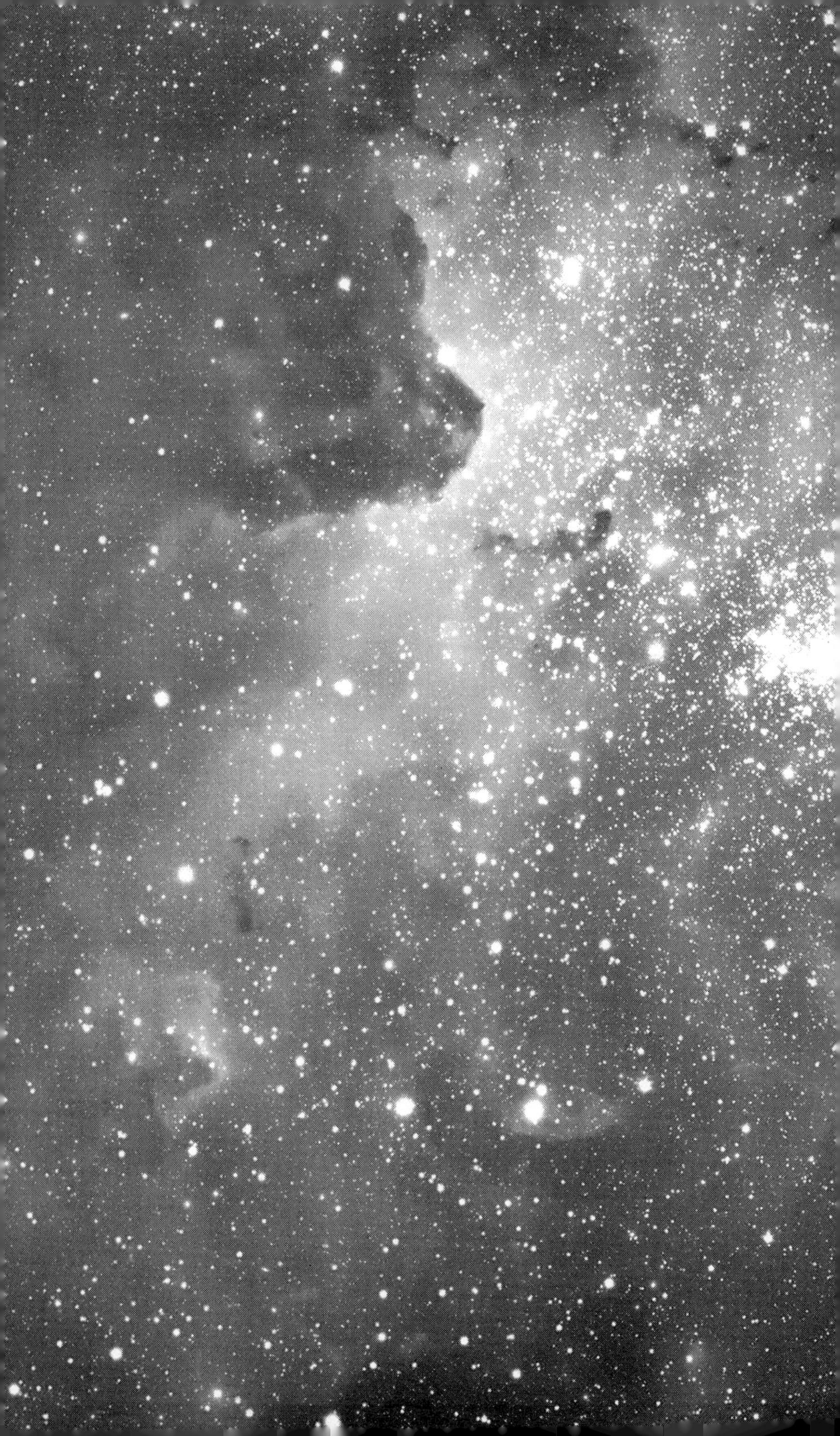

Chapter 13

Ambassador Aralias tugged his helmet off, his disdainful gaze snagging mine. "Captain Wexis," he snapped, his tone crisp. He was accompanied by two heavily armed UGFS officers whose faces were shielded behind visors. It definitely ratcheted up the intimidation factor, and to say that I was nervous would have been an understatement.

"To what do I owe the pleasure of your unscheduled visit?" I tried to keep my usual sarcasm out of my tone ... and failed horribly if the 'I just ate a lemon' look that puckered Ambassador Aralias' face was any indication.

He leaned forward into my personal space, which was very un-ambassador-type behavior in my opinion. "Do you have Ash? And the chip, do you have the chip?"

I blinked rapidly, taken aback by the almost desperate demeanor Ambassador Aralias was exhibiting. "No. I ...

we would have contacted you the moment we did. Why would you think that?"

Ambassador Aralias straightened himself, regaining his composure. "It was a logical assumption after you visited the Gartian territory. What other reason would one have to visit such a place?"

I slid a glance to Zula and noticed she was standing still ... too still. Her body language and lack of contribution to the conversation told me everything I needed to know in that situation. I should tread very carefully because something was very, very wrong. "We had a lead that didn't pan out. We don't have him ... yet." I smiled, dipping my gaze demurely as sweat gathered along my hairline. The demure act was a stretch, one that I hoped was semi-believable.

"And the upgrades on your ship?" he snapped.

"The Pittsburgh has long needed upgrades and maintenance. We—"

"You traded directly with the Gartians?"

My eye twitched. I wanted to tell him to shove it where no sun from any galaxy would ever shine, but my gut was tightening with the familiar warning of danger. Between the surprise visit, Ambassador Aralias' tone, and the very large Gartian I had hiding on my ship, I instinctively knew I couldn't let the UGFS know we'd had direct contact with the Gartians. "No. We happened upon a trader who had just stocked up on Gartian grade alloy, we were able to intercept him and ... convince him to sell us his supply. I have a very skilled Guaviva onboard who did the upgrades herself."

Ambassador Aralias' eyes narrowed as he studied me. Sweat trickled down my temples and built on my upper lip as I fought the urge to fidget under his scrutiny. I was isolated under the spotlight of his steady stare. It was as if everything had fallen away except for the two of us, and we were locked into a weird stalemate.

"Very skilled," he begrudgingly stated, although I got the sense that he wasn't buying what I was trying to sell one little bit. "Do you have another lead on Ash?"

"Yes," I lied. "I still plan on getting him and that chip to the UGFS before the deadline. I'm looking forward to spending that extra big payment." I smiled but was sure the humor didn't reach my eyes.

"How did you convince the trader to sell you the Gartian grade alloy when I'm sure you couldn't have offered him fair market value?"

It was time to put the nasty rumors about me to good use. I cocked my hip, gazing at him from under my eyelashes. "Well ... you know ... I sweetened the deal with a little something extra." I grinned coquettishly.

Ambassador Aralias' eyes flared with sudden interest. I blinked back my surprised reaction. With his thinly veiled disdain for me, I'd been positive that he'd never be interested in me sexually. Of course, I was a firm believer that you could still have amazing sex with someone you didn't like. Ash was case in point. My skin warmed at just the thought of the phoenix asshat.

"Captain Wexis, you intrigue me." The ambassador trailed his long index finger along my jawline. "Very much." He cleared his throat as his gaze roamed blatantly over my body. "I've heard you're very good at ... your job."

His words were like ice water being dumped over my head, all thoughts of Ash temporarily forgotten. "From who?" I croaked. I mean, seriously? I knew there were rumors about me, hell, I was the one currently fanning them, but I wasn't aware there were details about the quality of my ... work as well. I wasn't sure if I should be flattered or insulted. Especially because it was all a big fat lie.

"I've heard many speak of your ... talents. Maybe after you bring me Ash, we can discuss the furtherment of your career through UGFS exclusive contracts. I'd very much like for you to show me your particular brand of persuasion."

I stifled a shudder. I was repulsed and I wanted—no, *needed* to take a shower immediately. "Yes ... well, I'll be happy to discuss my career after I catch Ash. It's my top priority at the moment."

"Yes, of course." Ambassador Aralias turned abruptly and paused with his helmet over his head. "I look forward to Ash's capture and the conclusion of your contract then." He slid his helmet back on, clicking it into place. He and his entourage moved back into the airlock. I watched grimly as they traveled the short distance from The Pittsburgh back to their cruiser.

I turned to Zula who was eyeing me warily. "You don't have to tell me how fucked I am. I already know."

"Do you?" she asked softly.

I snorted. "Yeah, I'm well aware." I tilted my head back, cursing the Universe for not delivering, once again, on my good karma. In fact, I seemed to be marinating in the bad stuff instead.

I inhaled and exhaled a few times to calm myself. "We need to have a meeting between all of us. That means Dar as well. Fifteen minutes in the eating lounge." My boots pinged loudly on the metal floors as I stomped towards my quarters. I needed a scalding shower to remove Ambassador Aralias' slimy remnants from my skin.

WATER SPATTERED against the back of my head and shoulders, each drop weighing more than it should. I leaned my face against the warm metal of my shower stall needing to not only wash away the remnants of Ambassador Aralias but the events of the last few days. My inability to not be able to properly process the fear that was currently overwhelming me was paralyzing. It was an emotion that I normally excelled at avoiding, but my current situation left me no way out. I was trapped and therefore forced to face the insidious feeling of helplessness and the causes of it.

A simple job had turned into me picking up an unwanted mate, and now an unwanted, dangerous suitor.

When I ultimately turned down Ambassador Aralias, what would it mean for my career as a bounty hunter? Would he be able to stonewall me from the best jobs and ruin the career I'd worked so hard to build? The simple solution would be to just let him fuck me, but—I slammed my fist against the wall—I couldn't. I may have some questionable partners on my list of past conquests, but every single one of them I'd wanted—I'd chosen.

Yes, sometimes alcohol had been a prime motivator, but everything had still been my choice. Ambassador Aralias would never be my choice under any circumstances. I should have listened to Zula and forgotten about Ash when I'd had the chance. I wouldn't be in either predicament if I'd, just for once, not been so damned stubborn.

Switching off the shower dial, I stepped onto the auto-dry fan, quickly pulling on the same clothes I'd had on before my aquatic breakdown. I could be afraid—feel fear, but I would push through it. There was no other way.

My moment of weakness evaporated with the last droplets from my shower, leaving me lighter and more focused. There was no time for wallowing, or I really would end up floating out in space without any thrusters. There were always options. I just had to figure out what they were.

My determination began to crystallize as I made my way to the meeting I'd called … and was now late for. I knew I was going to get some attitude from my crew for that one.

As I entered the eating lounge I let my gaze sweep over Zula, Tamzea, Masha, and Dar. I stomped over to stand in front of the latter. Narrowing my eyes to slits, I crossed my arms over my chest. "Now would be a good time to start explaining why you felt the need to hide from the UGFS, and anything else you might think is pertinent to this shitstorm that's pouring down on me."

"Which you caused," Zula chimed in ... of course. I didn't expect any less from her.

"Yes, fine. I caused it by not wanting to let Ash go. It's kind of late for me to change my mind now, though," I grated, not taking my eyes off Dar. He glanced at Masha as if asking for her permission to speak. That fact pissed me off. "I'm the captain here, Dar. I tell you to jump and you say how high. Not ask Masha whether or not you should."

Dar's features hardened for a moment as he regarded me before they softened to something between deference and respect. "My apologies. You aided me without question before and now I do owe you an explanation."

"Yes, you do." I tapped my boot against the floor.

Dar spared one last glance at Masha before beginning. "We, the Gartians, are not the insane, unstable race that most believe us to be, which I'm positive you've already figured out for yourself." I rolled my eyes at Captain Obvious as he continued. "The UGFS can't be trusted. The only reason the Gartians, as a species, haven't been annihilated is because of two things. One, our grade of alloy makes us damn hard to destroy, not to mention our cloaking capabilities and other technological advances that most don't possess or are even aware of. And two, we keep to ourselves, not revealing the true nature of the UGFS. They don't engage us because it's not worth the risk of losses they would accrue. But if the status quo changed ... I'm sure that would as well. Finding me here on the ship would have meant you and your crew's death at the very least."

"What secret do the Gartians possess about the UGFS?" It was the only thing that made sense. It would explain why Ambassador Aralias was so nervous about us being in contact with them at all.

"They allowed the Denards to infect us with the G-Pox. The pox was an attempt by the Denards to wipe out yet another species that they deemed unworthy."

"Unworthy?" My mind was reeling. I hadn't fully processed the information Dar was giving me, but the need to have my questions answered was overruling everything else in that moment.

"We're not sure what makes them classify some species as tolerable and others unworthy, but they've been systematically wiping out entire races."

"No," Zula began in her professor-ish tone, as if we were all in her imaginary class. "Those times are in the past. The Denards killed the phoenix, the—"

Dar didn't let her finish her lecture though. "Those times are not in the past," he spat. "The Denards have just become more skilled at what they do. Things like the G-Pox are their weapons of choice now. The only thing in the past is their open extermination like with the phoenix."

"And what is it that they do?" I asked numbly. I found myself sitting without consciously deciding to. It wasn't like I was a big UGFS supporter in the way that I thought they were all good and shiny and perfect, but I was floored to find out that they allowed such things to happen right under their noses. I thought they existed to keep the peace and to prevent the extermination of planets and species from happening—bad things like the destruction of Earth from ever happening again.

"What do they do? Genocide of races without the mass population knowing about it. They are the true power behind the UGFS. Things are not the way you all are made to believe."

"It doesn't matter." I pulled myself to my feet, meeting Dar's shocked gaze steadily. "It changes nothing here for me or my crew. Or you, for that matter. You and all of the Gartians will continue like you've been doing and so will we. Once we bag Ash we can put all of this behind us."

"You're Ash's mate now," Tamzea said, the first words she'd uttered since I entered the room. "And what about Ambassador Aralias' interest in you? What will you do when—"

"I'll figure it out. I just need more time. Until then, all we have to worry about is tracking down Ash. Zula, you need to get on that containment contraption, or whatever you want to call it, immediately." I spun on my heels, heading towards my living quarters. I required alone time to think.

No one followed me, but I also knew my solitude wouldn't last long before Tamzea, Zula, Masha, or all three of them would be pestering me about my decision. I didn't have much of a choice though. After all, what could I do with the information Dar had just given me? Start some kind of uprising or revolution? I didn't think so. All I cared about was my ship, my crew, and myself. The rest of the Universe would have to take care of themselves, just like they always did.

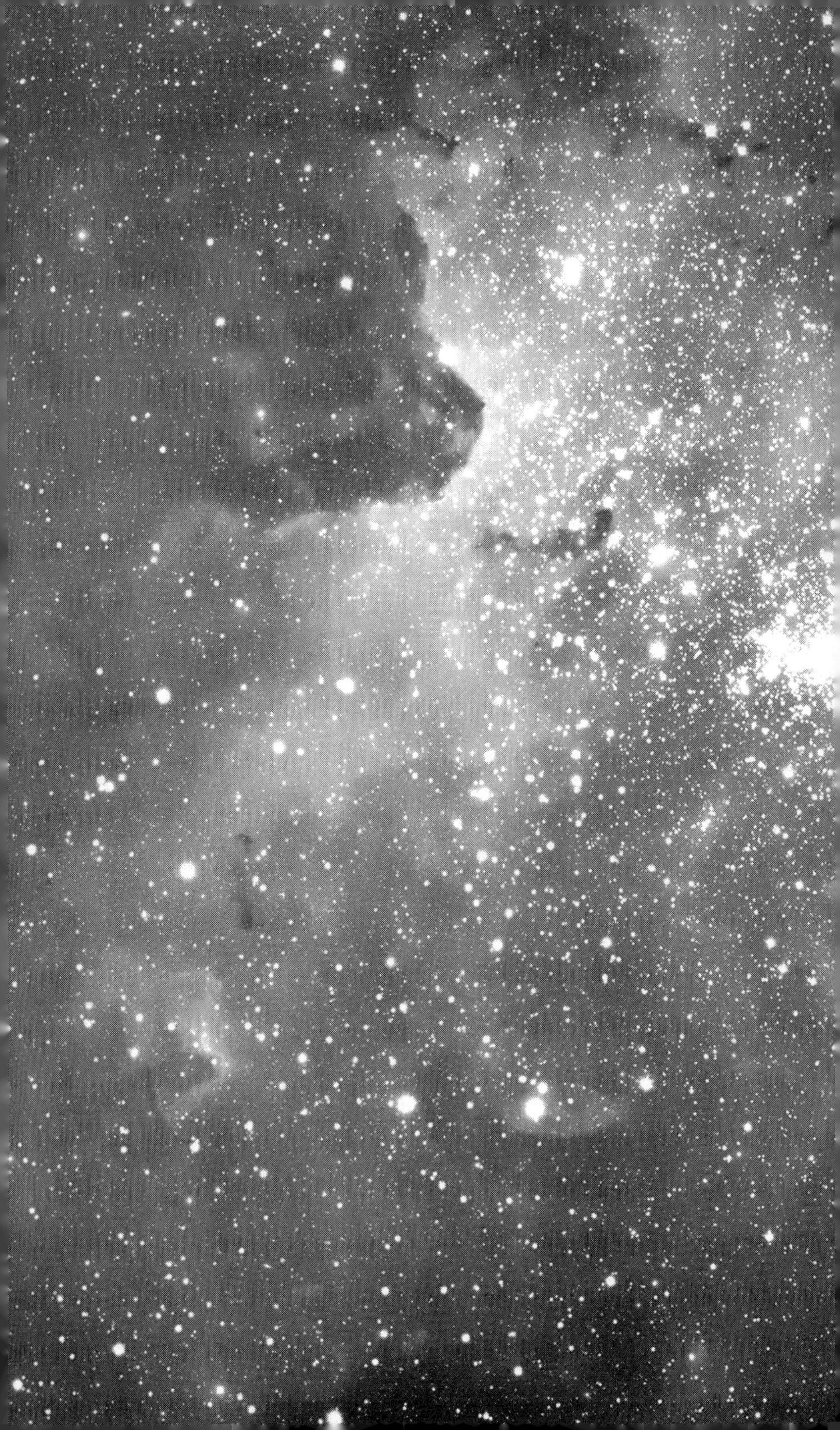

Chapter 14

I stood in my quarters with my naked back to the full-length mirror, my gaze locked straight ahead, unable to move over my shoulder. Apparently, I was missing the courage required to look at the mate mark that had been burned into my flesh when I'd let Ash claim me for his. There was a small part of me that felt that if I didn't see it then it didn't exist.

I clenched and unclenched my fists. My living quarters belonged to someone else now, the small space oppressive when it used to be comforting. My sanctuary was destroyed. There were no more Earth relics on my shelves holding up Earth history books. No more Earth artwork on my walls either. The sight was confusing, leaving me feeling lost. Sure, I'd been born well after the destruction of Earth, but for the first time since I'd been booted off of New Earth … I felt utterly and completely alone—isolated like never before.

My crew was my chosen family but none of them truly understood me. Hell, I didn't understand myself more than half the time. My identity as a bounty hunter was what I let define me and now I was terrified that it would be ripped away as well. *Who am I if not an Earth-obsessed, kick-ass bounty hunter?*

"Janey." Ash's deep voice crept over my skin, cocooning me in its warmth. Flames swirled around me, solidifying into Ash's rock-hard body. He wrapped his arms around me, pulling me against his muscular chest.

"How the hell did you get in here?" I willed myself to fight him, but he had me physically in his thrall. I arched my head back, inhaling his spicy scent. It made my mouth water. *I'm screwed, so screwed.*

"I am phoenix, I have no boundaries when it comes to reaching you, my mate." His full lips skimmed my neck softly, the movement achingly tender.

"Why? Why did you do it?" Would it make a difference if he bonded me to him because he wanted me or was using me? Perhaps it was another moment of vulnerability, but I just had to know. Not that his answer could sway me to not turn him over to the UGFS. It just meant that for the moment, I was transfixed by him, so I would take the opportunity to get some answers.

"I couldn't help myself. You're everything I could ever want in a mate."

Really? I chuckled. *How ridiculous.* He wanted a mate who would try to turn him over to probably be executed? *Yeah, that sounds helluva sexy to me.* "I doubt that."

"You may doubt it, but it's true. We're more evenly matched and suited for each other than you realize. Our flames burn at the same temperature, which is very telling for a phoenix."

His impressive erection pulsed against me, and I barely fought the urge to press my ass against his crotch in blatant invitation. *Resist. Resist. You must resist.* "Is it the whole twin flames thing you mentioned?" I sucked in a deep breath as he slid one hand to capture my wrists, dipping me forward. He traced his tongue along my back, over his mark, I was guessing. I shivered with delight. "Do you have a mark? A mate mark?" The thought of him baring a brand proclaiming that he belonged to me shot a sudden thrill through my system. *Yep, screwed, screwed, screwed.*

"Of course," he purred against my flesh, and I moaned, my eyes sliding shut.

"I want to see it," I rasped. "Please."

Great, now I'm practically begging. What's happening to me?

I should kick him in the balls and cuff him again. He may be able to turn into flame and escape but making him groan in pain would be gratifying—a symphony to my ears.

Ash flipped me around, letting me fall onto my bed. In one smooth motion, he removed his shirt, baring his skin to me. I stared in amazement. It was beautiful, the lines intricate and simple simultaneously, the way they flowed along the muscular plains of Ash's entire back was—suddenly I was on my feet. *I need to touch it.*

With my hand outstretched and trembling, I moved closer to him but somehow managed to keep a bit of distance. "It's so ...so ... " The words I needed to describe it didn't exist in my vocabulary. It was a visual masterpiece, the lines curving lovingly over his skin. In the center was a feminine-looking bird of flame, the design itself iridescent, changing with each refraction of light.

Seeing it there, etched into his flesh, made me feel connected, cherished ... loved.

No. No. Don't be stupid. You don't even like him, and he definitely doesn't love you. And yet, the emotions continued to churn within me, giving me the sense of connection and belonging that I'd always yearned for.

"It was your phoenix half that craved the connection," Ash offered as if he was reading my mind. "You never would have found it with anyone other than another phoenix."

No longer able to resist, I delicately ran my fingertips over the mate mark, tracing the pattern. I thought back to when Zula told me that she could have given me the true word for a phoenix mate and not the generic translation my interpreter implants forced me to hear. *I wish I could know that word. No. Stop. It doesn't matter.*

"I'm not a phoenix. Not really. I've only been spliced with phoenix DNA. I'm human."

Ash spun around, capturing my face between his large hands. His gaze bore into mine as flames erupted in his eyes. "You are mine, that's all that matters. We wouldn't have been able to bond as mates if you weren't phoenix ... or enough of one." His lips came crashing down on mine and I opened up for him, unable to resist. I reveled in the sharp taste of him, but only for a moment.

"No, stop." I pushed at his chest, forcing him to release me.

He backed up a few paces, studying me with obvious desire burning in his eyes. "I sense you want to talk about something?" He tilted his head, a smirk twisting up one side of his mouth.

"No shit. I feel like ... I feel—I feel violated is what I feel." I crossed my arms over my chest to hide my hard nipples. They didn't exactly confirm my statement. In fact, they were giving off the opposite impression. They were silently begging to be touched and suckled, bitten even. I shook my head to dislodge my pervy thoughts. *I'm pathetic. Pathetic, pathetic, pathetic.*

Ash quirked an eyebrow at me. "Really? I seem to remember you prancing onto my ship with seduction on your mind. Was it wrong of me to take you up on the offer?"

"No. That's not what I mean. I was talking about the whole mating thing. You claimed me without even asking!" I ground my teeth together, fighting the urge to punch him. "Why? Why did you do that?"

"I'm pretty sure I already answered that question. What is this really about? Are you afraid that you don't hate me as much as you want to? Or are you still steaming over the hit to your pride?" He grinned, and damnit the sight dazzled me. An unbidden image of me pulling him into a rough kiss where our teeth clashed together flashed across my mind. I forced myself to remain still.

His grin widened as if he sensed the true direction of my thoughts. "Or is it that you can't stand the thought of being out of control? Let me assure you, your fiery personality is very much like a phoenix. The challenge of mating is half the fun."

"You already mated me. So—"

Ash closed the scant distance between us, caressing the side of my face gently. I melted into his touch, hating myself for it. "No. The process is just beginning. There is much more to come."

Confusion washed over me as I stared up at him. "But we're already marked..."

"Which makes you mine and me yours. But the bonding process ... is just beginning. We hardly know each other." He hungrily devoured me with his eyes, letting me know he wasn't just talking about not knowing my favorite color.

"Then it's not too late to stop this insanity. Release me. You don't want me. If you let me go then I might even consider not turning you over to the UGFS."

Ash threw his head back, his deep laugh a physical touch. "I'm not an idiot. You'd turn me over in a heartbeat.

And it is too late, there's no going back for us. 'Til death do us part, sweetheart, literally."

Blood boiling, I took a wild swing at him. He caught my fist with ease as his gaze snagged, and remained riveted, on my jiggling naked breasts. My face heated, and I raised my knee to deliver him a painful ball buster, but he knocked me aside with his leg. "I don't want to be your stupid mate. And tell me, why the hell did you steal from the UGFS anyways? You had to know that you'd get caught."

Ash maneuvered so I was once again facing away from him with my arms held down by his steel band-like arms. His hot breath tickled the side of my face as he whispered in my ear, "Ah … but I'm not caught yet, am I? And you do want to be my mate otherwise you wouldn't be."

"You expect me to believe that? You mated me against my will. You—"

"I never could have marked you if some part of you hadn't accepted me fully. Mull that over in that pretty little head of yours. I—"

Just then my door slid open to reveal Zula. Her eyes rounded with surprise as she took in the situation, even so, her response was lightning fast as she lunged at Ash with what looked like a long, tubular wand attached to a small containment unit. Ash, as expected, instantly shifted to his flame form. A loud sucking sound filled the room. For a moment, I thought we had him.

I should have known better.

Ash's flame form circled me as he chuckled warmly.

He wasn't even the tiniest bit threatened by Zula's supposed secret infallible weapon. "You'll have to do better than that." He disappeared in a puff of smoke, and I was left half-naked staring at a very pissed-off Galvraron. Openly mocking her invention would not go over well, especially in this situation. Lucky me was left to deal with the fallout.

She slammed down her machine and swore. "That's it. We're done. I don't care how much money they're offering to pay us, the UGFS is on their own. I have no idea how to catch him. Me. A Galvraron has no idea how to catch him. How the hell did almost their entire species get wiped out?"

"Killing someone and catching them are two different things," I mumbled, pulling my shirt on over my head. "And we're not giving up just yet. I just—"

"Like hell we're not. You're mated with him. I saw what was going on between you two just now. You were half naked and he—"

"I was already half naked when he showed up!" I snapped. "He just *poofed* right in here and—"

"Started to seduce you … again!" Zula paused, dipping her head to gaze at the floor. "Look, I don't blame you. I don't know what kind of wacky things a mate bond can do to your hormones, but that's kind of the point. We're dealing with things that I don't even have a clue about. Me."

"So what do you suggest? Stay mated to a fugitive?

That puts me more at risk than anything else. Or maybe if we can catch him I can break this stupid bond."

Zula inhaled sharply, pinning me with her gaze. "You mean you would let them execute him just to be rid of him?"

No. "Yes."

"I don't believe you, Jane. And I need to do some more research before we decide to do anything else."

I crossed my arms over my chest. "We're kind of on a time crunch for the big payoff."

"I realize that," she growled. "Just give me a few hours."

"Fine."

"Fine."

Zula glided out of my quarters, leaving her failed machine on my floor. I kicked it, swearing when a sharp pain raced from my toes up my leg. *That was stupid. Of course, you've been doing a lot of dumbassery lately.*

Ash's words, about a part of me accepting him as a mate, echoed through my mind as I hobbled over to my bed. I rubbed my foot gingerly and tried to be honest with myself for once. Or maybe all it took was for me to accept Ash physically? I never denied my desire to be with him sexually. The man was the best sex I'd ever had. I mean, sue me. I was only human … or part human.

Something propped up on the pillow on my bed caught my attention and I swung my gaze over to—

"Oh, my God!" It was a small, stuffed animal version of an Earth animal called a mogwai. They had been completely wiped out with the destruction of Earth. Before I'd gotten rid of all my Earth relics, I'd had stuffed animals of a mogwai, a leopard, a kitsune, a koala bear, a dragon, and an elephant.

Picking up the fuzzy little toy, I saw that there was a note underneath it.

> *If you ask me, I can tell you all about Earth from firsthand experience. History books sometimes lie.*

I hurled the stuffed mogwai across the room. I wasn't going to ask Ash for anything. It didn't matter that for one millisecond, a moment in time, his gift, which was much more of a gesture, had touched some part deep inside of me. Not to mention that ... okay, I was seriously intrigued that he had actually been on Earth. How long was a phoenix's life span? Would the phoenix DNA allow me to live longer than the average human?

Well, *shit*. Now I had even more questions and I refused to ask Ash for anything ever again. He'd laughed at me when I'd practically begged him to release me as his mate. *Asshat.* My emotions were incredibly jumbled and I was beyond confused. I felt like I was having some kind of existential crisis. I wasn't even sure who I was anymore or who I would be after all the shit went down. Ash had somehow managed to obliterate my sense of self by revealing to me what my hidden genetics were. *Oh, the irony.*

I flopped onto my bed and curled into a ball. I would

force myself to put faith in Zula's brain and my ability to bounce back from anything. I just needed a little time to adjust to all the new information I'd recently received. After all, not much had actually changed. I was still the same Jane Wexis I'd always been. I just knew a little bit more about the non-human side of me.

No biggie. No biggie at all.

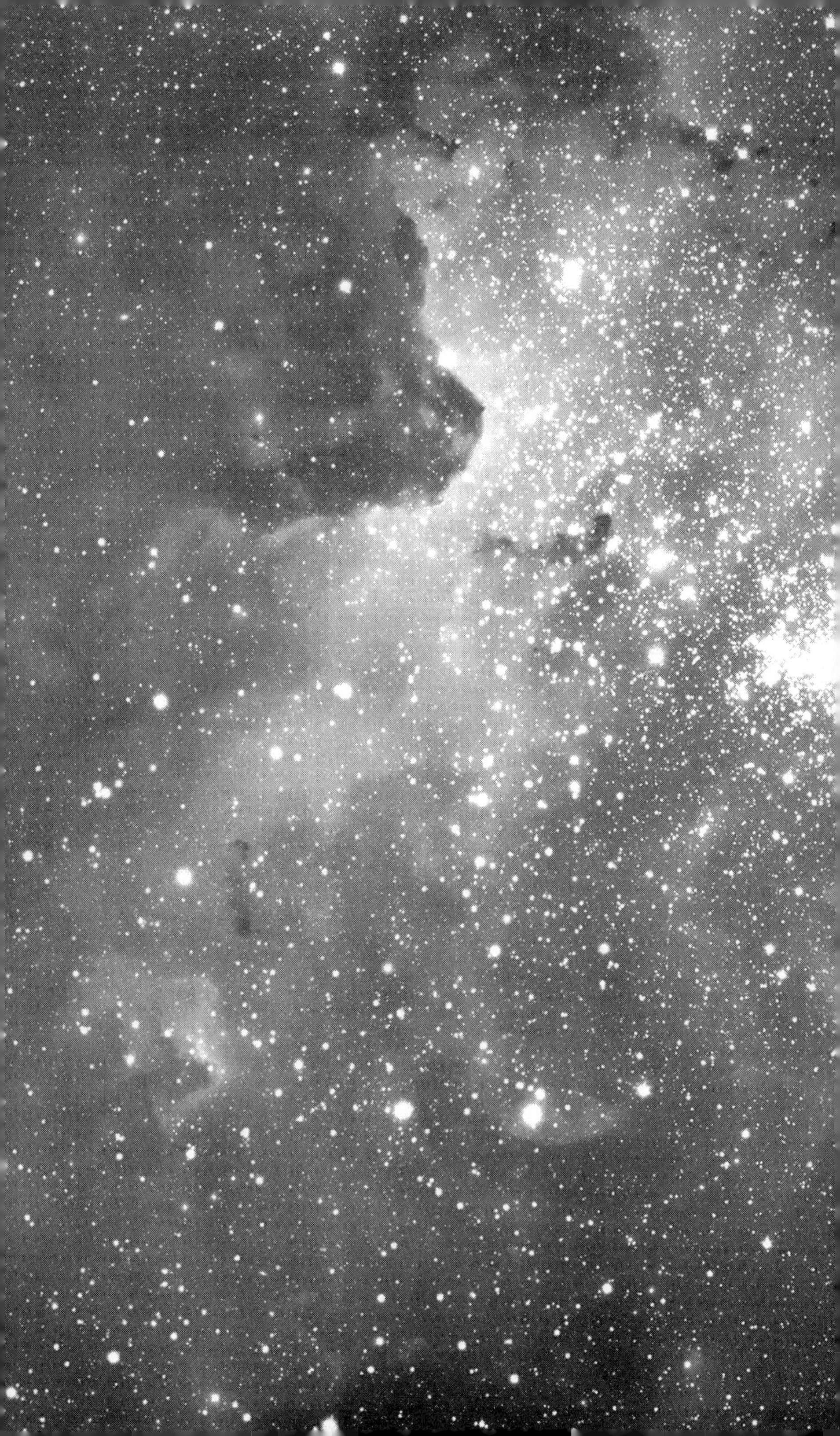

Chapter 15

"What do you mean, they're dead?" Ash's thoughts scattered, his emotions wavering between denial, anger, sorrow, and panic. "They can't be dead." An image of a woman and a small child flashed in his mind. "No, not them. Not them." He rounded on the bearer of bad news, a man who shared the same general features in construction and coloring. "Why didn't you protect them?"

"Brother," the man croaked, tears pooling in his eyes. "She was my sister, too, and my niece. I did everything I could, but the Denards ... they know our weaknesses."

"How? How can this be happening?"

"I don't know."

"I should have been there. I could have protected them. I would—"

"Be dead, too. They're targeting the royals. They thought you'd be there."

"We have to stop them, and we have to—" Sorrow and rage swelled up within Ash. "We have to make them pay."

My eyes snapped open. "What the hell was that?"

It felt like I'd been in a memory of Ash's—like I'd dreamt his memory. It was impossible, though. I wasn't sure why I'd had the dream, or really nightmare, but at least I'd been spared an erotic mental interlude with him again. Maybe that was a good sign? I was going to take it as one anyways.

Lurching to my feet, I punched the intercom button. "Zula, where are you? It's been a few hours."

When I got no response, I hauled my emotionally exhausted ass out into the main part of the ship in search of her. However, I didn't have to look for very long. She was on the ship's main computer, riveted to the screen as she scrolled rapidly through pages of text. "Ummm ... Zula?"

"Not now, Jane. I'm searching the Galvraron archives for anything I can find about the phoenix. So far I haven't found anything useful, but there has to be something somewhere that—"

"What would you do if you were me?" I slumped into the chair beside her.

Zula froze mid-scroll, turning slowly towards me. "Are you seriously asking me for advice about all of this?"

"Yes, I am. I admit that I may have been a bit ... pigheaded about going after Ash. But now I'm kind of stuck between a rock and a hard place. For the first time in a very long time, I honestly don't know what to do." I raised my hand to keep her from talking before I was finished. "Don't get used to this and don't get all smug on me or I swear to God I'll find another second in command so fast your ginormous brain will get a concussion from the whiplash."

Zula nodded, her expression remaining serious despite the twinkle in her eyes. "You should give up the bounty on Ash. Things are too complicated between the two of you. Maybe if you forfeit the job then it will sour the ambassador's attraction to you as well. What Dar told us about the UGFS does affect us, Jane. Or it does you. Or it could. The Denards hold a special hatred for the creatures of Earth, and you are part human."

Her gaze bore into mine. "You are part human *and* part phoenix. I'd avoid any attention being drawn to you as much as possible. I'm not sure how the scientists on New Earth even got a hold of phoenix DNA, but … Jane, this entire situation is too dangerous for you—for all of us."

Groaning, I dropped my head into my hands. It didn't take a brain the size of a Galvraron's to know she was going to tell me to give up the bounty on Ash. And she was right, even though it pained me to admit that he'd gotten the better of me in so many ways. Plus, if I couldn't catch him then who would? "Fine. Hail Ambassador Aralias' ship for me. I'll let him know the bad news."

The twinkle in Zula's eyes muted. "You're doing the right thing, Jane."

"Then why do I feel so shitty?" I grumbled. "By the way … you didn't happen to come across any tidbits about breaking the phoenix mate bond, did you? Because dropping Ash as a bounty doesn't do anything to solve that part of my problem. Not to mention ... what happens if the UGFS and the Denards find out that he mated me?" A lump formed in my throat. Ash really was like an STD, one that quite possibly could end up being the death of me.

"I'll do some more research. Let's deal with one problem at a time." Zula stood, and I trailed along after her so we could make the call to the ambassador.

A wave of shame threatened to drown me. I was supposed to be one of the best bounty hunters in the galaxy and Ash had bested me so easily. Now I was going to have to admit it publicly to someone who had the power to affect my career down the road. *Goodbye to any future UGFS contracts.*

As I stood in front of the screen waiting for Zula to make contact, I contemplated making a run for it like a friggin' child. *Maybe I should hide under the covers, too?* What the hell was happening to me? Since meeting Ash my entire world had been turned upside down. Or really ... I was feeling ... I was just feeling too much. And I didn't like it one bit.

My muscles coiled so tightly that my back ached by the time Ambassador Aralias appeared on the huge screen in front of me. I forced my lips into a smile and inclined my head slightly in greeting. "Ambassador Aralias."

"Do you have him?"

My eyes slid shut for a second before I met his eager

gaze. "No. In fact, I'm contacting you about the exclusivity contract. I'm going to have to terminate it. Ash ... well, we have no idea how to catch and contain him. We're officially out of leads, too. I've never dealt with a creature as ... as ... tricky as him before. I apologize for any inconvenience that this might have caused you. I would also like to—"

"You're supposed to be one of the best." Ambassador Aralias' features pinched tightly with unbridled anger. "You will bring Ash and that chip to me."

"Umm ... o-okay," I stammered. "It's not that I don't *want* to bring Ash to you and collect the price on his head but he's ... well, you know what he is, right?"

A muscle ticked in the ambassador's jaw. "We know what he is, yes."

"Okay, so unless you have any tips on how to catch and contain him, I really don't know what to tell you."

The screen flickered and went black. I glanced at Zula and she shrugged. "There's nothing wrong on our end," she offered after a moment of rechecking our settings.

"Did he just hang up on me?" Before I had the chance to ponder what that meant, the screen was suddenly filled with the ambassador's face again.

"Captain Wexis, I can offer you a way to retrieve the chip from Ash, and a way for you to collect on the bounty. We would have preferred to receive Ash alive for questioning, but under the circumstances, we're bendable on that point, like I previously stated."

I swallowed around the lump forming in my throat.

"You mean you want me to take him out and just bring you the chip?"

"Yes."

"But I don't know how to do that either. I know nothing about—"

"We shall provide you with the means to end Ash. A delivery will be made to your ship from a representative within the hour." The screen clicked off again and I stumbled over to my chair.

"Shit. What do I do now?"

"Isn't it obvious? You bring them Ash's dead body or you forfeit more than the bounty, Jane." Zula's tone lacked any emotion.

"You picked up on that, too?"

"It was hard to miss the underlining threat."

"What the hell is on that chip?" I slid my hands into my hair and tugged. Would I be able to kill Ash? I'd never taken someone's life in cold blood before. Even just the thought of Ash's lifeless body twisted my gut.

But it was now me or him, and I would do what I needed to survive. *I will always pick me.*

"It's probably best we don't know what's on that chip." Zula stood and left the room.

Despite everything, my curiosity was beyond piqued. "Well now I want to know more than ever what's on that damn chip," I mumbled to myself.

"WHAT IS IT?" I stared down at the bejeweled knife being presented to me by an official UGFS courier. I couldn't help but wonder why Ambassador Aralias hadn't made the trip himself. Not that I wasn't glad for the reprieve of having to deal with him in person again.

"I'm not sure." The courier then produced a small envelope with a UGFS seal on the back. "I was instructed to give the knife and this letter to you, that's it."

Zula reached for the knife at the same time I reached for the letter. "Thanks. Zula, how about seeing our guest out." I was already ripping open the envelope before Zula could respond.

"Yes, of course." She didn't let go of the knife, I noticed. Maybe she already knew what it was? Pulling the UGFS stationary out, I quickly scanned the letter.

Captain Wexis,

I have provided you with the means to deliver to me the creature known as Ash. The blade is an ancient and very valuable relic, and the only object known to have any effect on one such as Ash. Stab him in the heart with it when he's in his human form to complete the task.

I look forward to the completion of this job.

AA

Blinking rapidly, I struggled to process what I'd just read. Ambassador Aralias actually expected me to kill Ash. *Shit just got real.*

Zula snatched the letter from me when she returned, skimming it before handing it back to me. "I read about this set of daggers in the Galvraron archives. The metal is infused with something that attracts the essence of a phoenix. In other words, you stab Ash in the heart, and it will steal his flame, the thing that sustains a phoenix's life. Without his flame, a phoenix is no longer immortal."

Immortal? I gulped. Again, I couldn't help but wonder how being spliced with phoenix DNA would affect my lifespan. And did I have a flame? Suddenly I had the urge to step away from the blade. "How does it do that exactly? I mean, how does it steal the flame?"

Zula's lips twitched up, her eyes glittering with mischief. "It's magic."

I scowled. "Really? That's what you're going with—magic?"

"It's an age-old practice used to describe the unknown. I'm sure there's a scientific explanation, but no one is sure what it is. Therefore, I'm just going with magic."

"You have a twisted sense of humor. You know that, right?" For about the billionth time, I wondered if all Galvrarons shared Zula's weird sense of humor. I hoped it was just her, or that I never had to be around more than one of them at a time. That kind of non-humor humor was enough to drive anyone insane.

Zula studied the blade in her hands, turning it over slowly. "You're going to do it? You're going to kill Ash?"

"I don't have a choice, do I?" My chest tightened with a sense of foreboding. His blood wasn't something I wanted on my hands.

"You always have a choice. Always. You just have to be prepared to deal with the consequences."

I snorted. "Isn't that just the clincher, huh?"

"So what's the plan then?"

"I'll wait until he comes to me again and then I'll ... " How the hell was I going to be able to stab him when I couldn't even bring myself to say the words out loud? "You know ..." I wiggled my fingers. "So hand it over."

Zula extended her arm slowly and I snatched the blade away from her. My breath caught in my throat when the cool metal touched my skin. Without another word, I slunk off to my quarters. I couldn't help but feel like something on the bottom of someone's boots. Sure, I was a bounty hunter who would bring in practically anybody for a price. But cold-blooded murder? That was something I never thought I'd sink to.

Oh well ... I guess there's a first time for everything. Survival sometimes comes at the price of one's morals.

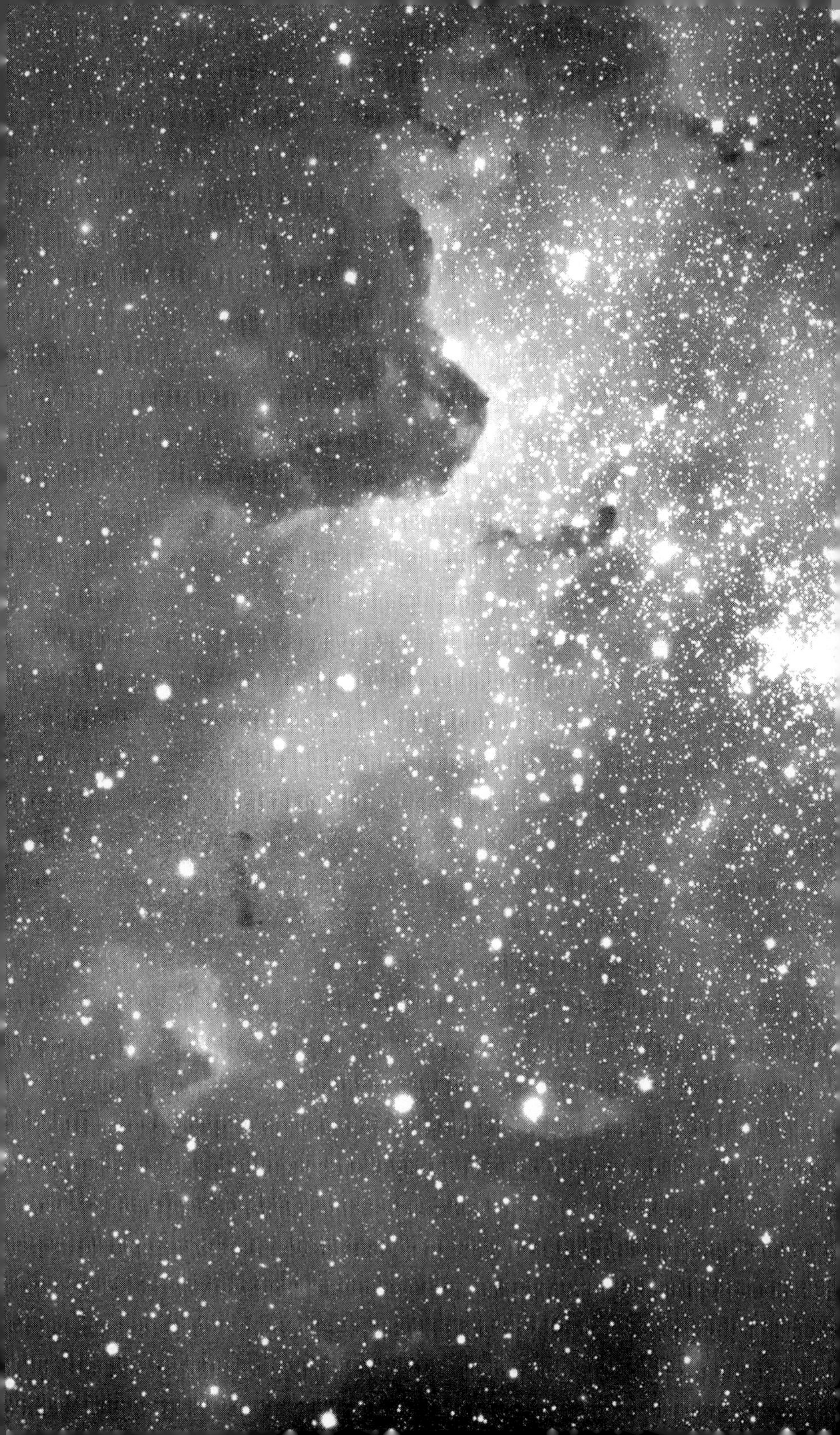

Chapter 16

It had been two grueling days since I'd received the means to kill Ash, and I hadn't heard anything from him. Not a dream, a whisper in my mind … nothing. Was there a possibility that he knew how I planned to betray him?

Betray him? I internally scoffed. I owed him no allegiance—no loyalty of any kind. Our pseudo relationship had only begun because I'd decided he was a hot piece of ass that I wouldn't mind taking for a spin before turning him over for the bounty on his head. It wasn't my fault he'd become infatuated with me. Just because you have sex with someone doesn't mean you're suddenly in a relationship.

"Zula!" I yelled into the intercom. "Are there any rules that say we can't take another bounty while we're waiting for the asshat to show up?"

"Yes," her voice buzzed back. "It's what's called an exclusive contract. It works both ways."

I slumped against the wall. "Great." I was a zeptosecond away from losing it. *I can't take the waiting. I just can't take it.* "Aaaaah!" I tipped my head back, screaming in frustration. "I wish I never laid eyes on him. Universe, you fucking owe me." I pressed the intercom again. "That's it. We need to stop at a supply space station ... or something. I can't take this for one second longer."

Tamzea seemed to just appear beside me. "Jane, do you want me to do something to help you?"

"Liiike what?" I slurred.

"Like sober you up. You've been hitting the firejuice hard for the past two days. Maybe—" She made a grab for the brightly colored bottle and I lurched to the side.

"No. What I need is to mingle with some people who are not on this ship. The non-judgmental kind."

"I don't think that's a good idea," Tamzea stated gently, still eyeing my bottle.

"Don't care. I'm the captain and I'll do what I want."

Tamzea perched her hands on her hips, her lavender eyes steeped in annoyance. "Yes, that sounded like the mature musings of a captain to me."

"Shut up." I hit the intercom. "Zula! We're stopping at the nearest space station port supply thingy!" *Wait, that's not right. Eh. Close enough.* I'm sure Zula could figure out what I meant with that big brain of hers. "That's an order!"

Tamzea shook her head, leaving me to my own devices when she exited in a huff. *Wise choice.*

I'D DONNED another outfit from my Earth Steampunk collection. This one was an all-leather pants and corset combo. I'd even taken the time to apply a full face of makeup. Hopefully, I didn't look like an Earth clown. The eyeliner had given me a bit of trouble, along with the lipstick ... and quite possibly the blush. *It's difficult doing your own makeup with a belly full of firejuice. Why have I never invested in one of those thingies that applied makeup for you? Oh yeah, because I hardly ever wear it. But still ...*

"Jane, please. I don't think you should go out in public in your condition." Tamzea worried her bottom lip between her teeth and wrapped her arms around her middle. Her lavender eyes beseeched me, but I turned the other way, ignoring her.

Dar and Masha lingered behind Zula, who was standing beside Tamzea with a scowl on her face. However, she was smart enough to remain silent. *Maybe she really is as intelligent as she claims.*

"If I'm not back in a few hours ... I'll be longer." I chuckled to myself.

I strode off The Pittsburgh, emerging in a supply space station. It was nothing special, the general appearance the same as all the supply space stations sanctioned by the UGFS.

I hastened towards the bar, the high-heeled boots and fuzzy vision combo making the trek a bit cumbersome. I got up close and personal with a few walls and the ground several times. And although my trip wasn't dignified, I did manage to reach my destination eventually.

Thank God. I need some more firejuice pronto because I think I'm starting to sober up. Stumbling for the counter, I poured myself into a bar seat.

"Jane," a familiar voice purred in my ear just as I'd managed to right myself.

"Jassen, you seriously are stalking me, aren't you?" I waved the bartender over, which wasn't a droid—a rare occurrence in a supply space station bar. I squinted up at the humanoid with orange scaly skin. "A firejuice." I slammed my palm down on the counter for effect.

"I think you've had enough," the bartender replied immediately.

"You've got to be fucking kidding me!" Leaning over the bar, I snagged the bartender's shirt. "I say when I've had enough, got that, buddy?" That's when a large hand palmed and then squeezed my ass. I stilled, shock rolling through my system before it was quickly replaced with anger. Releasing the bartender, I slowly turned around. "That better not have been you, Jassen." I ground my teeth together as I stared down at the large warrior who was still seated.

He grinned. *He seriously didn't just fucking grin at me.* "I couldn't help myself. It was right there in front of me begging for attention."

My chest constricted, all the frustration I'd been feeling for the past few days roaring through me. Before I made any conscious decision, I'd already launched myself at Jassen. I hit his stomach with my knees and his chest with my elbows. We toppled to the ground with me on top.

"Don't ever touch me without my permission," I hissed, sliding my hands up to encircle his throat. "You really don't want to mess with me right now."

Jassen's eyes darkened, and he reached up to cup my breasts. It took me much longer than it should have to process what was happening. My response was to bring my knees up to press into his chest as I dug my thumbs into the soft part on the front of his throat.

Jassen coughed, even as his lips hitched up at the corners. With one hand still around his throat, I slapped him as hard as I could across the face. *That should knock the smirk right off of him.* But it didn't make me feel as good as I'd hoped, so I decided to do it again ... and again, until I was hitting him with my fist instead of an open palm.

"Don't ever touch me without my permission again," I growled, while still beating Jassen's face. I knew I had to be right about him enjoying pain because I might have been drunk, but I wasn't stupid. If Jassen wanted to make me stop hitting him he could with ease. My skill set didn't lie in brute force, and I would never take down someone like him on my best day without using my weapons.

As I continued to pummel Jassen, venting my frustrations on his flesh ... warmth surged up my arms, and quickly morphed to heat only someone like me could bear. I watched in a dissociative state as flames erupted from my palms. Jassen screamed, throwing me off of him in the next heartbeat. My handprints were visible on him in the form of third-degree burns.

Jassen regarded me with wide-eyed terror, and I glanced around to see that the other patrons of the bar had suddenly given me a wide berth. "What the fuck, Jane?" Jassen croaked.

Pulling myself to my feet, I crossed my arms over my chest. "I told you not to touch me. Maybe now you'll listen."

Cursing loudly, Jassen hastily made his exit. I was guessing he was hightailing it to get medical treatment. If he got there fast enough maybe he wouldn't scar. Not that I cared. He should have listened to me when I'd said hands off.

I stumbled back over to the bar where the bartender gave me my firejuice ... finally. I slammed the whole thing down in one go.

"Since when do you have Class 3 capabilities?" yet another familiar voice asked in a sharp tone.

This one, though ... this one I hadn't heard in a very long time. Since I'd left New Earth to be exact. *Fuck me.* I was so not in the mood to deal with Maddox, my first and last real relationship. I thought I'd been in love with him until he turned his back on me when he found out I was only a Species Class 1.

"What the hell are you doing here, Maddox?

Slumming? The last I heard you were heading up the New Earth special ops task force. Protect and serve and all that bullshit."

He leaned over into my field of vision. His dark chocolate eyes narrowed in on me. "Why would you do it? Why would you keep something like that a secret?"

"It's new." I tried to ignore him as I waved my hand for another drink.

"Yeah, right." My arms were abruptly wrenched behind my back and laser cuffs clicked into place. "You know that I have to take you in, right? Hiding your true classification as a New Earth citizen is against the law."

"I'm not a New Earth citizen, remember? They didn't want me," I grated, as Maddox yanked me off of the stool and propelled me forward.

"We'll see about that. I should have known you'd try to shirk your responsibilities as a citizen." His fingers dug into my forearms painfully. "I'm taking you back so that—"

I really didn't hear what he said after the 'I'm taking you back' part. There was no way in hell I was ever going back to New Earth, and Maddox had no right to force me to. "If you don't let me go right now you're going to seriously regret it."

"I doubt that," Maddox snapped.

"You can't just kidnap me!" I screeched, twisting around in an attempt to bite him.

"You haven't changed one bit, have you?" Maddox's eyes flared with annoyance as he grappled with me. "I used to think it was cute when we were kids, but not so much now."

"Help!" I screamed. "Help! This man is trying to kidnap me!" Like I had a chance in hell that anyone in a place like this would do anything to help me. Unless—

"I'll pay anyone who helps me! I'm Captain Wexis of The Pittsburgh and I'm good for it!"

A chorus of chairs scraping on the floor stilled Maddox. We both looked up at the same time as almost everyone in the room ambled towards us in various states of intoxication. I grinned. "Should have let me go when you had the chance."

"Release the woman," a creature that resembled a big black slug commanded. I wasn't even sure he had a mouth, but I heard him speak clear as day.

"You think you're going to collect the reward?" a camo-colored humanoid who couldn't have been over four feet tall challenged.

"I'll wipe the floor with the two of you and still get to her before anyone else does," a mountain of a man with flesh-toned scales declared.

I've always had a sixth sense when it comes to bar brawls or just fights in general. It's a gift, really. And there was about to be a huge one at any moment. *Shit.* I hadn't thought that part of my plan through. I shook my head, trying to clear my vision. I was also still suffering from the effects of my firejuice binge. The truth was that I was lucky I was still functioning at all.

Maddox dragged me off just as my failed saviors began

beating the crap out of each other, the sounds of flesh meeting ... scales, and other various matter, meeting my ears. *Fabulous.* "I'm serious, Maddox. Let me go, now. I didn't hide anything from anyone and I'm not a New Earth citizen so you have no right to do this to me."

I twisted, kicked, and did everything in my limited power all the way to his ship. I would have burned him if I knew how I'd done it to Jassen. Fresh panic rose in me as his New Earth Cantrell grade ship loomed in front of me. "I'm not going back there, Maddox. I'm not!" I let myself become dead weight and I dropped to the ground. Once there, I rolled over on my back, trying to use my legs to fight him off. A few kicks later and I found myself flung over his broad shoulder. *He really has filled out since the last time I saw him.*

"No use fighting me, Jane," Maddox grunted. "I know all your tricks."

Really? I bet I still had a few he hadn't seen. Ash for one. *Desperate times call for desperate measures.* Ash was my mate, and we shared some kind of connection. I wasn't exactly sure of the extent, but weren't mates supposed to know when the other was in trouble or some shit like that? Or maybe that was just in the old romance novels I'd read from Earth. Either way, it was worth a try.

I closed my eyes and pictured Ash's handsome face in my mind. *"Ash ... can you hear me? Ash, I need your help."* I didn't get any kind of response. *"Please,"* I tacked on, just in case he was pissed at me or wanted me to beg. That was about as close to begging as I could get under any circumstances. After all … even drunk captains being carried over their ex-boyfriend's shoulder and hauled back to New Earth against their will should have some pride. "Aaaaasssh!" I hissed out loud.

"*Janey.*" Finally, his baritone voice slid across my mind, warming me. "*You think I'm going to drop everything to come rescue you when I know about the dagger? I know about everything.*"

"You can't just let him take me back there! You can't!"

"*I can. And I will.*"

"*I'm your mate!*" Wow. Had I really tried to use that card on him? What a joke. Unless it worked.

"*They won't kill you or cause any permanent harm—that kind of treatment I would stop. But I find I'm looking forward to you suffering a little bit, as long as your suffering is emotional only.*"

"Bastard!"

"*Maybe next time you'll reconsider when someone asks you to kill me,*" he spat. Okay, so he was pissed. "*If you're not free by the time I'm done with … my job, then I'll consider coming for you. Or at least telling your crew where you are.*" His deep chuckle resonated in my head, bouncing around and causing me to shiver despite myself.

Ash's words were still ringing in my head when a cell door slammed in my face. I was left with the soft hum of the security system and nothing else. I leaned over and puked all over the floor before passing out.

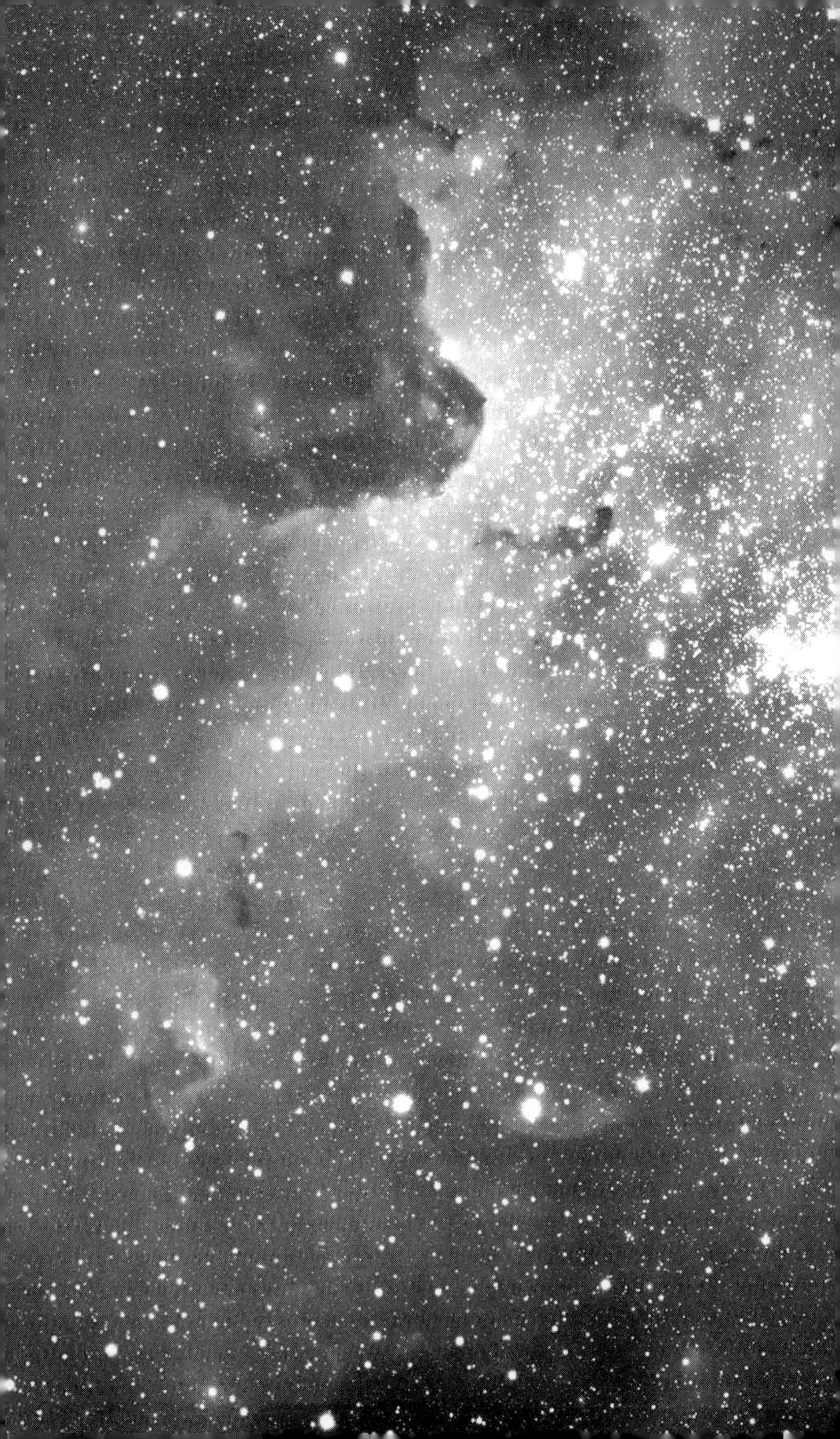

Chapter 17

Large, firm hands slid up my belly, pausing just under my breasts. I squirmed in an effort to continue them on their journey. "You want me to touch you?" Ash's deep voice tickled the side of my face and I arched towards him.

"Yes," I murmured.

But then it hit me ... I remembered his terse words, and how he'd let Maddox take me. I stumbled forward, breaking all skin-to-skin contact before whirling around to face him. "You think you can just waltz in here and try to seduce me after what you did?"

Ash's eyes blazed with a mixture of desire and anger. "You were planning to kill me."

I brought my arms up to cover my naked breasts. "Yeah, so? Maybe next time you'll think twice before mating someone against their will."

Ash was inches away from me in a flash, his hands

buried in my hair to hold me steady. "Sweetheart, you want everything I have to offer, even if you haven't let yourself acknowledge that fact yet."

"Arrogant asshat," I spat. "I don't want you, and I most certainly am not in any kind of denial."

"Liar." His lips twisted up into a smirk. He released my hair only to grab my hips. He held me steady as he ground himself into me. My breath hitched and I tried to stifle a moan ... very unsuccessfully.

"Me being physically attracted to you means nothing. I would have probably let you fuck me long and hard before I plunged that blade into your heart."

I wanted to hurt him, to piss him off as much as he had me. The thing that worried me, though, was that if I wanted to hurt him on that level ... did that mean his refusal to save me from Maddox had wounded me emotionally? And if that part was true, did that mean I was starting to care?

"Well then ... I guess I'm going to have to fuck you so long and so hard that you can't imagine ever being with anyone else ever again. When I'm done you won't be able to bear the thought of a life without me."

"Puuh-lease. You're good, but not that good."

"You already think about me when you don't want to. How many more times do you think it'll take before your want turns to true need? After all, I do have the mating process working on my behalf." He cupped my ass roughly and buried his face in my neck, inhaling deeply. "And I'll start—"

Loud banging shot me straight up, breaking me out of my apparent dream. I had officially lost the ability to tell the difference between reality and dream state with Ash.

"Wake up, Jane," Maddox's angry voice assaulted my ears. My head was pounding and nausea punched through my stomach.

I glanced up to see that Maddox had a large handheld gong in his hands. "Seriously? Whaaa—whyyyy?" I cradled my head and dropped my face down between my knees.

He set down his instrument of torture and addressed me. "If I give you something to cure your hangover will you take it?"

"I don't know. Will it kill me?"

"No," he snapped.

"Then probably not."

Metal on metal sounded as Maddox pulled a chair up close to my cell. "We need to talk."

"Nope. Well ..." I raised my head slightly to study my ex-boyfriend for a moment. He was broader and more muscular than the last time I'd seen him. Which made sense since it'd been years. He still had the same square jaw and high cheekbones, but his hair was cut into a short buzz as opposed to the longer floppy do he'd sported when we were younger. He looked every inch the New Earth soldier in his all-grey fatigues adorned with the colorful insignia patch on his chest. He was familiar, and yet a stranger. It was nice to know for sure, once and for all, that I felt nothing for him anymore. *Maybe that has something to do with Ash?* "How about just letting me go?"

"You broke the law, Jane."

Pulling myself into a sitting position, I regarded Maddox with blatant disdain. "No, I didn't. The whole fire palms thing is new."

Which now that I was awake and sober ... yeah, it kind of freaked me out. I mean, where the hell did it come from? It had to do with mating with Ash, it was the only possibility. Did the mate bond trigger innate phoenix-y powers, or was I somehow borrowing them from Ash because of the bond? Hell, I had no idea what a full-blooded phoenix could do except turn into flames. Now I had no idea what I was capable of either.

Maddox scowled at me, the hard lines of his expression making him appear much older than he really was. "You expect me to believe that?"

"Yeah, actually I do. Why would I have hidden something like that back when all I wanted," I leaned forward, perching my elbows on my knees, "was to be with you? Being Class 1 alienated me from everything I knew and loved."

He turned away from me, the muscles in his jaw feathering. "You're the one who left so suddenly. Just because—"

"You broke things off with me, and my parents decided I should be on my own, so, I what? Should have stuck around? Begged for scraps of love and attention?" Bitterness dripped from my tone. "Nothing about me changed that day. I just failed a stupid test."

Maddox stood and began to pace. "It wasn't a stupid

test—" He abruptly changed his path and came to stand directly in front of my cell, his face practically touching the bars. "If you didn't hide it then explain to me where the hell that little ability came from."

Staring at Maddox the man, I saw little to no traces of the boy I used to love ... or thought I'd loved. He was harder and ... jaded. His eyes held the look of someone who had seen too much, too quickly, and too soon in life. But that's what New Earth did to its people. It chewed them up and spit them out, sucking dry every bit of perceived usefulness from them.

Maddox was a Class 2. He could throw up an impenetrable force field around himself and sometimes one or two other people if they were close enough. It was what made him perfect for his job as a New Earth special ops agent. He could go in and do all the dirty work he needed with almost no risk to himself. He was born to be a soldier.

"What's wrong?" I taunted. "Jealous because I'm a Class 3 and you're just a Class 2?"

I couldn't help but press on that big red button. Maddox had been devastated when he'd tested out as only a Class 2. Special ops hadn't been where he'd wanted to end up. Special ops was a misleading term for their branch of New Earth soldiers. There was nothing special about them, unlike where they had originated in Earth history. I'd read that special ops used to be a coveted position in the military. Only the best of the best were a part of the regime. Now The New Earth First Wave was the job that all young New Earth boys dreamt about. Being a part of them not only meant top pay, but the chance for action and adventure. Maddox had been like every other little boy on New Earth with his desire to be part of the First Wave.

"Tell me where the hell it came from," he growled through clenched teeth.

I leaned back on my elbows to recline, regarding him with cool indifference. My head was still pounding but it was more manageable than it had been a few minutes ago. "What if I told you I wasn't sure?"

He hit the bars with the palms of his hands, producing a reverberating metallic sound. I cringed. "Then I would say I think you're full of shit, and I'm hauling you straight back to New Earth where they'll drag the answers out of you."

"Think what you want, but I don't owe you any explanations." My stubbornness had reared its ugly head. I knew I was cutting my nose off to spite my face by not at least attempting to make him understand the truth. But I didn't want to talk to him anymore. "You can leave me alone now." I waved my hand dismissively, turning away from him.

"Things have changed on New Earth." Maddox's voice dipped to a low rumble. "They won't merely question you, you know."

My nostrils flared and my stomach knotted, but I still refused to look at him. "What's that supposed to mean?"

"It means they'll poke, prod, and test you to get

answers. And they'll do *whatever* they deem necessary to get those answers about your ability. They'll want to know how they can duplicate it ... unless you can provide those answers for them."

Squeezing my eyes shut, I gritted my teeth to keep from responding to him. I wasn't sure I believed him, but there was a possibility that what he said was true. The gift of firepower would be a sought-after Class 3 result that the scientists on New Earth would want to duplicate in other offspring. The problem was ... I really didn't know where it came from or how powerful it was. For all I knew it was a one-time thing. Maybe I fizzled out already.

"Fine, Jane. I guess we'll just have to do it the hard way ... as always."

The lights dimmed to a soft glow and the main door slammed as Maddox left me alone with my thoughts. Not good since my mind turned to my parents and one of the last times I'd seen them.

As soon as I'd come home, I spotted the line of silver garbage bags on my parent's front porch. A sick feeling settled in my gut. I'd just gotten my results for the Species Classification and had been dreading even the thought of telling my father my disappointing results. It seemed as if there was more in store for me besides letting him down.

Before I could swipe my key card, the front door swung open and my father stepped out, his arms crossed over his chest. He wasn't a big man, but what he lacked in size he had always made up for with intimidation. My mom demurely followed in his wake.

Clearing my throat, I fidgeted nervously. "What's going on?"

"It's time for you to be on your own, Jane," *my father stated simply, as if it was the most obvious thing in the world.*

Blinking rapidly, I tried to process his words. They made sense intellectually, but emotionally? Not so much. "I was planning on moving out when—"

"We can't afford to support you anymore. Maybe if you would have pulled in an income from training ... but with you being a Class 1 you're not worth anything."

"John!" *my mother hissed.*

"What? It's true. Without her bringing in a paycheck then we can no longer afford to take care of her."

"I c-can get a job. I was going to move out soon to be with Maddox. I just need a few weeks ... a few days even." *Tears burned the corners of my eyes but I refused to let them fall.* "I'm your daughter! Don't you care what happens to me?"

My father had already turned to go back inside when my mother approached me. "It'll be okay, Jane. You know I love you, right?"

I nodded numbly. At least I thought she and my father loved me. I wasn't so sure anymore. Had I always just been a future paycheck or some kind of possession they could be proud of? I didn't understand how one little test could turn them from me so quickly. It was as if they were completely different people from a few hours ago. "I'll just go to Maddox, it'll be fine. I'll come back for my stuff later.

It hadn't been fine. When I'd gone to Maddox he'd broken things off with me. I'd been so upset that I'd shot him in the arm. I still wasn't sure how things had escalated to that point, though.

Later when I'd gone to retrieve some of my things they'd all been gone, probably incinerated with the evening's trash. I'd broken down right there in the street, begging for my parents to take me in because I had nowhere to go—no money and no possessions. My father had threatened to have me arrested if I didn't get off his property. That night I'd stolen away on a ship, leaving for destinations unknown. I didn't care where I ended up as long as it was as far away from New Earth as possible.

More memories washed over me, blackening my mood further. I hated that I'd let those people hurt me, that I'd let myself be vulnerable. All I'd wanted was love and I ... choking back a sob, I curled into a tight ball. *I won't let my past hurt me anymore. I won't.* But despite my best efforts, the memories continued to assault me, ratcheting up my self-loathing with each one.

At some point, I finally fell asleep.

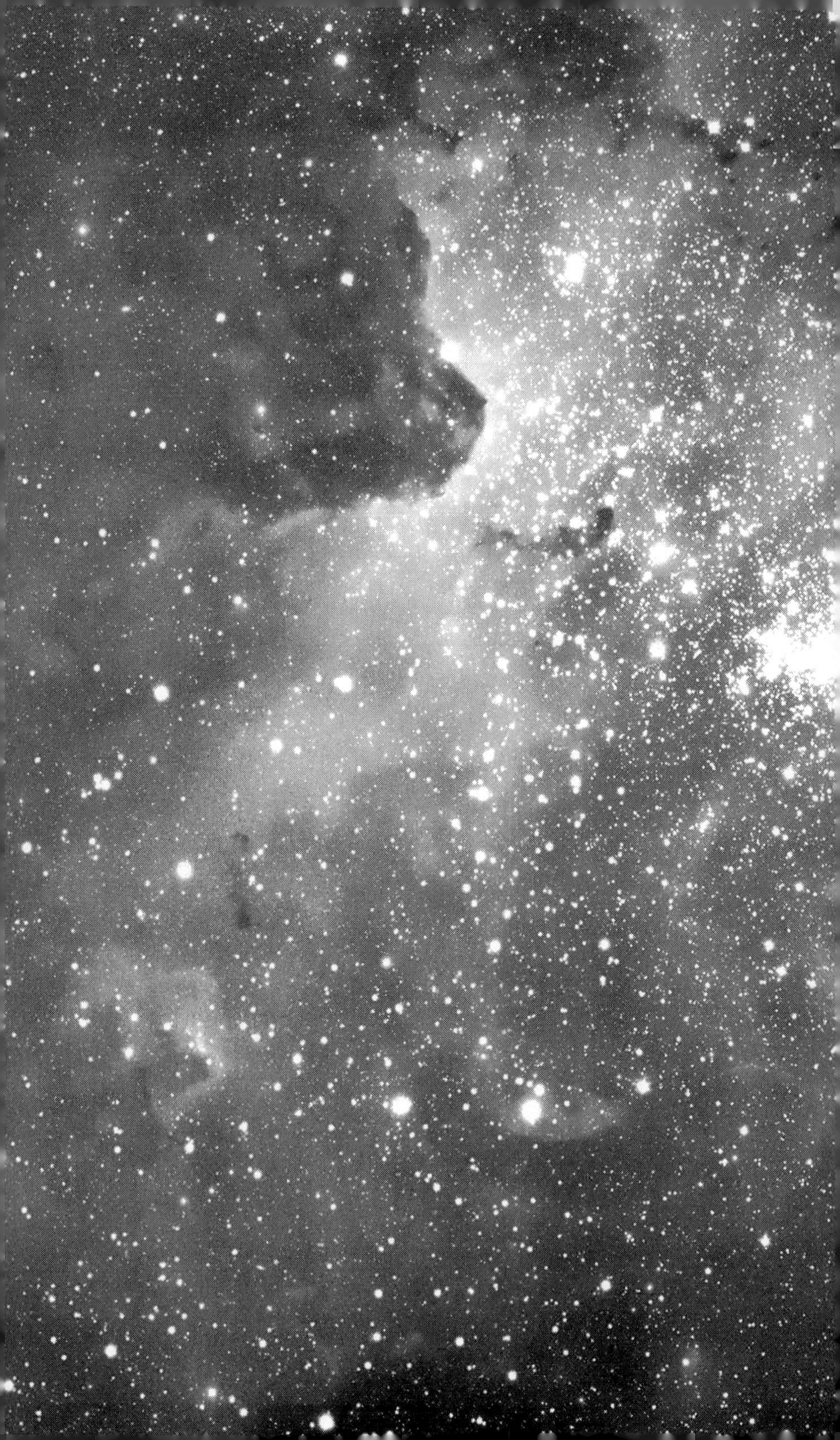

Chapter 18

"What the hell?" I sputtered, as a cascade of ice water hit my face. That's when I realized I was no longer in a cell on Maddox's ship. I was restrained in a reclining chair in a type of room that was all too familiar to me from my time on New Earth. A middle-aged scientist stood before me in a white lab coat.

Eyeing him with hostility, I bared my teeth. He merely spoke into his recording device. "Subject is awake. Questions will be followed with measures suited to answers." He lifted his gaze to regard me with cold detachment. "Please state your name for the record."

"I'm relatively sure you've already been informed of my name," I grated.

"Subject is being difficult," he said into his device.

"I'm not a subject, I'm a fucking human being!" Or at least part human. "And you have no right to detain me.

I'm not a citizen of New Earth. Maddox basically kidnapped me!" I struggled to get free, but the high-grade laser restraints didn't budge. Not that I'd expected them to, but I wasn't just going to lie there all complacent.

The door behind the scientist slid open and two others in lab coats joined him—one was a young female, and the other was a male who looked barely out of diapers. They both regarded me with the same cold detachment as the first scientist. "The subject is being difficult. I'm going to forgo the rest of the questions and move straight into the testing."

"Oh, hell no!" I screeched. "You people just can't kidnap me and then experiment on me without any consequences." The trio ignored me, like I wasn't even there, and busied themselves gathering various materials from cabinets around the room.

A tray with surgical instruments was wheeled right next to me. I trembled, my heart thrashing against my ribcage. "You can't do this to a non-citizen!"

My eyes widened as a huge needle filled with a greenish fluid was picked up by scientist number one. "I-I-I'm under contract with the UGFS!" I yelled. "Contact Ambassador Aralias! If you keep me from doing my job you're all going to be in big trouble!"

Why hadn't I thought to name-drop before? Of course, if they did contact the ambassador, I ran the risk of exposing my bond to Ash. Not the best plan, since I was sure that little detail wouldn't go over very well with him.

But then again ... I could lie my ass off. *I just have to think up a decent one first.*

The scientist trio was currently murmuring to each other, and I watched them intently, hoping they'd contact the ambassador before they decided to get needle happy with me. After all, it was not on my bucket list to become a pincushion.

The female scientist left the room and the other two busied themselves with more tasks that set me on edge. I attempted to steady my breathing and slow my heartbeat, but it was impossible with the pungent smell of chemicals assaulting my nose, and tons of shiny, pointy things being waved around.

The door slamming open stole everyone's attention. Maddox strode in, muscles rigid, and a pissed-off expression plastered on his face. "Is it all a big joke to you? You're on a job for the UGFS and you're just now mentioning it? Or is it another one of your lies?"

"I don't understand where all your hostility towards me is coming from." Okay, so I'd shot him once. But that was eons ago. *Get over it already.* It just served to illustrate how I always wore my heart on my sleeve. "When did I ever lie to you?" My face heated as anger washed over me. "And I didn't think to mention it because you have no right to take a non-New Earth citizen! I didn't think any of this would go so far!" I roared at the top of my lungs.

And what the hell was up with Ash? He said he wouldn't let anything physically bad happen to me. I was about to be experimented on and tortured, and I hadn't heard a peep from him. *So much for depending on my new mate ... who I barely know anything about.* I laughed darkly to myself, the sound demented even to my ears. *Just goes to prove that I can't trust anyone.*

"I always keep my word." Ash's voice glided through my mind just as a gigantic fireball exploded through the door, blazing into the room. The two scientific amigos exited as quickly as their legs could carry them, the younger male scientist screaming like a teenage girl.

Maddox threw up a shield to protect himself, completely unconcerned whether I was burnt alive because he had no clue that I could withstand any grade of fire. Clearly, he was only worried about himself. Would it have killed him to stand close enough to shield me, too? Apparently, there was none of the boy from my childhood left behind, not even a scrap of sentimentality. *I'll remember that asshat.*

Ash dashed into the room in his human form, snapping my restraints in mere seconds. He then scooped me up in his arms, shifting to his fire form. As we zoomed through the air, me weightless and cocooned in flame, something deep inside of me cracked open, spreading warmth through not only my body but my soul. Before I could contemplate what any of it meant, exhaustion weighed me down, stealing my consciousness from me completely.

WHEN I WOKE UP, I expected to be on Ash's ship or at least to have him close by ... But instead, I found myself in my living quarters on The Pittsburgh with my crew crowded in around me.

I guess Ash is still pissed at me.

Lifting my head, I swept my gaze over everyone ... I blinked. Correction: I was surrounded by my crew, plus Dar. Or maybe he was a part of my crew now? Had I picked up an official new member without knowing it? I shook my head and willed myself to focus. I was feeling a bit ... off.

"What happened?" I groaned, pressing my fingertips into my temples.

"Why do you never listen to me?" Zula demanded, her hands on her hips. "I told you not to go off ship completely out of your mind on firejuice. Even I hadn't expected for you to go and get yourself Jane-napped. We—"

"Had no idea where you were or what happened to you," Tamzea finished for Zula. Her face was scrunched up with anxiety, causing guilt to gnaw at my gut. I didn't want to be the source of her getting ulcers later in life. Unless ... could healers internally heal themselves? I'd have to ask her about that. *I can't believe I never considered that before.*

I sat up slowly and the room tilted a bit on its axis. "Look, I— Where's Ash?"

Zula flung her hands up in the air. "After everything the first thing you ask about is him?"

"Technically second," I grumbled. "I did ask what happened first."

Masha and Dar backed slowly out of the room, and when I glanced over at them they both spared me a shy smile. At least they seemed to only want to know if I was okay. Zula and Tamzea could take lessons from them. Maybe having Dar onboard wasn't such a bad deal after all.

"Tell us why you were taken to New Earth." Tamzea sat on the edge of the bed and Zula remained standing, her glare burning into me with the heat of a thousand suns.

"Ash didn't tell you anything?"

"No. He just appeared with you and disappeared again," Zula replied, annoyance lacing her tone.

"Oooh ... so the not knowing part is driving you crazy." I laughed. "But wait, how did you guys know at all about me being taken to New Earth?"

Zula scrunched her nose. "We questioned some of the ... riff-raff from the bar you were at."

"Riff-raff?" I laughed again. "That must have been a sight to see. I'm sorry I missed it."

"Just tell us what happened," Zula demanded.

I rolled my eyes. "Okay, okay ... "

I gave them the abbreviated version of what happened to me while I was gone, conveniently leaving out any unnecessary parts including Ash. When I was done, Zula fell deep in thought, her brow furrowed, and Tamzea wrung her hands, her nerves ratcheted up further by my adventurous tale.

"What are you going to do now?" Tamzea shifted uneasily, fiddling with her braided hair. "No matter what you do, I— How did you even end up in this situation?"

"She couldn't keep her damn legs closed, that's how," Zula stated absentmindedly, the majority of her attention still elsewhere. But before I could ream her out for trying to slut shame me ... yet again, she jumped to her feet with her eyes blazing. "We need to find out what's on that chip. It's the only answer."

"How did you arrive at that conclusion?" Could Galvrarons have mental breakdowns? Had I finally driven her to lose control of that big brain of hers? "I thought you said it was better if we didn't know what was on that chip."

"Things have changed."

"Okaaay ... And how exactly do you suggest we get a look at the info on the chip? You want me to just explain things to Ash and ask him to share whatever he's hiding?"

Zula tapped her chin, and Tamzea flicked her gaze back and forth between the two of us. "Yes, that doesn't seem like such a bad idea."

I snorted. "In case you forgot... Ash is helluva pissed at me. You really think he's going to come here when I have that blade?"

"Yes, I do actually."

I pointed dramatically at her. "You have lost it!"

Zula pressed her lips into a thin line. "No, I haven't. He did come to save you, after all. Just contact him. Explain to him what you want."

"No need." Ash's voice caused all three of us to jump as he appeared in the doorway. Giving me a cocky half grin, he leaned against the wall, arms crossed. "Well, I'm here. Let the groveling begin."

I pulled myself to my feet, slowly letting my gaze travel the length of him. From the first moment I'd laid eyes on him I'd been struck with an instant physical attraction. Unfortunately for me ... he seemed to be growing more attractive with each second I spent with him. He didn't even have the type of features that most women would find appealing, but he exuded the kind of raw sex appeal that made me want to climb him like an insane ape. Maybe it was the mate process at work, or perhaps it was that intangible thing that made certain people more attractive the longer you knew them, and others less so. Either way ... Ash couldn't be more appealing to me if he tried.

Ash's gaze met mine, flames swirling in their golden depths. "Now, Janey, it's not the most appropriate time for you to be undressing me with your eyes."

My face flushed. "I'm doing no such thing." I forced myself to look away from him. "And stop calling me Janey."

"I like Janey."

"Well, I don't."

"All right, Janey. You've let your feeling be known about it, Janey. I'll certainly take them into consideration, Janey."

Was I just pondering how attractive he is? Oops. I meant to consider how much of an asshat he is. I don't want to have sex with him, I want to smack that stupid face of his. "Why don't you just—"

"Jane," Zula said my name tersely, "talk to him about what's on the chip instead of continuing your New Earth first-grade level argument."

"Right." I dipped my gaze towards my boots while winding an errant strand of dark hair around my finger. "So, Ashby, care to share with us what's so important that no one finds out about?"

"Ashby?" He chuckled. "Call me whatever you want, sweetheart, as long as you're screaming it while I'm inside of you later."

My head whipped up, my eyes widening. "Uh-uh. Nope. Not happening. We're not having sex ever again and we're going to find a way to dissolve the mate bond. I just want to know how to get me and my crew out of the almost impossible situation we're in."

"Jane!" Zula hissed. "Give him whatever he wants for the information we need."

I whirled towards Zula my mouth hanging open. "You're suggesting I whore myself out for information? That's what your ginormous brain came up with?" I cursed under my breath. "You've got to be kidding me!"

Ash inclined his head, rumbling, "She seems pretty smart to me."

"I'm not whoring myself out to you!" My voice reached almost ultrasonic levels.

Ash was inches away from me before I could blink. He

captured my face with his large hands. "There's a big difference between being a mate and a whore."

Shoving at his chest, I managed to put a bit of much needed space between us. "You make me absolutely crazy, you know that? Nothing makes any kind of sense when you're around! And I just ... just— Why won't you leave me the hell alone?" Frustration wound its way through every cell in my body, and I fought the urge to simply throw my head back and scream. Mostly because I only partly wanted him to leave me alone. The other part ... well, the other part wanted to chain him to my bed.

Ash's eyes were completely consumed with flames. "Ladies, how about leaving me alone with your captain so we can come to some kind of agreement."

Tamzea rose from her perch on the end of my bed and moved quickly towards the door. Zula had to comment before her departure ... of course. "I have the blade, in case you were wondering, Ash. Jane is completely helpless against you."

My mouth dropped open once again, and I stared at the betrayer in complete disbelief. "That's it! I'm finding a new second in command as soon as this is all over!" It was the only thing I could think of to say to her. Plus— "Smurfette!"

When both of my traitorous crew members were gone, Ash stalked towards me. "We have a lot to talk about."

I inched back and kept going until I found myself pressed against the wall. Ash raised his arms to cage me with his large body. Inhaling a deep breath, I realized my mistake as I became immersed within his delectable scent.

My throat went dry and my knees weakened.

Despite my tenuous situation, I notched my chin up to glare at him. "Yeah, so start talking."

And he did.

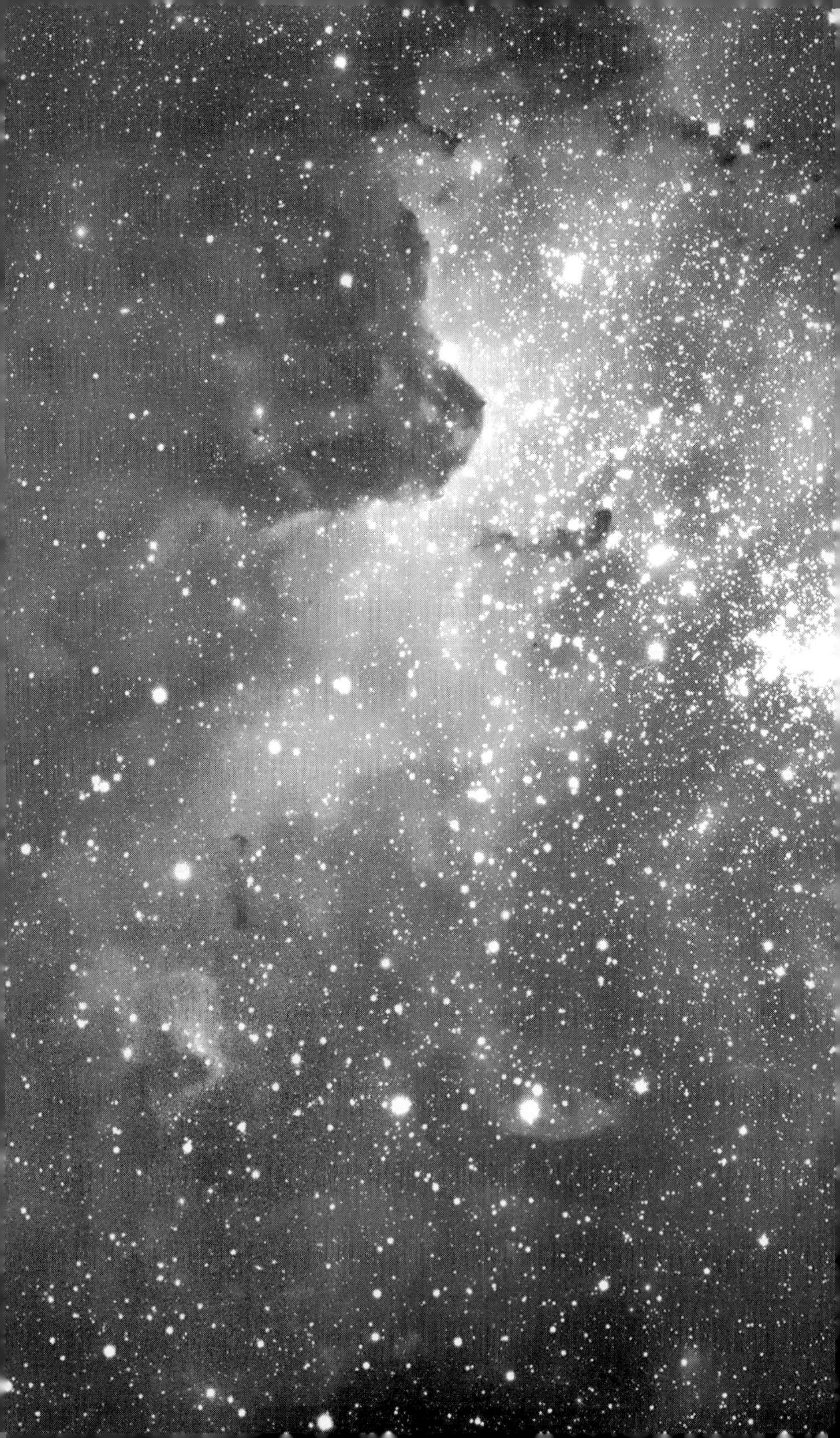

Chapter 19

"What good do you think it'll do to know what's on that chip? You think you'll be able to blackmail the UGFS?"

Hmmm ... I hadn't considered what I would do with the information from said chip, but now that Ash brought it up, blackmail didn't sound like such a bad idea. Maybe I could force Ambassador Aralias to leave me alone. "I don't know, maybe blackmail is the way to go."

Why the hell does my voice sound so husky? Just because Ash is standing so close doesn't mean I have to act like some kind of cat in heat. I'm a strong, independent woman who is in control of my own body.

"I wouldn't suggest it if you don't want to get yourself and your entire crew killed."

"The UGFS wouldn't ..." Ash's raised eyebrows caused me to falter. "Well, they wouldn't be able to just kill us. They'd have to answer to—"

"To who?" Ash challenged. "Let me break it down for you. The UGFS can do pretty much whatever it wants and it has been for a long time." His fingers whitened as he pressed them against the wall. "If I would have accepted that earlier then maybe I wouldn't be one of the last of my kind."

"What?" I shook my head. "No. The Denards are the ones who killed off the phoenix."

"And who do you think runs the UGFS? Why do you think the UGFS was formed around the same time that so many species were banding together to protect themselves? The Denards decided it would be easier if they made the public believe they were safe ... protected under a united government that had everyone's best interests at heart. It would just make what they were doing easier."

Ash's chest heaved as his eyes glazed over, his thoughts going elsewhere. Scrutinizing him, the realistic dream slash potential memory rose to the forefront of my mind. "I-I had this dream. It was about your ... sister and niece." I swallowed, nerves suddenly riding me hard. I was blunt and sometimes clueless, but I, at least, attempted not to be heartless, and if what I'd dreamt was true ... I didn't want to bring up such painful things just for the sake of it. But I needed to know if I'd made the whole thing up or not.

"Was that ... was that what happened? Did the Denards attack without warning?"

"The dream memories have started for you, too.

Good." He pushed off the wall and started pacing. I heaved a sigh of relief, even though I simultaneously felt bereft without his body heat. "And yes, we never knew what triggered the attacks. Hell, we still don't. But that's the way the Denards work. They hate and they destroy. But they do seem to have a special kind of hatred for any being that originated on Earth. After all, they're the ones who destroyed it."

I snatched at his arm, forcing him to look at me. "That's not possible! The history books say—"

His lips tipped up in a sad smile, stealing my words. "Haven't you figured it out yet? History is always written by the victors. Most Earth creatures didn't survive. They'll never be able to tell their tale or speak their truth. As for those that lived ... the Denards have systematically been picking us off. New Earth is somewhere on that list, I can guarantee it. And the elders of New Earth know it, too. Why do you think the focus has changed so much towards creating more Class 3s?"

I opened my mouth to protest Ash's claims, but my focus swerved off the dark topics of species genocide and the UGFS towards something I could easily wrap my mind around. "Phoenixes are from Earth? Is that what you meant by being there firsthand, and about history?"

My curiosity was officially piqued. And Ash had no reason to lie to me, or it at least seemed like he believed what he was saying. Plus, it fit in with what Dar mentioned about both the UGFS and the Denards. I'd brushed what Dar told me under the rug, even though it was similar to what Ash was saying. But now … now I had to admit, it made sense. It all made complete sense.

"Yes, I was born and lived many happy years on Earth. In fact, most fire species can trace their origins back to Earth."

An irresistible grin stretched my lips wide, glee simmering within me. As it turned out, both sides of my DNA were linked to Earth. Maybe my obsession wasn't so ridiculous after all. There was still much to consider though. "So what's on the chip, Ash? And what exactly were you planning to do with it?"

He resumed his pacing, tension evident in his stiff shoulders and furrowed brow. "This galaxy—hell, all of the galaxies—they all need to know the truth about the UGFS. There are plans and records on that chip. I'm going to make sure that information—the information that reveals exactly what the UGFS is actually about—gets out to the masses. United we stand and divided we fall. Ever hear or read that old Earth saying? The only chance the majority of us have in the long run is to band together like we started to do before the rise of the UGFS."

I swallowed around the lump in my throat. "If you're caught they'll put you to death."

Ash stilled and then turned towards me slowly. His eyes burned into mine, flames dancing within them. "There's no doubt about it."

"So why did you do it? Why did you put yourself on

the line when you could have kept hiding like you've been doing? You could have lived out a long and happy life."

"Because whenever I think about my niece and how her life was cut tragically short I just—" He bowed his head, jaw muscles jumping as he ground his teeth together. "I need to make sure it doesn't happen to any other children out there, no matter their species. I need to save more than just my own life."

"You're talking about starting some kind of revolution or uprising. Things will—"

He grabbed me around the waist, tugging me into him. I gasped in surprise. "Things will get a lot worse before they get better. And hopefully when the smoke clears ..." His golden gaze bore into mine once more. "Maybe I'll have the mate I've always dreamt of by my side."

My heart went into overdrive, doing a tap dance that echoed inside my skull. "I'm a bounty hunter, not a revolutionary or a rebel. I just want to live my own life. I just want to find some happiness wherever I can. And I have ... or I did before you came along and fucked it all up."

Ash's lips came to hover a hair's breadth from mine, his spicy flavor rolling down my throat and up my nose. "You weren't really happy, Janey. Stop lying to yourself. I felt the vast emptiness in you. The emptiness that every phoenix feels until they find their mate—their twin flame."

My fingers dug into his shoulders, and I wasn't sure if I was pulling him to me or pushing him away. "How many times do I have to remind you that I'm only part phoenix? I'm human, too."

"And how many times do I have to remind you that you're phoenix enough?"

"Phoenix enough for what exactly? The bond? The mark on my back? The—"

"For this." White-hot flame enveloped us when his lips slammed down on mine. I cried out as the heat stripped all sense of self—all sense of who I thought Jane Wexis was. No more did my past pain or current confusion define me. I was phoenix, and from pain and torment, I could and would be reborn stronger, smarter, and wiser. The man whose arms I was wrapped in—he was my mate—my other half. Together we would burn our brightest. Together we would rise from the ashes over, and over, and over again.

"Yes, Janey, yes. Give yourself over to our flame. It will heal and show you the way," Ash murmured against my skin, his scorching lips trailing down my neck.

Gripping his hair, I yanked him away from me, only to throw him to the ground. I growled some nonsensical things, my thoughts fragmented. My focus narrowed down to only him and the flame that surrounded us. The tendrils of fire were a loving caress—a soothing balm, and an inciter of my passion all rolled into one. I was happy, and at peace, and I allowed myself to let go—to be consumed by the flame ... and Ash. After all, they were one and the same.

IT WAS impossible to deny the dramatic shift in my feelings towards Ash anymore. It was official ... I cared about him. He'd gotten under my skin so quickly and so thoroughly. And as I lay with my head on his chest, nestled in his arms, I found myself wondering about him. I actually wanted to get to know him as more than a fuck. It was the first time for that kind of interest in any man since Maddox, and I'd been a doe-eyed teenager when I'd been in that relationship.

"What's between us, what I'm feeling towards you, it's the mate bond, isn't it?" I lazily circled my fingertips over his smooth chest. The last few hours had been a blur of carnal pleasure. The aftermath left me sore and tired, and yet strangely satiated on more than a physical level. It was something I'd never experienced before.

"Partly," Ash rumbled. "It merely speeds along a connection that would develop naturally."

"Speeds along? I'd say that's an understatement." The bond had pried open the doors to my heart and left me vulnerable. Did I love Ash? I didn't know, but I also didn't think it was impossible. What I felt for him was something I couldn't quite define yet. "Do you love me?" Yeah, it would be lightning fast but something else I couldn't deny ... I wanted him to say yes. I wanted to know what it felt like to have someone be powerless against loving me. I secretly craved the kind of love that all species spoke of, the kind that was envied by one and all. Or at least anyone with a soul.

Ash's large hand ignited my nerve endings as it slid down my back to rest possessively on my ass. "Maybe." I could hear the smile in his voice. He knew what I wanted him to say and he was denying me just to be a jackass.

I levered myself up so I could glare down at him. His golden eyes twinkled mischievously. "Maybe? It's a yes or no type of question."

"What is love? How can one define it? Can you?"

I opened my mouth to give him a witty retort but then snapped it shut. Did I actually know how to define love? Probably not. "You tell me then, Mr. Smarty Pants."

Ash grinned. "I really don't know. Is it when you can't stop thinking about someone? Is it when you always wonder what they're doing even when you're not with them? Is it the all-encompassing passion you feel when having sex with them? Is it the warmth that blooms in your chest when they're around? Or maybe it would be the fact that you would give your life to save theirs?" He paused for a moment, his eyes glazing over. "There are all different kinds of love. How can any one person define what love is?"

I exhaled slowly as I let his words roll through my mind. "I guess you can't. Or I can't."

"But I want you." Ash tugged me down to his chest, palming my head to keep me against him snuggly. "And I want to keep you. I wouldn't have mated you if I didn't feel that way."

I nipped at his chest. "So maybe you do love me? Or maybe you need more time for love to develop?"

"How can one say how much time is needed to cultivate an intangible emotion such as love? I think love can happen in an instant."

"Well, aren't you all deep with this love stuff?" I laughed. "I never would have thought you had so much going on inside that thick skull of yours."

"I've been alive a very long time. Which means I've had plenty of opportunities to ponder such things. Trust me, when I was a young phoenix living on Earth … there wasn't much going on in here." He tapped his index finger against his temple. "I think all the blood flowed straight to my—"

"Sssh. Don't say it." I giggled. "I think I get the point. Have you been with a lot of women? How many phoenixes and how many Earthwomen? What about other species? And I'm still waiting for you to tell me all about Earth."

I was rambling because of how excited I was to hear about Earth. And I was happy to live in the temporary bubble Ash and I had created. I knew there was a lot of stuff we had to deal with and soon, but I wanted to enjoy all the new emotions to their fullest while I had the chance. It wasn't like me to be so reckless with my heart, and I wanted to get lost in that carefree feeling completely. Plus, the truth was that Ash may not be alive for very much longer if he followed through with his plans. That thought twisted my insides with dread, so I pushed it aside, deciding to focus on the positive for the moment. There was no point in looking to the future when the now was probably a much better place.

Ash flipped me over and pushed my arms above my head. Goose bumps rose on my flesh from contact with the cold metal floor. We incinerated nearly everything in my living quarters besides what was protected by the Gartian grade alloy. Thank God my clothes were safely hidden away in the closet. Because with the look Ash was giving me, the metal I was pressed against wouldn't be cool for very much longer.

"I'll tell you all about Earth after." He dipped his head to steal a chaste kiss from me.

I frowned. "What about the women? Are you going to be one of those guys who skirts around telling me what your number is? I have no problem sharing mine."

It was Ash's turn to frown. "I don't want to know about your past. We all have one, but I don't want to think about you with other men. You're mine now."

"I guess I'm just weird. I want to know."

"I've been with many women, but I haven't kept track of the number."

I grunted my displeasure. "Make a guess then and stop trying to avoid the question."

"Your human is showing. But that's all right, I know exactly how to distract both your human and phoenix halves."

"Yeah?" I grated. *Why won't he tell me? It's not that big of a deal.*

"Yeah." He slid into me, and I threw my head back in delight.

Okay, so … yeah, he did know how to distract me. All was temporarily forgotten while Ash rode me hard, just the way I liked it.

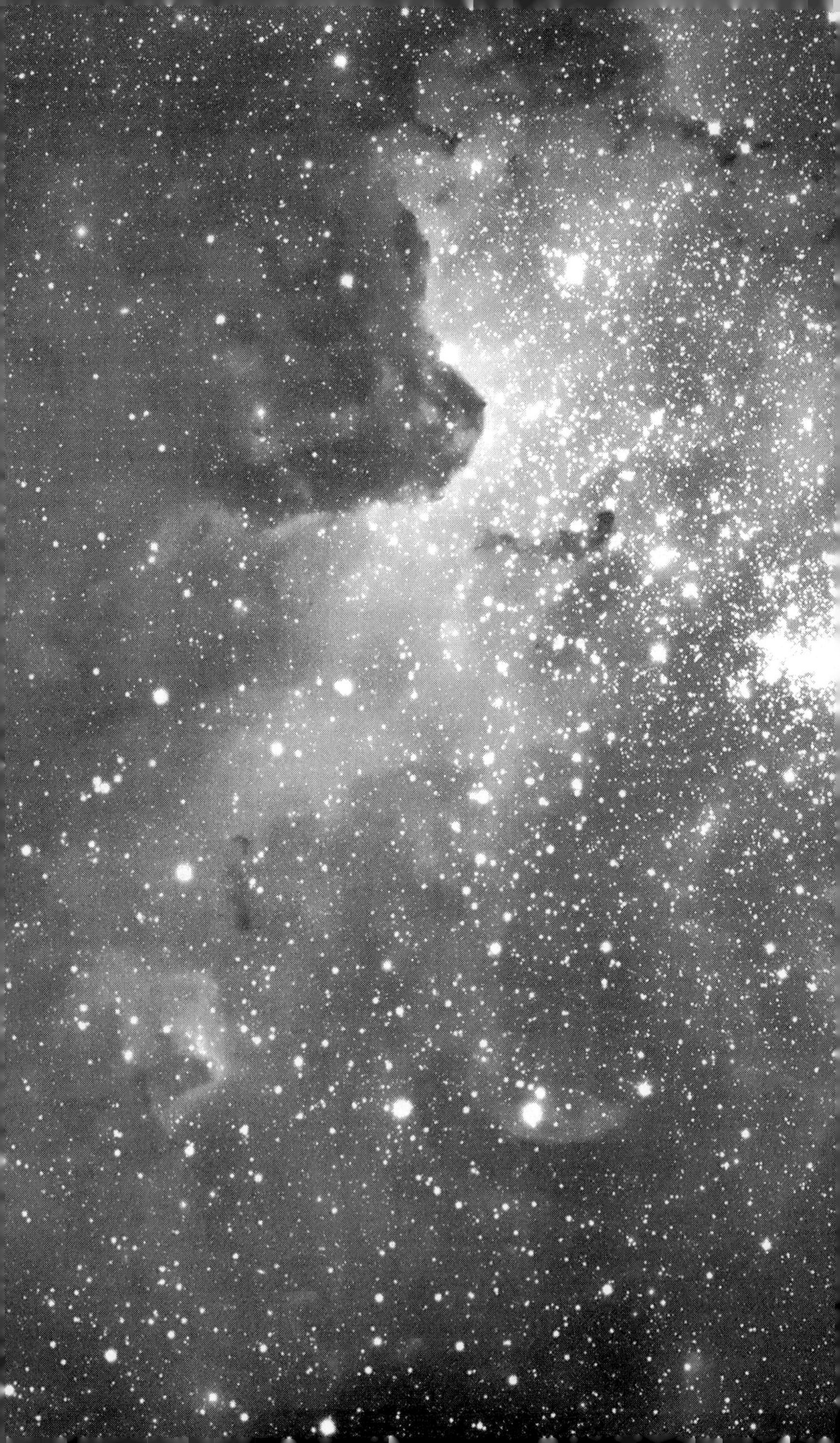

Chapter 20

Ash laughed. "Mogwais weren't real Earth animals. They were from a movie."

I glowered at him. "That's not true. I read about them in one of my Earth history books. I—"

"Are you sure it was a history book, or maybe it was a fiction novel?"

I punched his arm, twisting my knuckles into his bicep. "I can tell the difference. I'll have you kn—"

"Can you?" he interrupted. "Because Steampunk wasn't real either."

My mouth opened and shut several times without a sound. "No, that can't be true," I finally managed. "I got those clothes from an Earth museum that was closing down. Or at least some of them. The rest I got—"

Ash flipped me over, hovering above me, his grin stretching wide across his face. "You got them all from people who conned you. They could probably smell your desperation a mile away. Steampunk is fiction, just like mogwais. Although I will admit that you look fucking hot in your little leather outfits. Does it matter if they're a real part of history or not?"

"Yes, it does." My lower lip popped out forming a pout against my will. "How could I have been so stupid?" My face scrunched up. "Have you been laughing at me this whole time? Because so help me God—"

"It's not your fault. And they all did originate on Earth ... in a way. Just not the way you thought."

I mulled that over, chewing on the insides of my cheeks. "I guess." Whether Steampunk came from Earth fiction or not didn't really matter. Either way, the concept did originate on Earth, so close enough. Plus, I did look damn good in it.

"I have so much to teach you."

I cupped his face in a tender gesture that felt foreign to me. "Please don't go. I don't want to lose you." *Where the hell did that come from?*

Ash turned his face into my palm, nuzzling as his eyes slid shut. "What I'm going to do, it's bigger than me or you. It needs to be done."

"What am I going to do about the UGFS contract? Ambassador Aralias expects results. If I don't at least deliver the chip ... I don't know what's going to happen." If I could produce the chip, then maybe Ash would be forgotten or he could hide. Perhaps I could even fake his death. There were so many things that could be done if he just handed over that chip.

"I can see the wheels turning and I know what you're thinking. And no, Janey, I won't give you that chip."

"Please," I rasped. Yep, I was full-on begging. I didn't want Ash to die. I didn't know what I felt for him, but I at least wanted a chance to figure it out. Him being dead would kind of put an end to that plan. "We can spend lots more time doing this." I thrust myself up at him. "And just talking, too ... just being together. Don't give me a taste of something that I may want only to yank it away."

Ash stood quickly as he heaved a huge sigh, leaving me to feel bereft without his body heat ... yet again. "You could live with yourself? You could let things go on the way they are with innocents dying just so you can have a little slice of happiness?"

I shrugged. "I'm selfish. What can I say?" I tried to make it sound light but it didn't come out that way at all. Not to mention that it was completely true. I'd learned to put myself first over the years because no one else would. I didn't feel any guilt for being who I was, and who I always would be ... a survivor.

Ash drilled me with a hard look. It didn't matter that he was naked, it still made me regret my words a bit. Not the part where I felt that way, just the part where I'd shared what I really thought about the matter. "Is that what you truly want? For me to hand the chip to you so you can smooth things over with the UGFS, and then what?"

"I don't know, we could hunt bounties together and you could fly under the radar like Dar is doing."

He studied me for another few moments before coming to me in a burst of speed. "We'll talk more about this later." My body quivered with fresh excitement.

Fine. I'll wait. For now. But he's not going to make me forget or sex me into compliance.

I WOKE UP CHILLED, no Ash in sight. I rolled over to find an envelope propped on an uncharred pillow beside me. I opened it hastily, a small metallic object tinkling onto the floor. I picked it up, staring at it in utter shock. It bore the UGFS official seal—it was the chip. Ash left the chip for me. But then why did he leave? I pulled out the note that accompanied the small prize.

Janey,
Do what you must. I will find you when it's done.

Was this some kind of test? Or was Ash actually leaving the choice up to me? The possibility that he would do such a thing never crossed my mind. Sure I'd asked him to, but he'd seemed pretty adamant in his refusal.

Palming the chip, I refused to let myself think about anything else at the moment. With Ash gone, I felt fully myself again. The realization that I'd become almost like two separate people was headache-inducing. I was one person with Ash—and then the old me—the one that had existed before Ash when he wasn't present. I hadn't suddenly developed a split personality. Although there was no other way to describe the dichotomy of my actions, and even my personality when he was or wasn't around.

I pondered love and relationships while in his arms. I begged him not to go … I was open … vulnerable even. It was a contradiction to the person I'd come to think of as me. I'd let Ash past the walls I'd spent years building, and I wasn't sure I liked who I was when I was with him. Vulnerable was just that, weak and breakable. If I let him in much more, he would be able to destroy me completely. I could never allow someone to have that kind of power over me ever again. Maddox and my family had taught me that lesson very well.

Setting the chip down on the ground, I grabbed some clothes out of my closet. As soon as I was dressed, I stashed the chip in a pocket and scurried out of my quarters. My muscles were like jelly and my head was still a bit fuzzy, as if I'd gotten tipsy on Ash, but I had to talk to Zula and Tamzea ASAP. They were probably climbing the walls waiting to hear what was going on. They'd been suspiciously absent while Ash was there. They'd obviously been giving me privacy.

Panting, I burst into the med wing, which was where I knew Tamzea would be. I was lucky enough to find Zula there as well. My eyes narrowed, taking in the scene while I sucked in oxygen. The two of them seemed mighty cozy, sitting cross-legged opposite each other on a bed. They were playing cards and drinking glasses full of a liquid that looked suspiciously like firejuice.

What the hell? "What are you two doing? Don't you have a ship to run or something?"

"Oooor something," Zula sing-songed. "Masha and Dar have everything covered. They are quite the proficient ship-running pair."

I swung my gaze to Tamzea, who was grinning at me lopsidedly, as if half of her face was drunker than the other. "We were wondering how long you'd be," she raised her hands to make air quotes, "entertaining Ash." Giggling, she fell over.

"How much did the two of you drink? And I thought Galvrarons didn't stoop to drinking libations such as firejuice." I sneered. Zula was always fast to look down her nose at my firejuice preference and here she was. *Hypocrite much?*

Zula waved me off. "We were bored and Tamzea talked me into it."

I gazed at the two of them in horror. I'd come to them for advice of the utmost importance, not to mention that it was time sensitive, and they'd gone and gotten completely sloshed. *Just perfect.* "I got the chip. In case either one of you lushes were interested."

Tamzea rolled onto her stomach in a fit of giggles. "I can't believe you fucked it out of Ash. I thought he would be able to withstand your wiles."

"Nope." Zula smiled larger than I'd ever seen her do. It was kind of creepy. "No man seems to be able to resist our

Jane. That's her super secret bounty-hunting power. I'm sure you've heard the rumors."

"You know what," I stomped over and snatched both of their glasses, "that's enough out of the both of you."

Zula didn't believe those rumors and was just trying to give me a hard time, but I was in no mood. I needed her and Tamzea, and they were acting like complete idiots. But neither of them seemed to care at the moment so I decided to leave them to their own devices until they sobered up.

Swiping the almost empty bottle of firejuice, I headed to the control room. It looked like I was going to have to make the call by myself. I put the bottle to my lips, tipping it on end. *Shit. They could have left me a bit more for liquid courage.*

With shaky hands, I typed in the numbers to hail Ambassador Aralias' ship. Only a few moments passed before a connection was made and the ambassador's cold, yet handsome, face appeared larger than life on the screen in front of me. I straightened myself up, wishing I would've put some thought into what I was wearing. I probably looked like I'd just been on a sex bender. I wasn't sure whether that was a good or a bad thing.

"You have news?"

I nodded almost too demonstratively. "I have the chip."

"And Ash?"

I bit my lower lip, averting my gaze. "He got away … again."

"And how did that happen?" His voice was sharp.

"Ummm ... Well ..." Thinking on the fly, I realized the best thing to do was to tell him something as close to the truth as possible. That way there'd be less chance of a slip-up on my part. Also, it would explain my appearance. The best lies were usually saturated in truth. "I seduced him so that he would let his guard down. I managed to get the chip, but he wised up before I could use the blade on him."

"You seduced him?"

I met his hard gaze. "Yes."

A slow smile crept across his face. "I'm sending you rendezvous coordinates. We expect to see you there within the hour." The screen went blank. *How the hell does he know exactly where we are? Who am I kidding?* He'd known when we'd been in Gartian territory. He was obviously keeping tabs on our whereabouts.

"What happened?" Tamzea and Zula asked in perfect unison as they burst into the room. I was glad they hadn't shown up until after the call to the ambassador had ended.

"We have to meet up to hand the chip over." I patted my pocket, where I'd stashed it. I was hoping with the UGFS getting the chip back that they'd forget about Ash. I internally sighed. I'd lost that level of naivety a long time ago. All I could realistically hope for was that I wouldn't be the one they wanted to track him down again. *Yeah ... I'm seriously delusional if I believe that one either.*

"Can you manage to punch in the new coordinates or do I need to do it myself?"

"I can do it," Zula scoffed as if she wasn't drunk off her

ass. *She can probably do most jobs better than anyone while drunk.* That thought seriously rankled.

With a heavy heart and a churning gut, I headed back to my quarters to prepare myself for my meeting with destiny. It sounded corny as hell to even think that, but somehow it rang true despite everything.

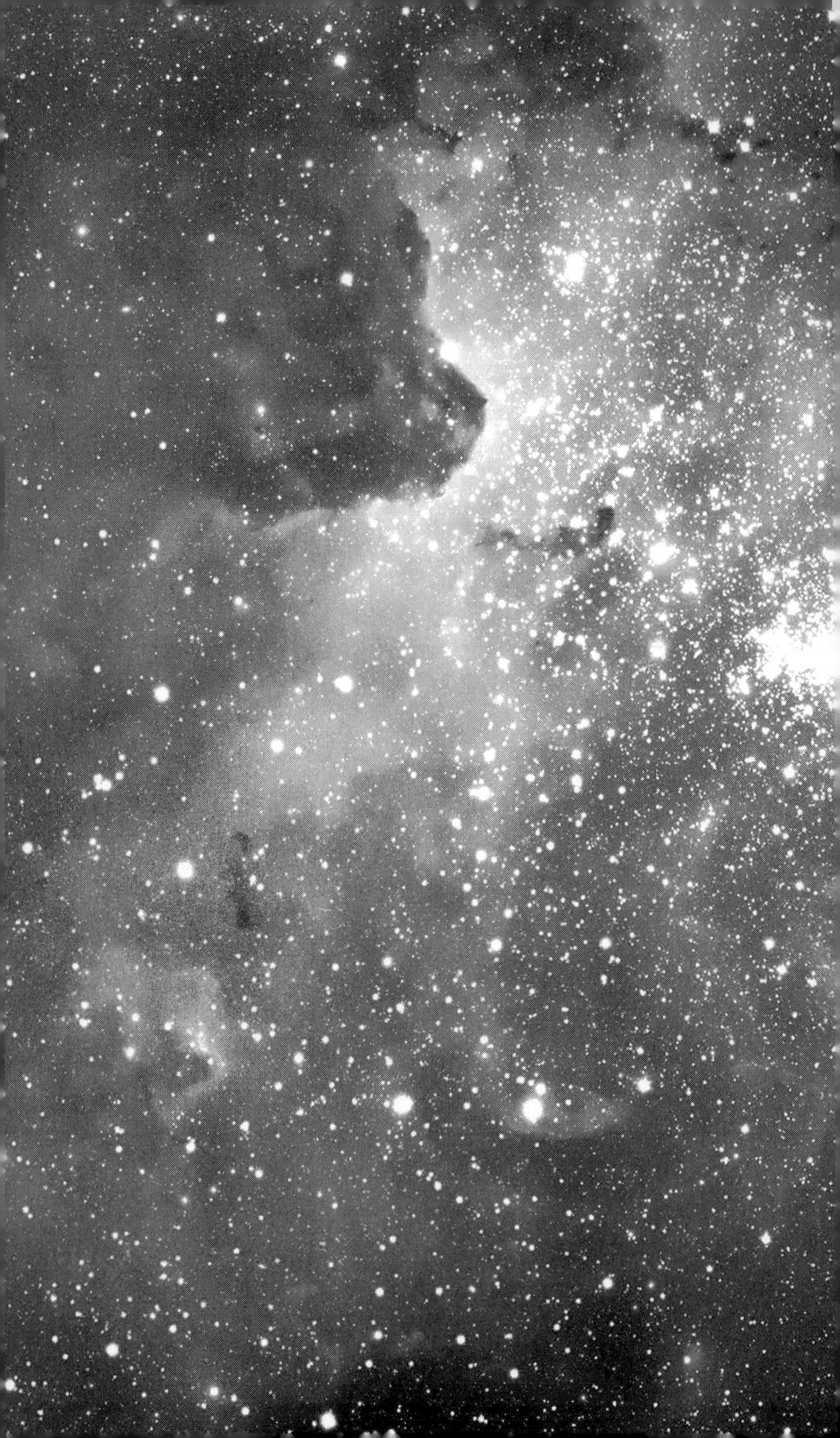

Chapter 21

My gut roiled as my heart ratcheted up to a dangerous speed. *And I thought I was tense the first time Ambassador Aralias boarded my ship.* But that was nothing compared to the current level of stress zinging through my system, all of it brought on by a horrible feeling of foreboding. I knew how I *wanted* things to go, but I also knew how they probably would. The two were not even close to the same thing.

I spent way too much time after my shower picking out my current ensemble, torn between wearing something skimpy, aka distracting, and something a bit more conservative. The last thing I wanted to do was encourage the ambassador's perverse attraction to me.

On the other hand, a woman in my line of work quickly learns that unlike what most believe, a woman should use all of her strengths, and a woman confident in her sexuality holds a special power, especially over men attracted to women. Straight men know this, which was why they feared and tried to control women's sexuality, using everything from slut-shaming to birthing rights. They knew, deep down, if we didn't have to fight those constant battles, if we so chose, we could rule them all.

Sometimes showing a little skin or using a perfectly timed wink could put a certain type of man under a woman's thrall. That type of man was easy to manipulate and were the kind I dealt with most of the time. Putting all of that into consideration … I'd finally decided to wear a leather pants outfit, which split the difference. The truth was, if I was wearing a burlap sack and the ambassador got it in his head that he wanted to try something … he would.

Dar and Masha were hiding out again, and thankfully Tamzea had some kind of tea that sobered both her and Zula up. I was beyond relieved not to be facing Ambassador Aralias and his UGFS bodyguards alone.

I gulped audibly as the UGFS trio made it safely into the airlock. I glanced back at Zula and Tamzea, who both gave me encouraging nods in turn.

I can do this.

Unlocking the second door to the airlock, I stepped back, my head bowed slightly in deference.

"Captain Wexis. The chip." Ambassador Aralias' tone was beyond eager. I reached out my hand, the chip resting in my palm. He snatched it away immediately. "Good. It carries the correct code. Do you know if he made any copies?"

I winced. I hadn't even thought to ask Ash that, although I was assuming no. *Unless that's why he gave the chip up so easily.* "Ummm ... I don't—"

"The seal would have changed color if it had been copied on anything but official UGFS equipment," Zula offered. "The seal appears intact, so therefore the creature known as Ash did not have a chance to copy the chip."

Silence reigned for a moment before I cleared my throat, my eyes still locked on my boots. "I know you must be disappointed that Ash got away, but I do remember you saying the chip was more important ... " My voice wavered despite my best efforts. I hated not being in control. *I want the ambassador the hell off my ship already.*

"I did say that. And it is true," he snapped. "But Ash cannot be permitted to live knowing what's on this chip." My head snapped up, my gaze meeting the ambassador's. It was a mistake. I quickly glanced away again, but I already knew it was too late. "You don't want to kill him, do you?"

"I—"

Ambassador Aralias closed the scant distance between us in the blink of an eye, his hand sliding around my throat. "Don't think we don't know what's going on." His hateful eyes filled up my vision as I reached up to clamp my hands around his wrist. He wasn't choking me ... yet. But the act of force wasn't one I'd expected from an ambassador. "Now let me tell you what's going to happen. You're going to come with me, without protest, and I'll let

213

your crew live. If you do your job and kill Ash ... I may let you live as well."

"He'll never come to me on your ship," I croaked.

My mind was reeling. I knew if I somehow managed to get my laser gun free that the two UGFS guards would take me out in a zeptosecond. I also knew that even at my best, maybe I could take down one, but the other would most definitely put a hole through my skull. Fear shot through my system, my heart thrashing against my ribcage. Trembling, I sucked in shallow breaths, struggling to get enough oxygen. I was trapped, trapped, trapped. *There has to be a way out! Think, Jane, think!*

"Shit!" Ambassador Aralias reared back from me as my palms spewed flames. Not enough to kill him, but enough to burn him just like I had Jassen. His eyes widened as his guards swung their laser rifles to point at me. "How did you do that? I've read your records, you're Species Class 1. Part human and ... " His eyes narrowed in on me, understanding dawning within them. "You're part phoenix and wholly an abomination. Cuff her!" he roared.

All chaos broke loose. I pulled my laser gun, dropping down to my knees in one fluid motion. I squeezed off a few shots before one of the guards tackled me fully to the ground. Even though I was trying to take them out, they were still attempting to take me prisoner, otherwise I would have already been dead.

I can't let them take me on that ship! It was my last thought before everything went dark.

"WAKE UP, Captain Wexis. Or I think I'll call you Jane since we're going to get to know each other very well soon," Ambassador Aralias cooed right next to my ear.

Revulsion caused me to shudder, my eyes flying open. I found myself laser chained to a chair in front of a large viewing window on the ambassador's cruiser. The Pittsburgh was right there in front of me, appearing to hang perfectly still in space. "I wanted you to know the full scope of your situation, and therefore you needed to witness this firsthand."

"Fire when ready," he commanded, a small smile curling his lips up at the corners.

My breath caught in my throat, my mind blanking as the laser shots tracked across the sky in seeming slow motion. Fire erupted and then ... then The Pittsburgh was just gone—as if it had just disappeared into thin air.

Completely numb, I stared for who knows how long before tears began to track down my face. It wasn't just my ship that was gone ... Zula, Tamzea, Masha, and even Dar, were gone. I'd gotten them killed. They were all dead because of me. It was my fault. All of it was one hundred percent my fault.

Sorrow morphed into rage, boiling my blood. "I'm going to kill you!" I heard myself screech as I fought my bonds. "I'm going to kill every last one of you!"

"You see," Ambassador Aralias said to his crew, "this is

why their kind should not be allowed to live. Look at her. So volatile. Drug her and then bring her to my quarters."

My chest heaved with exertion, fire streaming from my palms. I bared my teeth, watching as the flames grew. "I'll burn you alive, Aralias," I snarled. "Your screams will be music to my ears. A fucking symphony."

He shook his head, watching me with disdain. "You know what to do," he said to one of his guards.

"Yes, sir."

My flames were doused with some kind of liquid that wasn't water, and my neck was jabbed with a needle. I lost consciousness moments after that.

"LET me show you what it was like. At least a small piece of it," Ash said, his voice both sad and proud.

I seemed to step into another memory of his ...

And suddenly I was flying. Lush green lands, treacherous and yet beautiful mountains, vast seas, and oceans stretched out before me. The landscape was much like New Earth, but I immediately knew it wasn't. I was seeing—really seeing Earth for the first time. It was something I never thought I'd experience on any level.

A joyous giggle burst forth from me as I—we continued to soar over the once great planet.

Yes, it resembled New Earth, but it was crystal clear what the scientists had failed to reproduce when creating humankind's new home. New Earth lacked a soul. Earth was alive with an energy that seeped out from the ground itself. It was a living, breathing entity. I wished I could have walked on those lands, swam in those seas, breathed in that air ... even for just one day.

"*It's why we have to fight so that no other creatures lose their home. We can't bring Earth back, but we can save countless other planets and species from the same fate.*"

My eyelids fluttered open, and I gasped as a sharp sting bit into my cheek. I wiggled my jaw as I eyed Ambassador Aralias. He smacked me across the face again, the copper tang of blood blooming in my mouth. I took the opportunity to drop my head, scanning my surroundings from under my lashes.

I was in lavish quarters, dominated by the dual blue tones of the UGFS. I remembered his words from before I'd been knocked out and knew I was in the ambassador's living quarters. Unfortunately, I was chained to his bed. Everything about my situation and what it implied terrified me in ways I'd never felt before. But I refused to succumb to the base instinct since it wouldn't do me one bit of good.

There were so many questions dancing through my mind, none that I would ask. Ambassador Aralias seemed like the type who would enjoy talking about himself and his plans, so I refused to give him the satisfaction. His hand collided with my face a few more times, and I remained stoic, managing to keep any reaction contained.

"Jane, you keep surprising me. I would have thought you'd be giving me the third degree by now." I let the hatred for him shine through my eyes as my only response. He chuckled. "If you won't speak, I'll make you scream."

He reached behind his back, drawing out a long, thick leather whip. *Fuck. Just my luck. He's some kind of sadist.* Now it made perfect sense why he was interested in me sexually even though he held such disdain for me. Of course a sadist might prefer getting someone they didn't like in bed so they could feel doubly good. But who knew? I wasn't privy to the inner workings of what made a sadist tick. And in the end, it didn't matter. I would just have to make sure I didn't scream. The thought of him being turned on by my pain both sickened and infuriated me.

"Do your worst." The words tumbled from my mouth unbidden. The answering gleam in his eyes told me that I'd just inadvertently served him a challenge. I silently cursed myself for my lack of control and stupidity.

The whip sang through the air, landing on my leather-clad thighs. It stung but hardly had the kind of impact that would be dragging screams from me against my will. "Oh, dear. You have too many clothes on. We need to rectify that immediately." The ambassador smirked.

I tried not to roll my eyes. I mean … seriously? I'd seen that coming a few hundred miles away. As if any decent villain of any kind can do proper torture when their victim is fully clothed, and wearing protective leather to boot. He was merely playing with me and we both knew it. I bit my tongue to remain silent.

With the same blade that he'd given me to steal Ash's

life, Ambassador Aralias cut off my pants and top, leaving me in only my undergarments and boots. When he was finished, he roughly flipped me over with ease, the laser chains keeping me completely at his mercy.

A string of foul obscenities filled the air when he got a gander at my back. I knew what was causing his reaction: Ash's mate mark. "You let him claim you. I knew you were part phoenix—a hu-mutt, but for this to be possible ... I can't soil myself with you."

Did I just hear that right? Did just the mere sight of the mate mark save me from sexual torture and rape? I turned my face into the bedding to hide my grin.

Pain raced up my spine and I screamed into the mattress, taken by surprise. "I'm going to peel it from your flesh," he snarled, raining blow after brutal blow down on me.

I'd been lying to myself. I wouldn't be able to contain my screams. This pain—what he was doing to me, was on a level I could never have fathomed before. It was raw and sharp, the intensity never shifting or receding, nor did it fade into numbness. Every hit was worse than the last, making me fear for the state of my back as I pictured the flesh hanging from my bones.

Tears poured down my cheeks, my throat hoarse from my pain-addled wails. Even so, I sublimated my urge to cry out for Ash, to beg him to save me, because I knew if he attempted to come here, surely, he would die right alongside me. And if this was going to be what ultimately took me out, I didn't want him to know the agony I suffered in my last moments in this mortal coil. I wanted him to remember me fondly, basically, before I'd screwed everything up beyond repair.

Despite my unwillingness to summon him, as darkness pushed around the edges of my vision and the pain became too much for my body to bear, his voice echoed through my mind as he screamed my name.

I should have listened to him ... about everything. It's too late now.

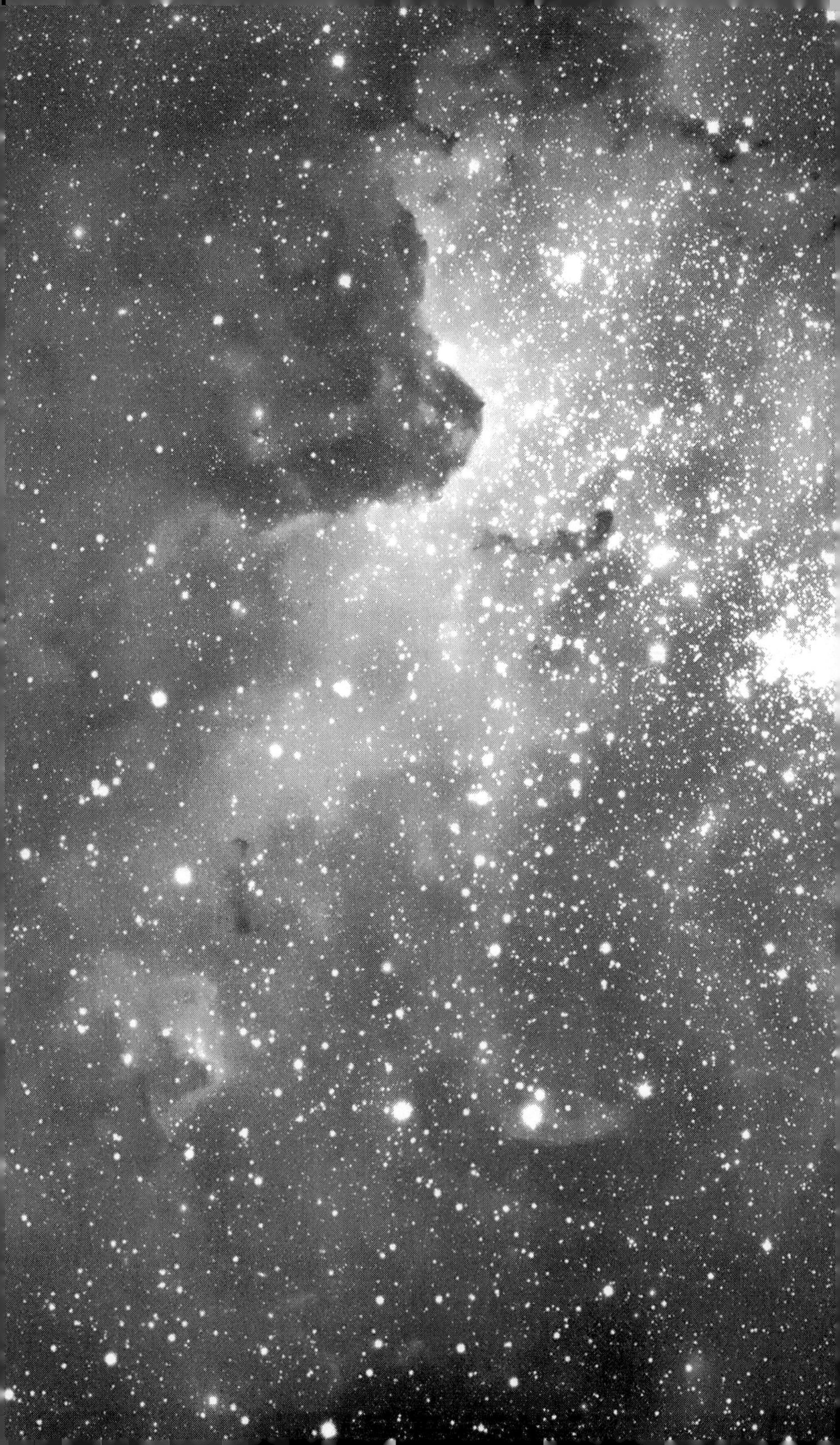

Chapter 22

Consciousness found me slowly as warm water trickled down my spine. I bit the insides of my cheeks, stifling a groan. I was no longer chained to Ambassador Aralias' bed, but instead, my arms were stretched over my head and my face pressed into a wall. I wriggled a bit, realizing after a moment that I was completely naked. I wasn't digging that fact one little bit.

"Be still," a female voice commanded from behind me. "I'm merely washing the blood off of you. No harm will come to you … while you're in my care."

Ah, so this stranger knew that the same couldn't be said with Ambassador Aralias. I decided to try to get some information out of her. "Who are you?"

"That is none of your concern."

"What's going to happen to me after you're finished cleaning me up?"

"Probably more of the same of what you've already

experienced. The ambassador has a predilection for giving pain, and you are half human and half phoenix."

"Yeah, so?" I grimaced when it felt like a sponge swiped over the raw flesh on my back.

"Your mate mark is healing you. In no time at all you'll be good as new."

I snorted. "I'm thinking in this situation that may not be the best thing." Was that why the pain had been so intense the entire time I was being beaten? Was there some kind of magic in the mark that had been trying to heal me? I had so much to learn. *Too bad I probably won't be alive long enough to learn any of it.*

"You should have killed Ash. You exchanged your life for his."

"You certainly seem to know a lot about my situation. Again I'm going to ask you, who are you?"

I was roughly flipped around, and a surprised gasp was ripped from my throat. Before me stood a small humanoid female of unknown species classification. Her pale face was littered with scars, the kind that were inflicted by a blade intentionally. It was clear that she'd been beautiful once. And in some ways she still was. Her long, flaxen hair gleamed with health, and her luminous blue eyes were clear when they met mine with defiance. "I'm someone who understands."

"He did this to you?" It came out as a question, but I already knew the answer. "Maybe I should be asking, who is he exactly? He's not just an ambassador, is he?"

"No, he is not. He is so much more."

"I should have known."

I glanced beyond her, noting that I was in a shower stall, the walls and floors metal, several sets of chains in various places hanging empty. *What kind of person installs chains in a friggin' shower stall?* Of course, I already had the answer: the sick and twisted kind. How many creatures had bled in the very same spot as me? Blood of different colors washed away so easily from the metallic surface. *As if none of us ever existed.* I stared at the drain, the pink-tinged water swirling around my feet.

A sponge scraped down my arm, the female speaking again as she continued to clean me. "There would have been no way for you to know the truth. So few have that information anymore. The Denards are so much cleverer than most think. They've even fooled the Galvrarons, which is no small feat."

My heart fisted when I thought of Zula and how I'd never see her blue, sarcasm-spewing face again. Her words belatedly sunk in. "Are you saying that Ambassador Aralias is a Denard?" It was possible. I had no clue what one even looked like. I guess since they were spoken of like some kind of Boogieman, I'd assumed they wouldn't be humanoid. *Seems like I'm wrong ... again.*

"Yes," she hissed. "They hide in plain sight among the UGFS. And they have plans—plans for us all."

My head flopped down from the weight of my shame. I'd wanted Ash to just hand over the chip and run away from all of this. On some level, I never accepted that it was as bad as he or Dar described.

"*You can make it up to me later,*" Ash whispered in my mind.

"No!" I exclaimed.

My scarred attendee eyed me with curiosity as she flipped me back around. "*No, Ash! You can't come here. You'll get yourself killed! I'm being used as bait,*" I yelled in my mind.

He didn't respond, which caused terror to race through my system. Terror for him. I'd already accepted that I was as good as dead. I was a survivor, selfish to the core, but even I knew when the jig was up. There was no point in both of us dying.

Besides, maybe he really could bring down the Denards one day. But he wouldn't be doing anything if he was dead. I couldn't allow my involvement to screw things up further.

I know what I have to do, and it's going to royally suck. But hey ... maybe I'll get to die with a little bit of dignity after all.

"I KNOW WHAT YOU ARE," I spat as Ambassador Aralias loomed over me.

I was once again laser chained to his bed. He wasn't even trying to hide what he was doing with me, which made me wonder how many of his crew were Denards as well. I'd been paraded back to his room stark naked, and no one had even batted an eye. It'd been humiliating, and extremely telling.

"Ah, Nina has a big mouth. I can never seem to punish her enough, though. Her time with me may finally be coming to an end." He perched himself at the end of the bed, smiling warmly. "You know what I am and I know what you are. I suppose that's only fair."

"I don't know why you—the Denards—are doing this. Why? Why do you want to wipe out species and planets? What good does it do?"

He tapped his chin, regarding me thoughtfully. "I suppose you're expecting some kind of full disclosure about me and my kind's motivations. You want me to explain all of our plans, spell it all out for you?" he asked snidely.

"Yeah, that'd be nice," I growled.

He wasn't going to tell me shit, but it was worth a try. With his extensive knowledge about the phoenix he probably knew that whatever he told me, I could share with Ash directly into his mind through our mate bond.

The thought of Ash brought me full circle back to my plan. Time was of the essence so I couldn't dilly-dally any longer. "By the way, if you think you and your Denard buddies are going to get away with whatever you're planning, then you're dumber than you look. Ash is going to bring you down."

I plastered a jovial smile on my face. My goal was to taunt him into losing his temper to the point where he'd end me quickly before he could reconsider. Then Ash would no longer have a reason to put himself at risk by attempting to rescue me. I wasn't the self-sacrificing type, but if I was going to die anyways, I might as well make it worth something.

"You don't know what you're talking about." His expression said I hadn't managed to rile him up, not even a little.

I'm just going to have to try harder.

"Just because you fooled me doesn't mean shit. Ash knew the whole time—I just didn't listen. Do you really think he just handed that chip over to me without some kind of backup plan?"

The ambassador's eyes hardened. "You seduced him. He mated you. I know how the phoenix works when it comes to such things. He wouldn't have been able to resist you."

I quirked my eyebrow. "Really? That's what you think?" I smirked with satisfaction. "Good to know."

He grabbed my chin roughly, lifting my head off the bed. "What's his backup plan? Tell me!" He backhanded me and I recoiled into the soft mattress. The metallic tang of copper bloomed in my mouth. I merely smiled up at him as I watched a mask of rage fall over his features. *That's right. Lose your temper and then you'll be right where I want you.*

"And is there a reason why I'm naked? I mean, we both know you can't get it up. It has nothing to do with me being part phoenix. That's the real reason why you like to beat women. You're just pissed because you're not enough of a man." Most species didn't like their masculinity questioned. Hopefully the Denard culture wasn't one of the weird ones that didn't give a crap about such things.

The ambassador's fists pummeled into my middle. *Score! I insulted his stupid male ego.* "You're nothing but a hu-mutt whore. I'm going to get much more satisfaction from making you bleed than I ever would between your legs."

"Yep, that's right. Make me bleed," I grunted as my eyes slid shut. I just wanted it to end. "I wish I could see the expression on your face when Ash ruins all of your carefully made plans." I forced myself to laugh. "You're all going to look like such idiots."

The sickening sound of bones breaking and flesh tearing met my ears. I was somehow removed from it; I forced myself to be. A twisted sort of laugh echoed in my ears. One that lacked humor, and instead was filled with dark satisfaction. I was about to die, and I wouldn't be begging for my life. No, I would laugh in death's face until the end.

I just wish it didn't hurt so much, not my body, but my heart and soul.

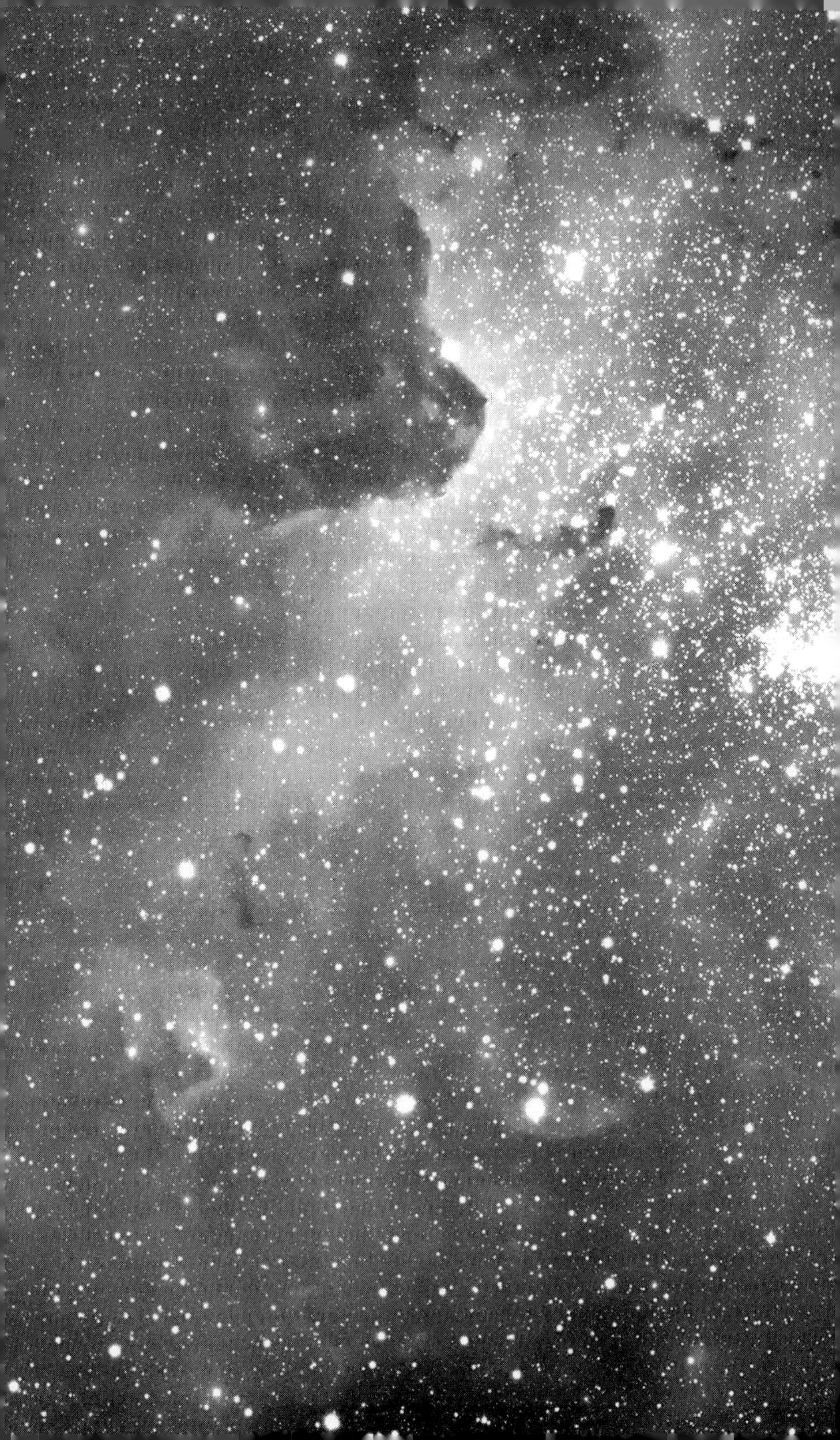

Chapter 23

Despite my less-than-perfect life, I'd never so much as contemplated suicide. I was not a quitter. It simply wasn't in my genetic makeup. And because of that, I went from scavenging garbage at supply space stations to being the captain of my own ship. I rose from my ashes and persevered.

So what am I doing now? Why am I willing to essentially commit suicide by Ambassador Aralias? It's a copout—I'm giving up. I can save Ash ... and myself.

No. I will save myself, save Ash, and make Ambassador Aralias beg for his life like a little bitch.

Or maybe it's the head trauma talking? I am getting knocked around quite a bit. But even if I was delusional ... I'd just faced down the idea of death in my mind, so I had nothing left to lose. And no one is as dangerous as someone out of options and not afraid to die.

Flames burst from me, defending and protecting, as if

my newfound determination had taken on physical form. A startled cry from the ambassador registered in the distance, but my focus was turned inward as I guided my fire to regenerate the damage done to my body, its warm embrace cocooning me. There was a peace in communing with the fiery part of my soul that I'd never known existed.

When I was fully healed, my eyes snapped open, and I watched in startled amazement as I slipped free from the laser chains. I didn't fully transform into a flame like Ash could, but I blinked into a less substantial form for an instant in time. It was all that was needed.

Ambassador Aralias studied me with malice as I approached him, no fear, though, which set my nerves on edge. With his knowledge of the phoenix species, he could have a deadly ace up his sleeve that he was just waiting to pull. My revenge would have to wait, a dish best served cold, as the old Earth saying went. I wouldn't make the mistake of being overly confident in this situation, instead, I would run and live to fight another day.

Still engulfed in flame, I swung around and dashed for the door. I was faster than normal, but not fast enough for my tastes in the given situation. I slid into the corridor, flaming down the hallway, my path suspiciously empty. I faltered for a moment, though, not knowing what direction to go when I reached a fork at the end of the hall. *Left or right? Left or right?*

"Go right at every turn and then down one of the small ladders into a micro escape pod. The activation code is

399, and you'll need this key." Nina reached her hand out to offer me an old-fashioned, notched metal key. "You'll fly under the radar since Ambassador Aralias meant them to be for his secret escape if he ever needed to make one."

I stared in shock at Nina, my scarred yet beautiful guardian angel. "You could come with me," I suggested. "I don't know exactly where I'm going since they destroyed my ship, but it has to be better than here."

"No." Her large blue eyes met mine with determination. "Someone has to stay here to run a distraction just in case."

"Why? Why would you do that for me?"

"Not for you. For those you'll save. Now go."

I understood. Even if I wasn't, it turned out that Nina *was* the self-sacrificing type. I followed her impeccable directions, finding myself at the micro escape pods not too long after. They were named that for a reason. *Talk about tiny. Good thing I'm not Dar's size or I'd be screwed.*

My flame receded and then was snuffed out with barely a thought as I climbed into a pod, the space ridiculously tight. I had to pull my knees up to my chest to fit into it properly. *How the hell would the ambassador fit into one of these?* Unless he had shrinking powers, I didn't think it was possible.

I pulled down the control panel, which was a small pad no bigger than my hand and typed in the code 399 before sliding the key into place. The pod activated immediately. The hum of the air filtration system clicked on, and after a few moments, the door slid smoothly shut. A flight helmet with a built-in breather dropped down and I pulled it over my head. I liked that I was doubly ensured to be able to breathe. That was never a bad thing.

"Destination?" a computerized voice asked in my ear.

Destination? Now that was an excellent question. I couldn't exactly say *to Ash*. He wasn't a destination. I had no friends and no allies besides him. Or did I? I was left with only one viable choice. "To the Gartian planet."

The pod initiated the command quickly, jettisoning me out of the ship, and plastering me against the wall painfully. I was still naked, after all. Wiggling, I attempted to get comfortable, but the effort was futile. Anxiety pinged through my system, the lack of windows in the pod denying me any way of tracking my progress, so I had to simply hope I'd end up where I intended to go.

After only a few minutes, exhaustion took over. I let my eyes slide shut. Of course, my thoughts turned to Ash. Did he know I'd escaped? Or was he even now heading towards danger in a useless attempt to rescue me?

"Ash," I mumbled. "Ash, I'm okay. I got out. Please don't go there. Please don't die for nothing."

When I got no response of any kind, worry began to eat at me. *Why isn't he answering me? Did something already happen to him? No. The Universe wouldn't be cruel enough to have us just miss each other or something as equally ridiculous as that.*

Or maybe it was?

I kept calling out to him as sleep pulled me under.

"JANE! Why does it seem like you're always naked lately?" Tamzea stood beside an unfamiliar Gartian who was holding the door to the pod open.

I blinked a few times and swore under my breath. "After all that and I still died somehow." I snapped my fingers. "I bet it was lack of oxygen, huh? That would be ironic. That stupid micro pod should have had a third backup air system. Third times the charm and all of that."

Tamzea frowned. "Jane, you didn't die. Did you hit your head?" She addressed the Gartian beside her. "Can we get her some clothes please?"

"I don't need clothes in my afterlife," I groused. "I thought everyone just walked around naked." Tamzea offered me her hand to help me out of the cramped pod. "And why is your face the first one I'm seeing? I would have thought they'd give me some hot guy or some—"

"Janey." Ash's deep voice rumbled from behind me.

I spun, eager to drink him in with my eyes. He wasn't naked, to my disappointment, but he was more gorgeous than ever, like every time I saw him. His eyes danced with flames, and I couldn't help but launch myself into his arms.

I slanted my lips over his, plunging my tongue into his mouth, my nerve endings igniting. Grinding my naked body against his clothed crotch, I protested his state of dress while still ravaging his mouth. I needed him inside

235

of me so I could be as close to him as possible. I needed to feel him—

"No one wants to see that!" Tamzea exclaimed.

"Janey." Ash pulled away from me, somehow managing to disentangle himself from my grip. "You're not dead." His eyes twinkled with mirth. "And as much as I'd like to get reacquainted with you right now, I'm not really up for putting on a show."

"Not dead? But I saw The Pittsburgh ..."

His lips twisted as he swallowed back a laugh. "It was fitted with a Gartian cloaking system. So when—"

I smacked my hand over my mouth as tears pricked at my eyes. "Not dead. Not dead." I whirled around to face Tamzea. "Not dead!" I cried with glee as I rushed to engulf her in a crushing hug.

"Jane. You're naked." Tamzea slipped out from under me and took a few steps back.

"Shit!" I tried to cover myself with my hands and arms while pressing my legs together in an odd, standing cross-legged position. I'm not sure why I bothered since it did no good.

"Here." The Gartian from before returned, offering me a stack of clothes. I hastily pulled them on. Even though they were a bit big, I was happy to no longer be naked in public.

"S-so ... I feel like I have a lot of catching up to do since you are all somehow here." I eyed Tamzea and Ash. "How are you both here?"

"Come on. Zula and Masha are waiting for you. We'll

fill you in on our end, and I have a feeling there's some stuff you need to share, too." Tamzea offered me her arm. I took it but glanced back at Ash. He smiled at me, the sight warming my heart. I guessed everything was okay between us again.

He leaned forward and whispered in my ear, "What you did back there ... we're going to have a little chat soon."

Okay, so not one hundred percent fine. I guess he's a bit pissed. Eh. I shrugged. "Whatever you say." I let Tamzea lead me to the rest of my friends, and for the moment, I couldn't keep from smiling.

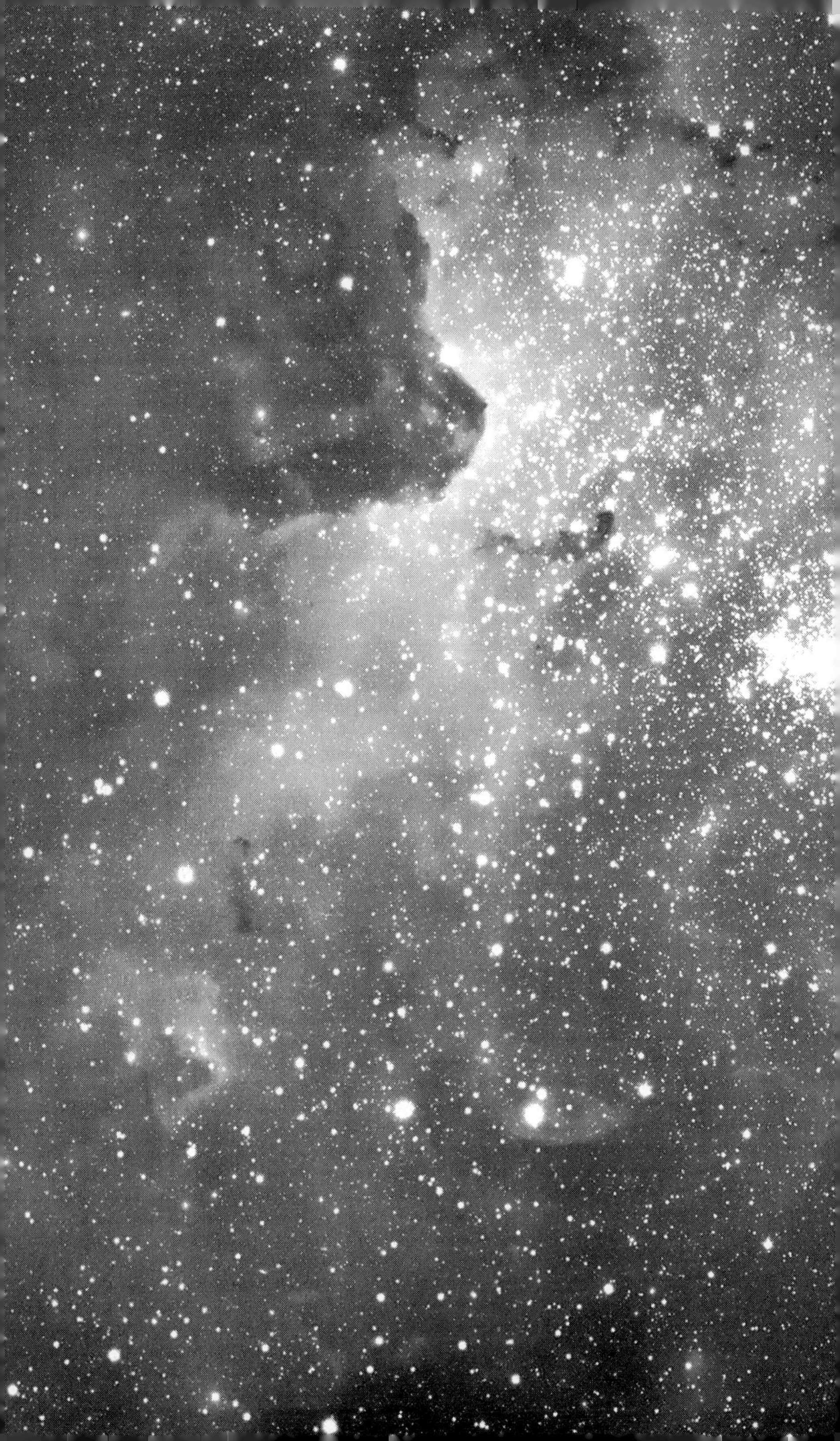

Chapter 24

The room was packed with all different shapes and sizes of Gartians. I hadn't expected to be thrust into some kind of impromptu meeting, since I'd been under the impression that I was just going to meet my friends. They, of course, were there, too. I'd captured first Zula and then Masha in crushing hugs, much like the one I'd delivered to Tamzea. I was so happy to see everyone that I even hugged Dar. At least I think it was Dar, it could have been one of his brothers. Not that I cared in the moment. After I was done greeting my not-so-dead crew, I found myself seated between Tamzea and Ash at a large table.

All attention, including mine, was stolen by a super-sized Gartian as he entered the room. He made his way to the head of the table, his footsteps echoing in the abrupt silence.

"Who's he?" I whispered to Ash.

"Their leader."

With a nod, I returned my full attention to the Gartian bigwig. Not only was he larger than even Dar, but also more intimidating. Who would have thought that was possible? Bigwig's face was almost completely made of their special grade of alloy, as was his entire left arm. His long dark hair was pulled back in a leather cue, much like how I'd seen Dar wear his. Human-looking, dark blue eyes met mine briefly before roaming over the rest of the room. I shuddered despite myself. It was creepy seeing such soulful eyes peering out from metal, trapped behind a permanent mask. I forced my thoughts away from the jarring sight and the G-Pox that had caused it.

"My people, we have waited a long time for our chance to repay the Denards for the creation of G-Pox, and that time has finally arrived. Our friend Ash has made this fact possible." He nodded at Ash, who pulled himself to his feet beside me. I tilted my head back, surprised that he was going to speak. *He lost the chip, what leverage does he still have against the Denards?*

"My friends." Ash reached into his pocket to produce a UGFS official chip. He spared me a glance long enough to wink. "I have here all the information we need to bring down the UGFS, and therefore the Denards. Ambassador Aralias believes he has this very chip in his possession again. It will buy us some much-needed time. The most important part of our plan—"

I zoned out for the rest of what Ash was saying. I already knew his grand plan. I'd just been under the impression that he was going to do it alone. He'd led me to believe that, and he'd tricked me into believing he'd given me the chip.

Was I bait? I could have died on the ambassador's ship. Was Ash even planning to come for me at all, or was I disposable to him? Maybe he mated me so easily because he thought I would die soon? Was it all a lie? I stood abruptly, metal sounding upon metal as my chair flew back. Not meeting the eyes of anyone in the room, I dashed out into the hallway and blindly kept running.

I couldn't contain the raw emotions that rose up within me. I'd been betrayed... again. Used and discarded by someone who made me believe I was worth something to them. What was left of my heart disintegrated instantly. Darkness grew inside the empty cavity where it once dwelled. Is that all I'd ever be—a pawn—a thing that could be used by the men in my life to get what they wanted?

Both Maddox and my father's faces flashed in my mind. What was wrong with me that no one loved me the way I wanted... needed? And just when I'd been willing to admit to myself that I might love Ash, he'd gone and betrayed me. Sure, the whole thing was fast. But it didn't matter now because he'd used me just like everyone else had. *Of course*, after all these years, I would catch feelings for the one creature who would do such a thing. It was an apparent pattern with me.

"Janey." Ash appeared in front of me in his fire form for a mere instant before solidifying. "You have it all wrong." He attempted to wrap his arms around me, but I shirked out from under him.

"No, I don't. You used me." I hit his chest, feeding my anger so I wouldn't cry. "Is it because you thought I could kill you? Were you still mad? Is that it?" Maybe he didn't trust me. If that was the case then I couldn't blame him. Much. And I was ... or at least I thought I was going to kill him. When I looked back at the situation, I didn't think I would have been able to go through with cold-blooded murder ... especially of Ash. I'd been lying to myself the entire time.

"No. That's not it." He pulled me to him. I tried not to breathe in his spicy scent or feel the way my body was already begging to be touched by him. "Let me explain."

"I was tortured on that ship," I rasped into his chest. "I was going to die for you. And the whole time you were playing me for a fool."

He pressed his lips to the top of my head in a tender gesture before he spoke against my hair. His breath washed warmth over me, and I forced myself to resist the urge to melt into him. "I didn't think it would get that far. I didn't think Ambassador Aralias would take you on his ship. I thought he'd accept the fake chip and give you some ultimatum about tracking me down. I figured—"

"You lied to me. You made me think ... you made me think that I was worth more to you—more than the chip and more than this uprising."

"Oh, Janey." He stroked his hand through my hair and

down my back. "You're not as jaded and tough as you pretend to be, are you?"

I pushed at him again, stumbling backwards. "Maybe not, but I can work on it. I don't need you or anyone. I never have."

He captured me within his embrace once more, his arms like steel bands. "You need me."

"No, I don't, you arrogant asshat!" I thrashed against his hold, hating that I didn't want to leave his embrace.

"Yes, you do. And I need you."

"Because you have to? Because we're mates?" I spat.

"Because I love you. And I'm pretty sure you love me."

His words sucked all the air out of my fight. *He loves me? No. Not enough, though. Not nearly enough.* "You almost let me die."

"You were going to kill me. One of us didn't know the consequences of their actions—that would be me. The other was going to seduce me and plunge a dagger into my heart afterwards."

Okay, so maybe he had a point. I bit my lower lip and curled my fingers into his shoulders. "I suppose when you put it like that ... We're even?"

"Not yet. We still have to sort some things out between us."

"What's left?"

"How about the fact that you don't trust me? We can start there."

"I trust you ... enough." Hadn't I just thought that he

didn't love me enough? How much different was it that I didn't trust him enough?

Ash took me by the shoulders, his golden gaze bursting into flames as it bore into mine. "There is no such thing as *enough* between mates. It's either all, or we'll end up nothing."

"We practically just met!"

He sighed heavily, exhaustion pulling at his features. It was only then I noticed the smudges of purple under his eyes. "Let me get this straight ... You want me to trust you, to be completely open and honest with you about everything, but it's okay for you not to trust me one hundred percent just yet? Because we haven't known each other long enough?"

"I have issues." I averted my eyes sheepishly. When he said it out loud it almost sounded silly. His words almost made me sound wishy-washy. *As if.*

"Not with me you don't," he growled as he slung me over his shoulder.

"What are you doing?" I wasn't sure if I should get excited about some possible impending naked time or fight him. My brain and body were carrying opposing votes. I decided to go for some halfhearted hits against his back. He palmed my ass and squeezed. "Hey!" I protested even as I smiled to myself. *There's definitely something wrong with me.*

"We are going to do the final step in the mating process. I had hoped to wait until we'd have more alone time together and things weren't as tense, but it's clear it needs to be done immediately. I won't lose you now that I finally have you."

I thought about all we'd already experienced as mates. I'd been both fucked and branded. Hell, we could even communicate to some degree telepathically. What was left? "There's more?"

"Yes."

"Are you going to tell me what this last and apparently dramatic final step to our mating is? And do I get a say in it at all?"

"No to both of those questions."

"Well, then we aren't doing it!" I started pummeling the muscular expanse of his back in earnest. "That's not how this relationship is going to work! You can't just tell me what to do! I'm your equal or you can just forget about it, asshat!"

"For God's sake, woman. That's what I'm trying to do—put us on equal footing. Now if you could just shut that alluring and yet utterly infuriating mouth for five seconds this would all go a lot smoother."

Since I'd been staring at his back I hadn't registered where he was taking me. Suddenly I was airborne before I hit a soft mattress. I glanced around warily, taking stock of a small living quarters. Before I could say anything else, Ash was in his flame form and flowing towards me.

"Don't be nervous. It won't hurt ... much."

His flame engulfed me like it had so many times before, but that part only lasted for an instant. The blaze pushed past my lips and rushed down my throat, and I let loose a startled scream.

"Ash?" I gasped, my entire body exploding into a white-hot blaze. I was no longer surrounded by fire. I was the fire. I had become like Ash. I'd gotten a slight taste of it on Ambassador Aralias' ship, but I'd assumed because I was only half phoenix that was all I'd get. I'd never been so happy to be wrong in my entire life.

I realized in that moment that I'd never truly understood the elusive connection I'd craved. It was freedom and intimacy with none of the smothering feelings I'd feared. Ash was everything I needed, and I was the same to him ... always. We were mates—separate and yet one. I was his home and he was mine. All the remaining walls around my heart burned, and I rejoiced instead of regretting the bond.

Once I'd idly mused how I was like two different people: one was Ash's Janey, and the other was Captain Wexis. The lines of those identities blurred and then united. And maybe that was a better way to describe what was happening between Ash and me. We weren't one, not really. We were united. That's why we remained separate, and yet permanently aligned. I'd been terrified of losing myself in a relationship, especially in one with a mate bond. I finally understood that it would be different with Ash. He didn't want to control me; he craved a partnership, just like I had demanded. That I could do— that I wanted more than anything. And I was finally going to have it ... a home that was more than just a place, but a feeling of belonging.

I belonged.

I belonged with Ash.

We belonged together.

I'm not sure how long we remained as flames, swirling around and through each other. Quite possibly it was until we burned away to nothing. Then were reborn—reborn from the ashes just like phoenixes were meant to do. Ash and I were reborn to each other.

Eventually, I found myself back in Ash's very human arms as he made love to me. The transition had been seamless. One moment we were being born again into flame, and the next we were enjoying one of the best parts of being flesh. We continued the final step in our mating process for what seemed like hours until exhaustion pulled us both under and we fell asleep in each other's arms—the way it always should be—and would be, if I could help it.

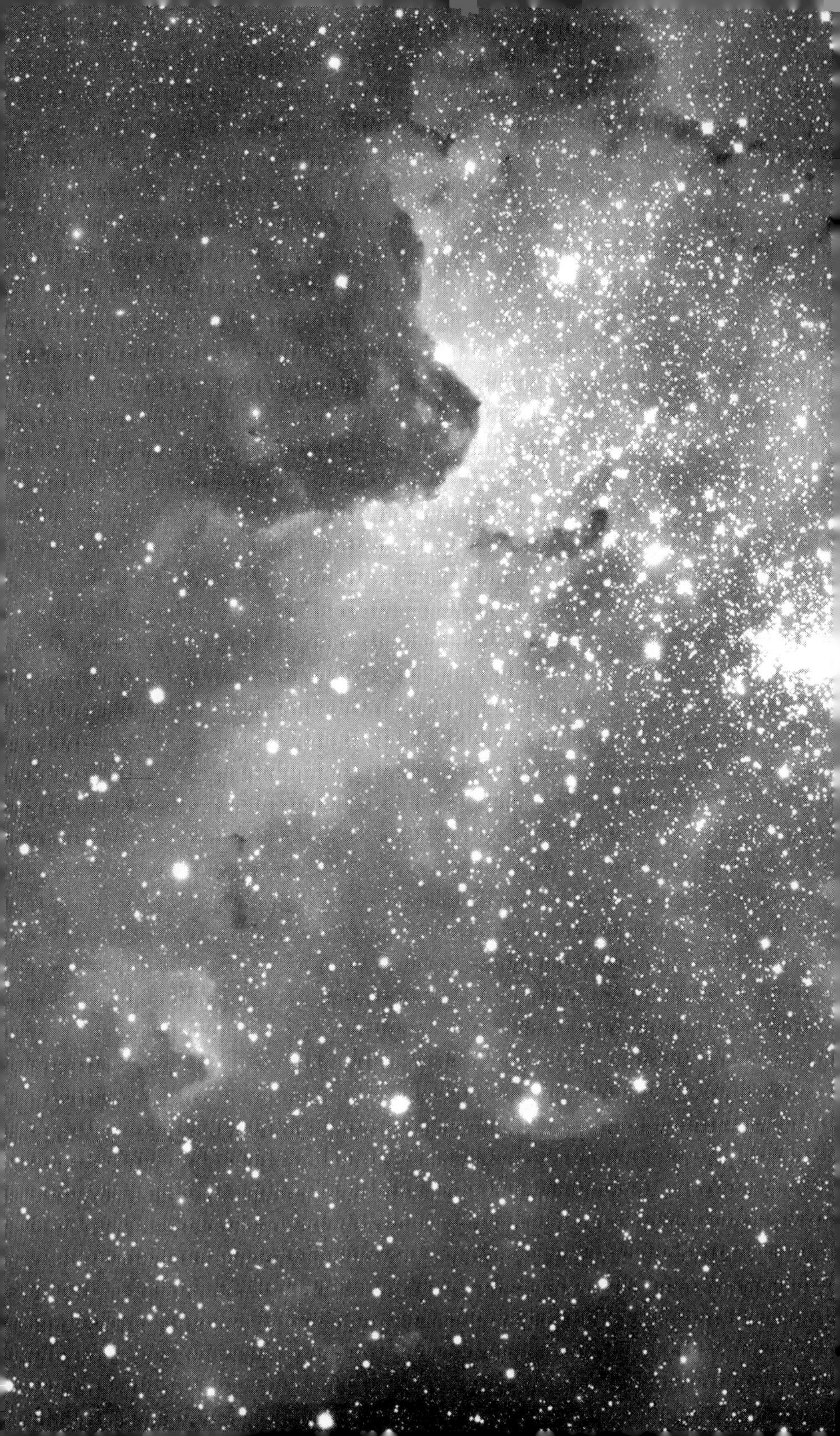

Chapter 25

"Janey, it's time to wake up." The delectable aroma of food wafted up my nose, pulling me from my fitful slumber.

Sitting up, I smiled at Ash as he slid a hover tray in front of me. Although the food smelled delicious, I wasn't quite sure what I was looking at. There was a stack of round, tan, kind of gooey-looking things. Or they were covered in something gooey. It was kind of hard to tell. Beside them was something yellowish with bits of green in it. My breakfast trio was completed with crispy, wavy-looking things. "What is this stuff? Not that I'm complaining, it smells great."

"Zula told me that you've been trying to sample Earth food ... very unsuccessfully for some time. I thought—"

"Oh, my God!" I clapped excitedly while bouncing in place. "This is Earth food!" I started shoving bits of the fare into my mouth with my fingers. The flavors burst onto my tongue and I groaned with delight. "It's amazing!"

"Maybe if you chew it you'd get a better gauge. Also, you're not supposed to eat it with your hands." Ash sat on the edge of the bed and chuckled.

"No time for anything but hands!" My cheeks were puckered out to what I'm sure was a comical level, but I didn't care. "By the way," I said while stuffing more food into my mouth, "how come this room isn't a big pile of ashes? You know, like my living quarters on The Pittsburgh."

"Flame retardant materials. Sometimes I forget that not everyone has such things. The Gartians fit my guest quarters for the needs of a phoenix."

"I need some flame retardant ... everything, I'm thinking." I continued to eat, deciding that the round, gooey things were my favorite. Or maybe the yellowish thing, or ... Okay, I liked everything I was eating. "What is the food called that I'm eating?" Which was almost all gone. *Oops.* Hopefully, it wasn't a meal meant for two.

"Pancakes, an egg omelet, and bacon. Good thing I already ate," he said as if he'd read my mind. *Can he now?* God, I hoped not. It's one thing to be super close to someone, but it was an entirely different thing to have someone be able to stomp around in your head anytime they felt like it. A girl had to have some private thoughts sometimes.

"Can you read my mind now?"

"No. We can communicate with each other

telepathically, which you already know. And we'll both be more in tune with each other's emotions. It's almost as good as mind reading." He smirked, and the twinkle in his eyes told me that he was well aware I didn't think mind-reading would be the greatest thing.

Relief surged. *Thank God he can't read my mind!* "Whatever. So what's the plan ... with everything?"

"Same as before. Of course, your involvement with Ambassador Aralias has probably propelled you to the top of the UGFS most wanted list, right alongside me." I stopped chewing. Ash slid his hand down through my hair. "You're not going to be able to bounty hunt anymore, Janey. I'm sorry."

I knew it was coming, but the words being said out loud caused my stomach to drop. I pushed away the hover tray even though there were just remnants left on my plate. "So what should I do, for money ... and to keep from going insane from boredom?"

Ash scooted forward, tipping my chin up with his index finger. "You can help me free the Universe from the tyrannical rule of the UGFS, of course. We'll figure out the money thing. Trust me." He smirked.

I rolled my eyes. "How exactly am I going to help? It seems like you and the Gartians pretty much have it all figured out."

"Things are more complicated than they seem. We'll work it all out, don't you worry." He stood, taking the tray with him. "Now go get showered and dressed. I bought you some new clothes to tide you over until you can get into your stash on your ship." And with that, Ash left me alone to stew with my own thoughts.

I dragged myself from bed, my mood darker since being faced with the demise of my bounty-hunting career, but I still wasn't as down as I thought I'd be. After all, I'd picked up a mate, one that I loved, even though the process had been ridiculously fast, and I also still had The Pittsburgh and my crew … who were more than crew. They were my family.

My heart swelled. Ash anchored me in a way that allowed me to feel more in tune with myself. It may not sound like much, but when you figure out how to love and accept yourself, then and only then can you let the rest of the world in all the way.

I quickly showered and dressed, smiling to myself as I pulled on a brand-new Steampunk outfit. It was the little things sometimes. Like having Earth food delivered to me in bed by an incredibly sexy man that was mine, and having that same man provide me with new clothes in line with my peculiar fashion sense. It didn't matter that Steampunk was a part of fiction from Earth. It was still a part of Earth culture, and the fact that Ash was encouraging what others thought was a weird fixation just proved that he got me. *Maybe if he had started off with Earth food and fashion I would have softened to him a lot sooner.*

I searched for my bank cuff and other jewelry but came up empty. My mind conjured images of the wavy metal Zula had been working with and I swore under my breath. Ash's room may have been made up of flame-retardant materials, but my accessories were not. I'd have to talk to Dar about if it was possible to make all my things with Gartian grade alloy.

Tapping behind my ears, I sighed with relief. My interpreter implants were intact. I wasn't sure what materials were used to make them, but apparently, they could withstand a phoenix flame, and the transition between my forms. *Interesting. I'll have to look more into that later.* Although it may have been nice to hear the word for mate in the phoenix language, I didn't relish the idea of not being able to understand any species I came across in the future. But then again maybe it wouldn't have mattered. I still had no idea the kind of 'magic' I was dealing with as a phoenix. Would I be able to understand species all on my own now? I had a near-endless list of questions for Ash, and I tacked that one on. If only I could concentrate on anything beyond getting him naked when he was near then maybe I could get some answers sooner rather than later.

Once I was done getting ready, I aimlessly wandered in search of … Ash, Zula, Tamzea, Masha? Someone … anyone? Ash hadn't said where I should meet up with him or anyone else for that matter. And I was currently directionally challenged being that I didn't know my way around the Gartian planet.

Hesitantly, I opened door after door, hoping to find a clue of some sort to point me in the right direction. What I found behind door number, I'm not quite sure what, shocked me to my core.

Holy shit! Masha!

It was Masha, but she wasn't Masha. She was instantly recognizable to me as the small engineer from my ship, but she'd changed. No longer was she small and childlike. In fact, she appeared to have more curves going on than me. And she was currently locked in a passionate embrace with Dar. At least I assumed it was Dar.

I involuntarily squeaked, catching their attention. They broke away from each other hastily, and Masha approached me awkwardly, her cheeks flushed.

"Captain Jane?" Her black eyes studied me with confusion. "What's wrong? It's perfectly normal for—"

"What happened to my cute little cherub-faced engineer?" I croaked. "How did you ... when did you ... you were normal last night!" I raised an accusatory finger. I wasn't really sure what I was blaming her for, but I was blaming her hard.

"I'm still your—"

Ash's warmth suffused my back and I pressed into him. He wrapped his arms around my middle, resting his chin on my shoulder. "Give it up, Masha. We completed the bond. She now has all my powers, which means she can see past your glamour, like I can."

Masha hung her head and scooted back towards Dar. "I never meant anything by it, Captain Jane. Please don't make me leave my engine." She lifted her head, the familiar black eyes in a very adult face filling with tears.

"But I thought Guavivas were all childlike ... I thought —" I threw my hands up in the air, narrowly missing Ash's face. "You have some explaining to do, Masha." Accusatory finger went back on display.

"It's what my kind does. We throw off glamour to make us appear small, childlike, and non-threatening to other species. Only a select few can see past it."

I frowned at her. "You totally worked me over."

"It's in my nature. I can't turn it off. Please don't be mad!"

I eyed Dar, who looked torn between wanting to defend Masha and letting her speak for herself. He knew I posed her no real threat.

"How can I not be mad? You lied to me! Does everyone lie to me?" I pinched Ash's arm. "And you could have told me!"

"I knew it would be easier for you to find out this way," Ash murmured against my hair.

"We're going to have some words later about that," I snapped at Ash, but didn't leave his comforting embrace. I could still be angry with him and love him at the same time.

Dar stepped forward, his head tilted as he raised his hand to his ear. Masha glanced over at him and then did a double-take. "What is it?" she asked.

He lifted his gaze to meet mine. "Another pod like the one that brought you here has just entered our territory. We are unable to communicate with it. We are sending out a team to retrieve it and its passenger. Do you have any idea who it could be?"

I did. The only possible option was Nina. However, I

wasn't sure what it could mean if it was her. "Where are they going to take the pod when they secure it?" I tilted my head back to look at Ash. "We need to go. It might be Nina, she's the one who helped me escape," I said loudly so Dar could hear, too. "And if it's not it could mean trouble. Either way, I want to be there."

"It could be a trap," Masha chimed in. "What if someone or something was planted on the pod to kill you or explode when opened?"

I stared at Masha for a moment before responding. It was still weird seeing her as anything but a small, childlike creature. The bright side was that I didn't have to be freaked out by her blossoming relationship with Dar anymore. *Silver lining.* "Good point. We'll take precautions. Aaaand—" I narrowed my eyes at her. "We're having a long talk later." Her shoulders tensed and her black eyes widened. I was still angry with her, but after thinking she was dead I couldn't stand the thought of losing her. "Don't worry, I won't take your precious engine away," I grumbled.

She grinned, jumping up and down. *Waaay weird.* She still had the same mannerisms, but was all grown up. Maybe it would help to simply think that instead of the alternative. "Weeell … who's showing me the way? Let's go already!"

Dar moved past us with Masha trailing along behind him, her slender hand captured within his. I fell in line behind them, dragging Ash along for the ride.

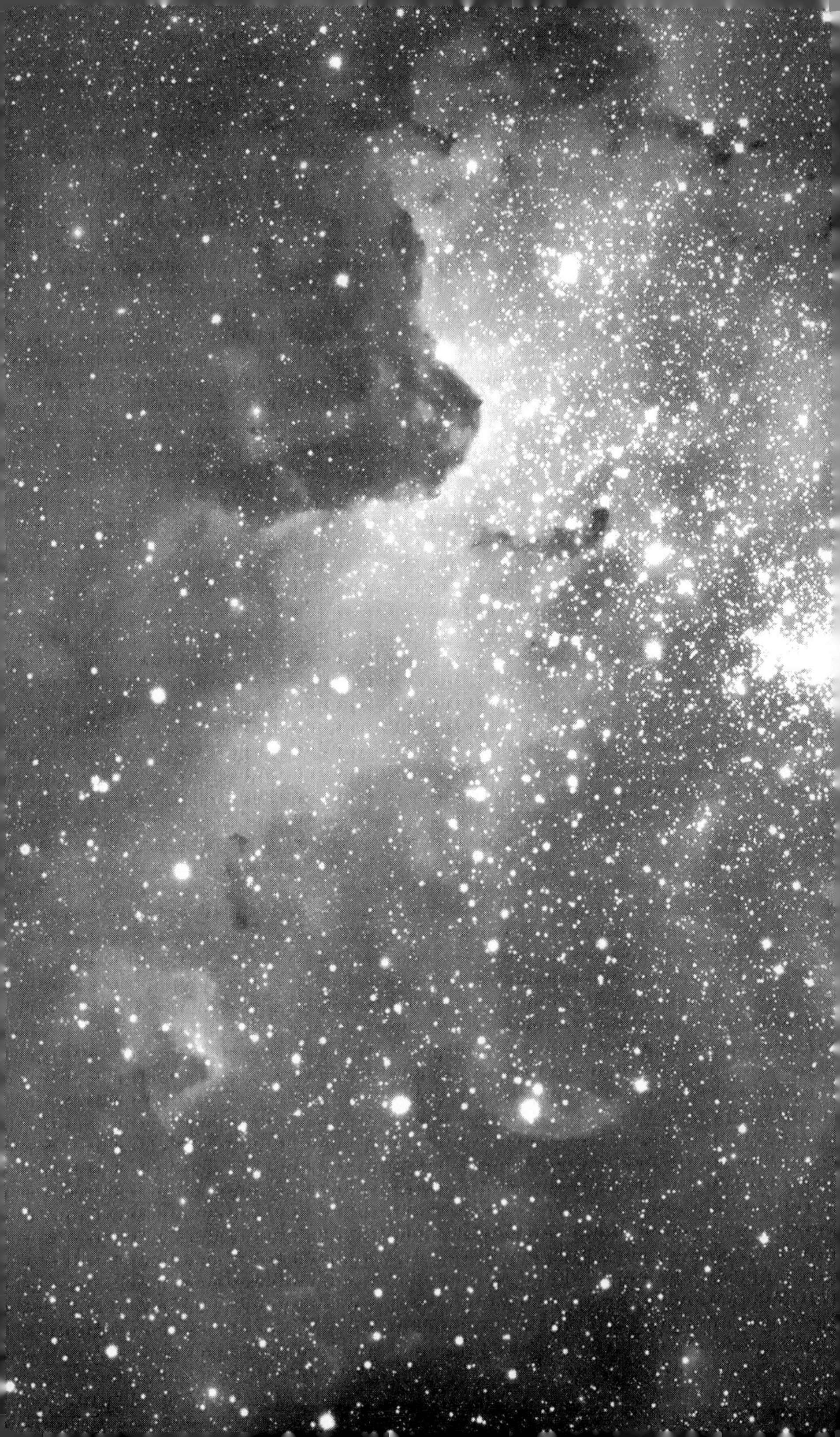

Chapter 26

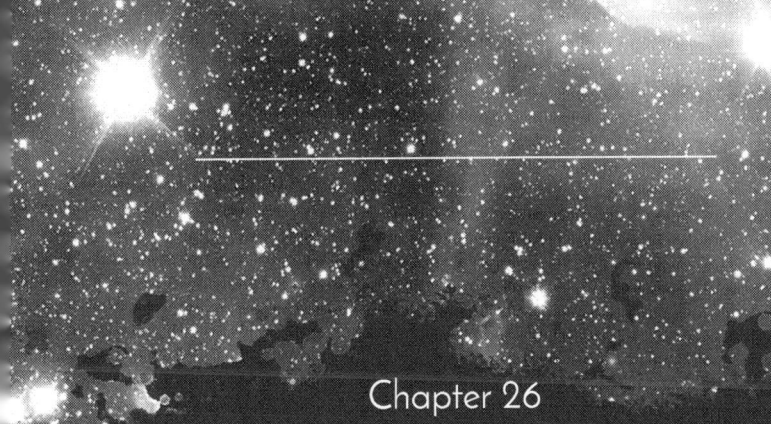

"Is this necessary? Flames can't hurt me." I pulled at the padded, metal-lined suit, complete with a shielded helmet made out of Gartian-grade alloy. "You're not wearing one." I glared at Ash, who was standing beside me in his normal everyday clothes. No bulky metal-enforced suit for him, apparently.

"Yes, but I have the common sense to stay a safe distance away. You'll probably go rushing right up to the pod before it even pops open. Flames may not be able to hurt you, but other things can."

I lifted my head to try and see the sky as the pod was brought slowly down to the docking deck. The helmet shifted and thumped against my forehead. "Ouch!" I said demonstratively. The helmet was a tad too big for my head. The lender was the size of a mountain, and I was the size of a hill.

"Calm down, you can take it off soon. At least I'm not like Dar and making you stay back completely like he is with Masha."

I awkwardly folded my arms over my chest. "As if you could make me do anything." He'd coerced me into the suit with guilt, not exactly the same thing as being forced. The same outcome though. Fidgeting, I stared up at the sky, the pod was only a few yards up now. The curiosity of who or what was in it was killing me.

"My point exactly. Hence the suit." His gaze darted to me from the corner of his eye, a smirk tipping his mouth up.

That smirk is going to be the death of me. I simultaneously wanted to smack and kiss it off his face. *Maybe one right after the other?* "Shut up already." I hated how he kind of had a point. I probably wouldn't be able to contain myself by the time the pod was on solid ground. I might have the urge to rush it just like Ash claimed I would. He already knew me so well. It was both annoying and endearing at the same time.

The pod finally touched down, and I held myself in check for close to a whole thirty seconds just to prove Ash wrong. But as soon as the same Gartian who had extracted me made a move to peel open the door, I was propelling myself forward. My thoughts were whirling around possibilities. If it was Nina, how did she know where I'd gone? And if it was a trap, why were the Denards only now attempting anything hostile against the

Gartians since the G-Pox? Maybe they'd use the fact that they were technically harboring fugitives against them. There were so many possibilities.

I was pressed up against the Gartian's back trying to see around him when Ash pulled me away. "Let the man work."

"Thank you," he rumbled to Ash.

"Well?" I ignored Ash, and began doing an extremely awkward bobbing and weaving dance to try and see what was going on. "Who or what is in there?"

The big Gartian hesitantly stepped back as Nina pulled herself from the pod. She'd already removed her helmet and also had enough good sense to not travel naked like I had. Not that I'd gotten a choice.

Her blue eyes immediately found mine, and she strode confidently towards me. "Jane."

I ripped my helmet off, letting it clatter to the ground. "Nina. What are you doing here and how did you find me?"

"Don't trust her," Ash commanded.

"Why not? She's the one who saved me."

"She had ulterior motives. Ambassador Aralias probably sent her. She's his little lackey." Ash's voice oozed disdain—hatred even.

I shook my head to disagree, but then I thought twice about it. She had been the one that bathed me after my beating. And she'd just appeared out of nowhere, all conveniently with the codes and key ... and now she was here. "Stop where you are, Nina. Why should we trust you?"

Nina halted mid-stride and brought her foot down. She reached into her pocket and placed something on her palm in offering. Unfortunately, she was too far away for me to see exactly what it was. "Because I brought you this."

"What is it?" Ash asked with blatant suspicion.

"The chip. I brought you the chip you need."

Ash and I glanced at each other. Obviously, Nina didn't know that it was a fake, and neither did Ambassador Aralias. He'd be tracking her now. "Shit. He's going to come after all of us with a vengeance. Especially you."

"No, he will not." Nina's lips tipped up into a tight smile. "I killed him. I killed them all."

My jaw dropped. "Whaa— How?"

"I've been biding my time and waiting for the opportunity to present itself. I—"

"I don't believe it," Ash growled.

"Ash," I chastised. "Let her speak." I silently tacked on, *"What the hell is wrong with you?"*

The Gartian who had opened the pod, joined by three others, approached Nina quickly from behind. Before I had time to register what was happening, Nina was in laser cuffs and being led away. She'd let the chip fall to the ground as an offering and didn't so much as make a peep in protest at her treatment.

"What. The. Hell?" I had no idea what was going on. "What do you all seem to know that I don't?"

Ash came to me and started undoing the locks on my ridiculous suit. "She's a Denard."

What? "Impossible." *Are they all so pretty?* There was no denying that if it wasn't for his … flawed personality, Ambassador Aralias would have been swoon-worthy. And Nina was still stunning despite her scars.

"No, it's not." I heaved a sigh of relief as Ash pushed the suit off of me and it clanked to the ground. He turned me around to face him. "She is, or was, depending on whether or not you believe what she said about the ambassador, his wife."

Wow. And the surprises just kept on coming. "But I thought—he did that to her—the scars on her face?" I guess I'd just assumed with Ambassador Aralias' predilection for giving pain to other people that Nina was some kind of abused servant slash sex slave or something.

Ash intertwined our fingers, tugging me along as he made his way back to the building we were guests in. I dragged my feet. "He did do those things to her. But it doesn't change the fact that she is, or was his wife, and a Denard."

I halted, causing Ash to almost pull me over. "It makes every difference in the world. *Every* difference in the world." I snatched my hand away from his and glanced over my shoulder in the direction Nina had been led off in. "I need to talk to her. Please, Ash."

The muscles in his jaw flexed. "At least let us confirm or deny the status of Ambassador Aralias before you do anything." He raised his eyebrows. "Okay?"

I scrunched my nose. "Fine. But now. I need to know *now*."

Shaking his head, Ash rolled his golden eyes. "Zula is right. You were born without any patience."

I trudged past him, scowling. I wasn't a fan of the fact that Zula and Ash were discussing my negative personality traits when I wasn't around—even if they were true and they had every right to complain. If you love someone, you bitch about them to their face. Everyone knows that. I pushed my annoyance aside, focusing on the more important task at hand. "Are you coming or what?"

"Of course I am." Ash smirked.

Damn smirk. I will smack it and kiss it off. Both.

"IT'S HIGHLY possible that such abuse could have made her hate Ambassador Aralias so fully that it didn't matter anymore that she's a Denard, too," Zula stated.

Ash and I both ignored her but for different reasons. Ash, because he was already over Zula's information drops and lectures. It was evident by the glazed-over look in his eyes. Me, because I was fidgeting behind the Gartian who was on a little fact-finding mission.

"Anything yet?" The Gartian ignored me. Most Gartians weren't that friendly, I was noticing. Polite, yes. Friendly, no. Most of the time they didn't bother to introduce themselves, and I was starting to have to refer to a lot of them with job descriptions tacked on to keep them straight in my mind. Like ... Computer Gartian, Pod Opener Gartian, Cook Gartian, etc.

Finally, Computer Gartian responded, "I have just confirmed the death of Ambassador Aralias ... and his wife, when their ship exploded a few hours ago. The incident is still under investigation, but it's thought to have been an engine malfunction combined with some extremely bad luck."

Relief washed over me. If the ambassador was dead, did that mean what I thought it could mean? I looked over at Ash with elation. "I don't have to stop being a bounty hunter!" I shrieked. "He's dead!" I threw my arms around him and gave him a big, wet, sloppy kiss. "He's dead!"

"Are you sure?" Ash asked Computer Gartian around my head, as I peppered his skin with kisses.

"Yes."

"Eeeep!" I let go of Ash and happily skipped my way around the room. "This is amazing news!" I stopped short abruptly. "We need to go get Nina out of wherever she is because she didn't lie, and she faked her own death. That has to mean something, too."

"All right. I'll see what I can do. It's ultimately not my decision, I just want you to realize that."

"I know, but who can deny what she's saying now?"

Ash sucked on his teeth. "We'll see."

Yes, it seemed anticlimactic that Ambassador Aralias had been killed so easily. But the Universe owed me. I'd definitely take his death as payment for all the crap I'd been through recently. Things were starting to look up again. At least I hoped they were. *After all, the Universe has played tricks on me before.* I pushed my pessimistic thoughts aside. This was real life, not fiction, and no matter who you are ... death can come easy.

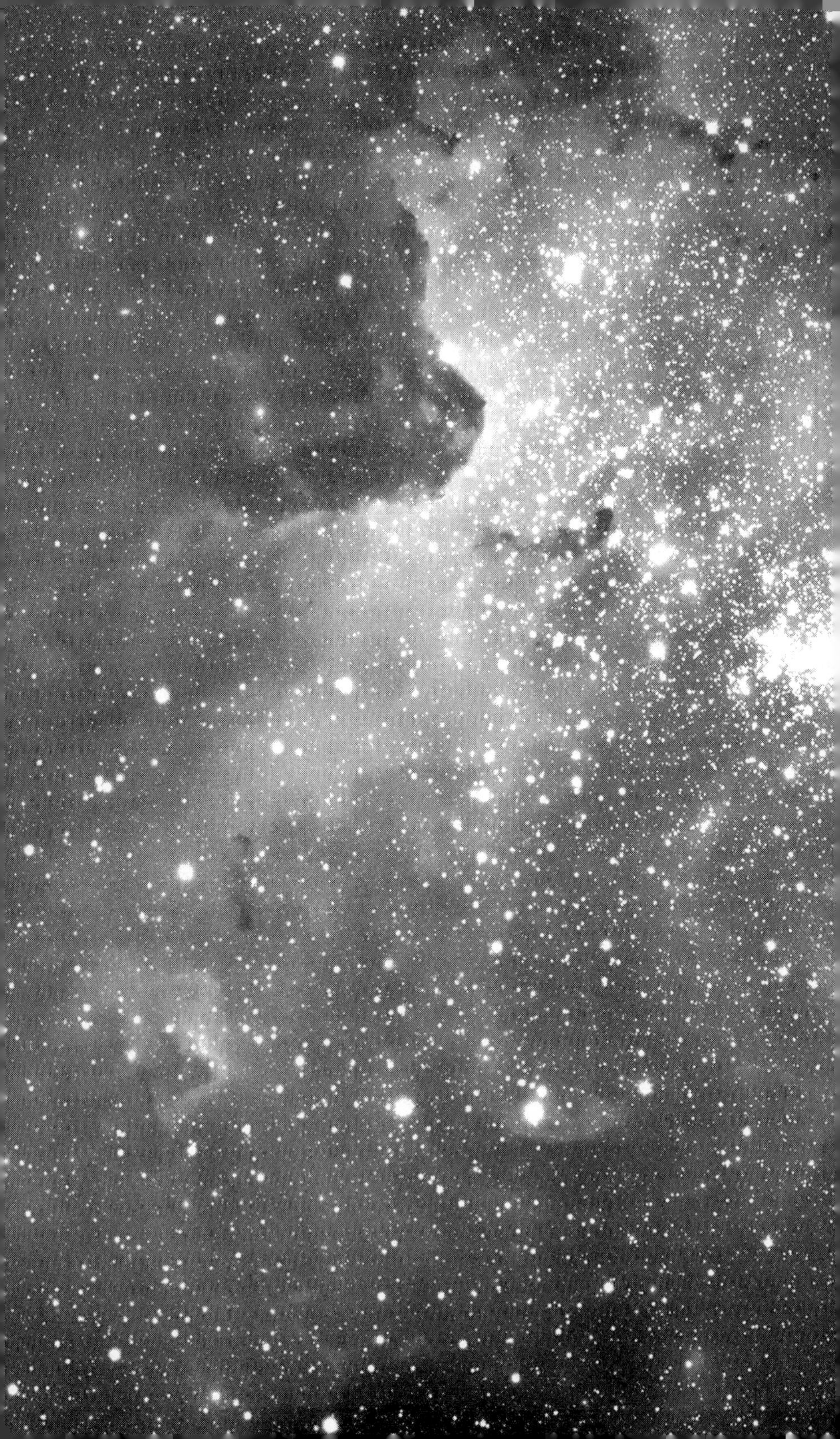

Chapter 27

"Nina, I can never fully repay you for all you've done for me. Killing Ambassador Aralias was just the icing on the cake."

I peered at Nina through the bars of her cell. I'd managed to wrangle my way into seeing her while she waited for her fate to be decided. Ash thought it was best that he be the one to argue for her release since he had a history with the Gartians, and they considered him a friend. Plus, I'd probably just start making demands. Unfortunately, he was right again.

Nina lifted her head, meeting my gaze. "I didn't do it for you. I'm sure you're now aware of what I am?"

"Yes. But I'm confused. The ambassador did that to your face? Why? I thought Denards only hated, I don't know, everyone but themselves."

Nina leaned forward, perching her elbows on her

knees. "I loved him once, and I do believe he loved me. Until he found out a secret from my past."

It was difficult for me to wrap my mind around Ambassador Aralias loving or being loved. Therefore, my curiosity was officially piqued. I needed to know Nina and the ambassador's story.

"What happened?" Biting my lip, I waited for her reply.

"Like I said, he found out a secret from my past. You see, not all Denards hate everyone and everything outside of their own species, as you have stated. True, the vast majority do, but some of us are more open-minded."

I was utterly riveted. *Her secret is going to be juicy. I can feel it.*

"I had a relationship with a hu-mutt."

"You mean a genetically altered human, or spliced human, or altered human. Not hu-mutt." I couldn't help but correct her. *I mean, seriously ...* "I'm standing right here."

"Yes, sorry. I sometimes forget that your kind finds that term offensive. I'm so accustomed to using and hearing it."

"Yeah, yeah, you're forgiven. Now tell me about your relationship with this altered human."

"I loved him," Nina stated without any preamble. "I loved him as much as any young woman can love. The relationship was ended by my mother. She was right to do so. My father would have done much worse than mangle my face if he found out. Years later I met and married the man who became Ambassador Aralias. We were happy for a time."

Tears welled in her eyes. "Until … I still don't know how he found out, but he did. He said he couldn't stand to look at my face anymore … " The tears spilled, trailing down her cheeks. "He said he wanted to kill me but couldn't because of who my father is." She swiped her face with the back of her hand. "He—he—" Sobs shook Nina's thin body. "He deserved to die by my hand."

I couldn't begin to imagine what it must have been like for her. Sure I'd felt betrayed by Maddox when he'd dumped me, but what the ambassador did to Nina took things to an entirely new level beyond fucked up. "I'm sorry, Nina, you're safe now."

"And so are you. I'm tired of my kind's blind hatred. We're raised to believe we're better, and we have the right to dictate who lives and who dies. But what I saw in my husband … my kind is not better, we're worse. So much worse."

"*You're* not," I whispered. "You saved me."

Nina sat up, baring her teeth while her tears continued to flow freely. "Not for you. For me. I wanted revenge. And I want more. I can help you. I can help you bring down the Denards." She ground her teeth together. "They are no longer my people."

"Well, I'm all for revenge. I was planning on getting it on your recently deceased hubby so I have some time on my hands. I think you need to tell all of this to the

Gartians, though. Can you really blame them for not trusting you?"

"No, I can't. I wouldn't blame them if they executed me."

"They won't. I'll make sure of it." I turned to leave but paused. I didn't know how much beauty meant to the Denard culture, but obviously, it had to mean something or Ambassador Aralias wouldn't have scarred Nina's face as punishment. "We can get your face fixed. I know a great plastic surgeon. He owes me a huge favor and he has all the latest equipment. You could look good as new in a matter of minutes."

Nina smiled. "I will wear these scars as a reminder of what was done to me. It will fuel my need for revenge. When I've done all I set out to do—if I get that chance, then and only then will I consider taking you up on your offer."

"Sounds fair enough. So I'll leave the offer as an open-ended one for whenever."

"Thank you."

"No. Thank you. Regardless of why you did it, you still saved me by helping me escape. And for that, I will forever be grateful." Nina fell into silence as I left the room. I couldn't help but wonder what was taking so long to set Nina free. I decided to go ahead and check out the situation.

As I made my way out of the Gartian prison, I passed several guards who nodded at me politely. Not one of them spoke to me. *Polite, non-friendly bastards*. I practically ran into Ash on his way into the prison, obviously searching for me. His face was lined with worry, his eyes slightly wild.

"What's up?" I nibbled on the inside of my cheek.

"There are several military New Earth ships just outside Gartian territory. They're here for you, Janey."

"What? I don't understand. Why the hell am I so in demand lately? What did they say exactly? And how the hell does everyone know I'm here?" I never did find out how Nina had pulled that one off. I'd have to ask her later just to have my curiosity slaked.

"They're claiming you're an escaped New Earth criminal. They're demanding for the Gartians to hand you over."

"Not that again. Tell them to fuck off. I'm not a New Earth citizen. I—"

"There's more. Their claim has been sanctioned by the UGFS. If the Gartians don't cooperate then an embargo will be placed on them. They can't let that happen, trading their alloy is how they survive."

"They can't expect us to agree to me just going with them?" I gulped. Although, I couldn't fault the Gartians if they did. I was just one person. We were talking about an entire species being affected by what could possibly go down.

"They need us to leave, Janey."

"They'll snap us up the minute we cross out of Gartian territory. And why the hell is the UGFS backing New Earth's claim on me?"

"You keep forgetting about the cloaking capacities of The Pittsburgh. We can make a successful run for it if we do it just right."

Oh, yeah. The cloaking system the Gartians installed. Duh. The Pittsburgh could now be invisible, thank God. "Again, why the hell is the UGFS backing New Earth's claim? I'd guess it had something to do with Ambassador Aralias but he's dead."

"It really could be that they want you for your fire capabilities. They have legally petitioned the UGFS for the return of someone they're claiming as a criminal."

"Then maybe I should face this claim head-on." If I was on the run from a UGFS arrest warrant then I would again be back in the situation of not being able to be a bounty hunter. *Come on, Universe! I thought we talked about you owing me. Multiple times! Now you're just being a bitch!*

"No, it's better if we put a safe distance between you and them before we look into the matter. This is the kind of thing that's always better to be safe than sorry about." Ash's eyes implored me to listen to reason, for once, instead of simply running off half-cocked.

"Yeah, okay. So we head out immediately then? What about Nina?"

Ash was already turning to head back out of the prison. "We don't have time to worry about her now. We need to ready ourselves for departure."

I dug my nails into Ash's muscular forearm. "Like hell we don't have time. I owe her my life and she's already proven she's not lying."

Ash's muscles flexed under my fingertips, but he didn't pull away from me. "Unless you want to take her with us—"

"Done. Let the Gartians know that I will be taking her into my custody on The Pittsburgh."

"Janey," Ash warned.

"Nope. There's nothing you can say to change my mind."

He snorted. "That's what I'm always afraid of. Damn stubborn phoenix women."

It was my turn to smirk. "And I'm only half phoenix."

"That seems to be plenty enough for you."

I slid against him, standing on my tiptoes. "It's one of the reasons you love me."

"Damn straight." We gazed into each other's eyes for a few moments before he pressed his lips to mine for a brief, but intense kiss. My senses narrowed down to him and only him until he pulled away, causing me to grumble in protest.

"Come on." He wrapped his arm around my waist, propelling me forward. "We'll have plenty of time for that later."

I nodded but couldn't push aside the worry that suddenly took root. Wasn't it usually the male of the species who put sex first? Ash was being too rational and reasonable, which could only mean one thing: He was more distressed about the current situation than he wanted me to believe. *Not good. Not good at all.*

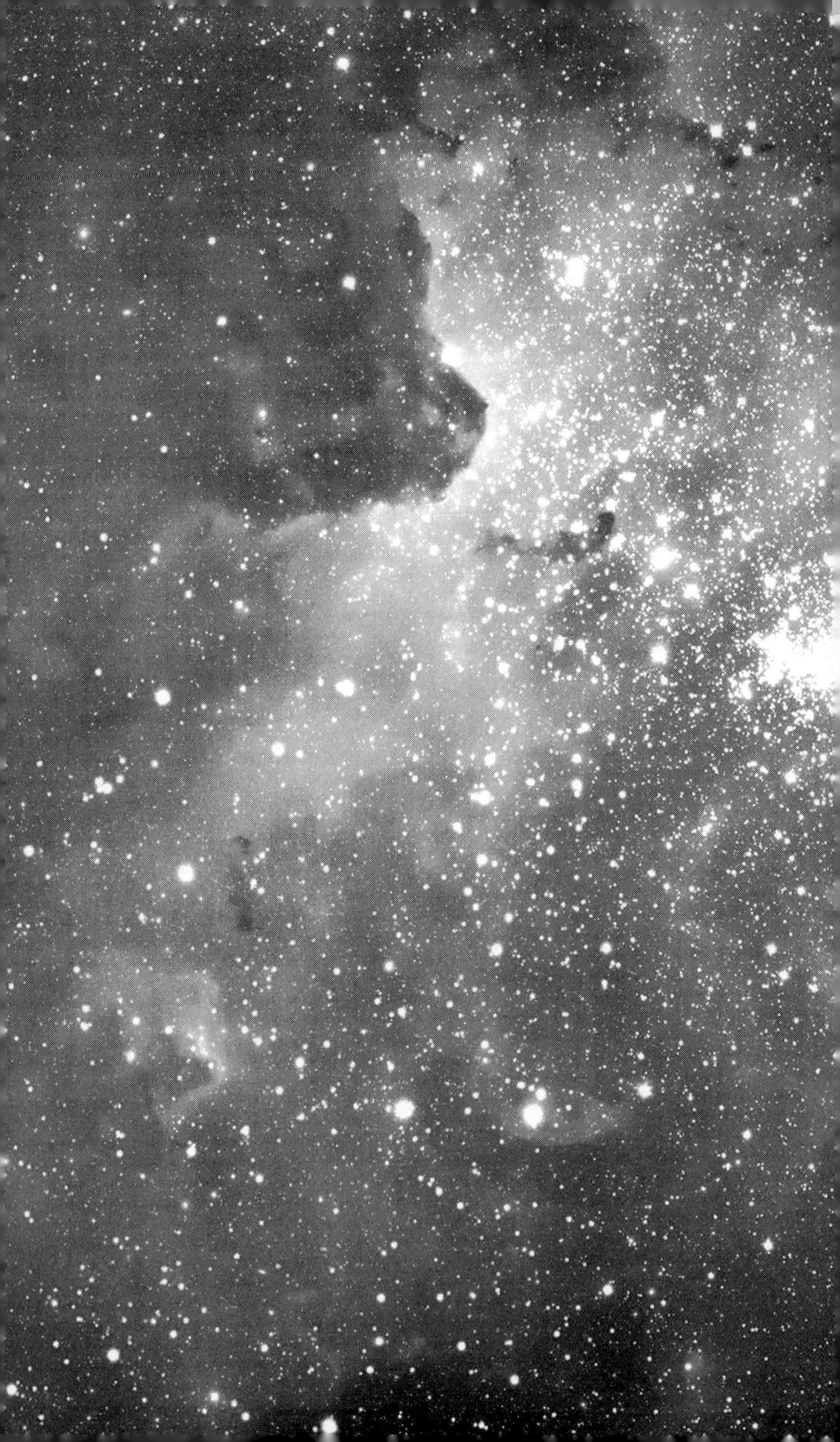

Chapter 28

I sat ramrod straight in my captain's chair on The Pittsburgh, my nails digging into the leather armrests. Zula was in her flight chair, opting to do the flying herself instead of trusting the auto-pilot in this situation. Tamzea was ensconced in the med wing, while Masha and Dar were manning the engine room, making sure everything was running at top capacity. As for Nina, she was in her new living quarters.

But Ash ... I'd wanted him with me on my ship, a fact that I'd assumed was just going to happen. Much to my dismay, he'd insisted on running a distraction for us. He was going to fly out of Gartian territory on The Phoenix, hoping it would just be assumed that I was on that ship. Then The Pittsburgh would just slip under the radar ... literally.

I hadn't understood why we couldn't just leave, but Ash insisted we had to offer some kind of plausible deniability for the Gartians. And I'd eventually agreed. The Gartians had been good to us and I didn't want them to have to suffer because of me. It didn't mean I wasn't upset about the plan nonetheless. Being separated from Ash again, especially with such a risky plan, already had my nerves at an all-time high.

I'll see you soon. Ash's voice briefly touched my senses before disappearing.

"You ready?" Zula glanced over at me.

"As I'll ever be," I grated.

"He'll be fine. The plan is about as sound as any of yours."

I winced. I wasn't known for my spectacular success rates when it came to my crazy plans, especially lately. "Let's hope that's not true."

"Ash is not the focus of this hunt."

"No, but he is wanted by the UGFS."

"He may not be. That may have gone up in smoke with Ambassador Aralias. We don't know the situation as it currently exists."

"Exactly." We didn't really know anything. Which, by the way, the Universe had been behaving lately, was probably a bad thing.

"I'm ready when you are." Zula changed the subject, obviously annoyed because I wasn't listening to her well-thought-out reasons. Or that's the way she usually saw it anyways.

"Has Ash already launched?" I was stalling. I knew he had. That's what his message in my mind meant.

"Yes."

"Ok-okay ... well, I guess let's go."

Zula turned and raised her blonde eyebrows at me. "Was that a command? You want me to go?"

"Yes! Just go!"

"Going," Zula muttered.

The Pittsburgh roared to life, and we surged out of port and into the air. I bit at my thumb as the darkness of space loomed before us. Sure enough, several large, military New Earth ships could be seen off in the distance hovering in wait. The sight was very disturbing to me. In between us and the New Earth ships was The Phoenix. It was headed straight at them going at a pretty good clip. I wondered when Ash would hop to a light slide. I dropped my hands to the armrests on my chair again, digging my fingers in.

"Come on. Just do it. Come on." But The Phoenix continued to hurtle straight at the New Earth ships. "If he doesn't jump soon they might think he's planning to attack or crash into them. They could shoot first."

Zula didn't respond as we continued to track across space at a much slower speed. "He needs to go to a light slide ... now." My heart was thrumming in my ears, and sweat was accumulating on my face.

"Ash, what the hell are you doing?" I screamed at him in my head. But of course, the jackass ignored me.

"Oh, my God!" I rushed over to the window to get a better look. The New Earth ships were angling themselves so they could—

"They're going to fire!" Red lasers tracked across space, and The Phoenix exploded right before my eyes. It was déjà-vu with what had happened with The Pittsburgh, but this time I knew what to look for. Fragments, debris ... it was all there. "NO!" I screamed. *This can't be happening. This isn't real.* "Ash!" I dropped to my knees, breaking into sobs.

"Get back to your chair, Jane," Zula commanded. *"We need to hop into a light slide."*

I curled in on myself, letting my despair rip at me. I should have known. I should have seen it coming because the Universe just didn't seem to want me happy. I could have been happy with Ash, and that's why the Universe ripped him away.

"Get back to your chair—NOW!" Zula roared.

I'd never heard her yell before. Not on that level. I numbly crawled back to my seat and strapped myself in. A moment later I felt the familiar pressure of a light slide. After another moment it was over. Dark space without any New Earth ships glowed before us. I slumped over, despair taking hold of me again.

"Glad to see you would miss me," Ash said, humor in his tone.

I inhaled sharply as I lifted my head to see him standing directly in front of me. "How?" I narrowed my eyes at him as his smirk registered. It had all been a part of his plan. He just didn't want to tell me in case it didn't work out for some reason. Unbuckling myself, I stood slowly, wiping at my already-drying tears. "You are the biggest asshat that I've ever come across in my entire life."

Ash pretended to ponder my words. "I doubt that."

"How could you? How could you do that to me? It was dangerous! I want to kill you with my bare hands!" I wrapped my arms around him, needing to be near him—needing to assure myself of his very real presence, and yet I couldn't resist the need to hit him as well. I beat my fists into his muscular back, wanting to hurt him for scaring me in such a manner.

He gave me a lopsided grin. "Only you would threaten to kill me over putting my life in danger." His face dropped into serious lines. "I did it to protect you. And it worked. Now we can mov—"

"I hate to interrupt your special little moment, but we have a problem," Zula said sharply. I glanced over to see her white-knuckling the edge of the control panel as she leaned over her rear-viewing screen. "A small New Earth special ops ship just dropped in behind us. I don't think it's a coincidence."

"Shit." I scuttled over to have a look past Zula's shoulder. Sure enough, what she said was true. Not that I doubted her, but I guess I just wanted to see it with my own eyes. "How much longer can we maintain the cloaking without starting to drain power from something else?"

"Just a few more minutes. It sucked up a lot of power going into a light slide while still cloaked, but we couldn't risk not doing it."

"There's no way they could have followed us. How could they have followed us?" The evidence was undeniable, but how? How did a special ops ship know what was going on?

"New Earth special ops ships are equipped with top-of-the-line heat trackers for when they do search and rescue," Ash said. "It's possible if someone knew what to look for, they could have tracked my flame when I came onto The Pittsburgh."

"And once they were locked onto you they could have tracked us by way of your heat signature," Zula finished for him.

And who did I know that was a New Earth special ops agent and had also seen what Ash could do? *Fuck me.* "Maddox."

"Exactly what I was thinking," Ash agreed.

"So now what? As much as I can't stand him I don't want to have to kill him."

"We invite him onboard," Zula said.

"What?" Ash and I exclaimed in unison.

"Show him that your powers come from your mate bond and not from hiding your abilities. What are they going to do? Even if New Earth scientists can duplicate your DNA, they can't make spliced humans bond with a full-blooded phoenix, especially since they're practically extinct."

Ash raised his eyebrows. "She has a point."

I couldn't disagree. If I admitted the truth, then maybe I could get everyone off my tail and I could go back to being a bounty hunter. I really, really ... wanted that. "Looks like we're about to prepare for a guest." I caught Zula's gaze. "Tell him whatever lie to get him onboard, and try to get him to come alone."

"Got it."

I grabbed Ash's hand. "I'm still mad at you, but we'll deal with that later. For now, let's go get ready to entertain my ex-boyfriend." *Oh joy.*

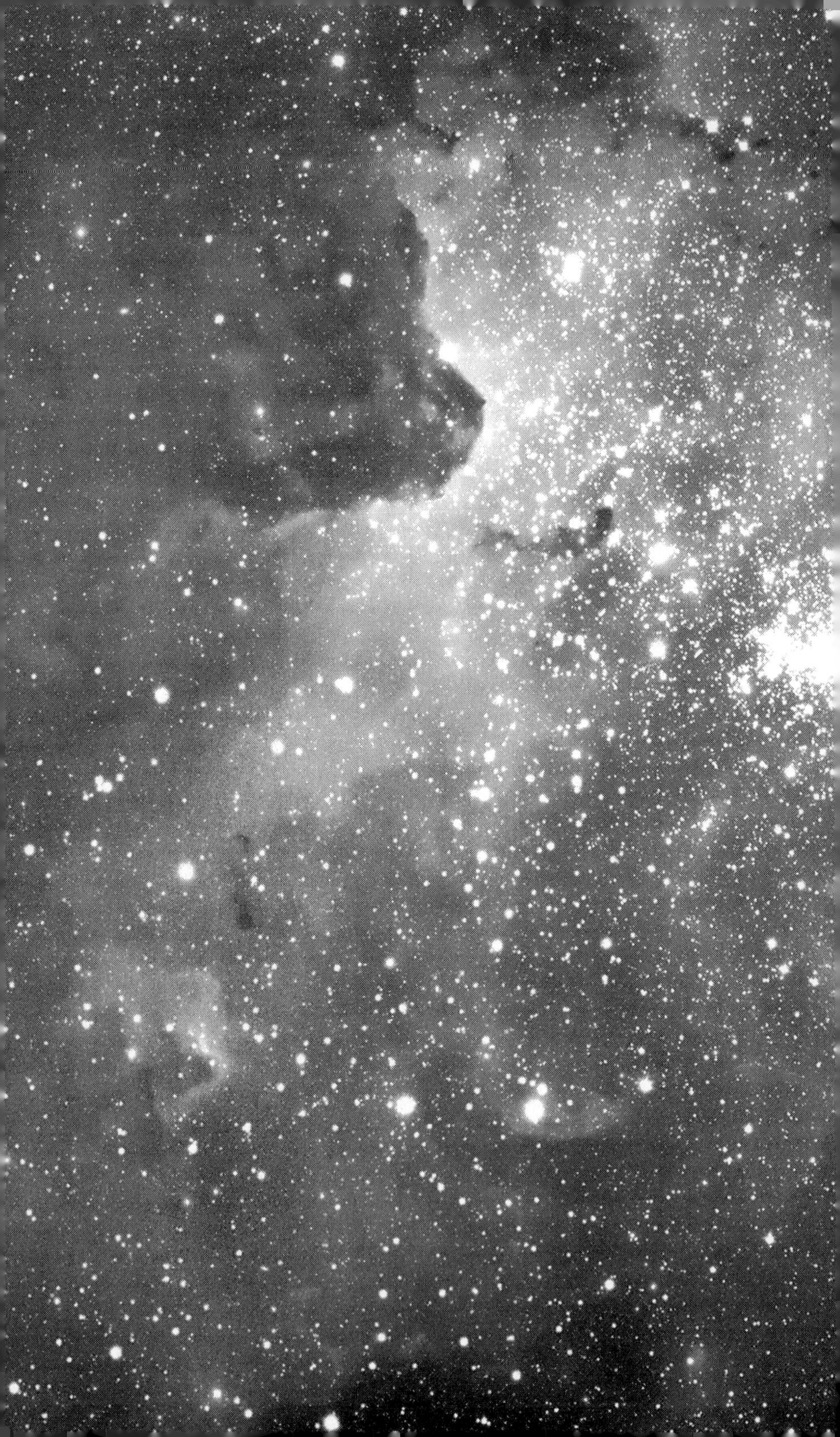

Chapter 29

"You *had* to tell him that my crew decided to hand me over?" I glared at Zula as she snapped the laser cuffs in place on my wrists. "I think you're getting way too much enjoyment out of this."

Zula, wisely, stayed mute on the subject. Ash was biting the corner of his lips on one side to keep from smiling. He was also getting too much enjoyment out of me in laser cuffs. I had no doubt it was because of how I'd kept trying to ensnare him in them when we'd first met.

"I can slip right out of these if I want." At least I thought I could. Ash claimed I had all his powers now that we were fully bonded. I'd experienced the going full-out flame thing but I wasn't exactly sure how to control any of said powers just yet.

"He doesn't know that," Zula stated, with yes, a glint in her eyes.

"How can he be so clueless and still have managed to track us?"

"Not much is known about phoenixes. Plus, he doesn't even know what you are. He knows nothing which is why we need to enlighten him." Ash pulled me to him, dropping his mouth to my ear. "I wouldn't mind using those on you later when we're alone, by the way."

I tried to ignore the warmth that bloomed within me. The cuffs wouldn't hold me, but it still didn't dampen the sexiness of being dominated by Ash. I could switch it up sometimes if he wanted. I didn't always have to be in control. I could let go in that way—with him. My mind hummed around the concept of Ash naked and me handcuffed with—

"Way to distract me." I scowled.

"Here he comes," Zula announced as she peered out the small window into the airlock.

I let myself lean into Ash for a moment before pushing off of him to stand up straight. "Go hide," I instructed.

Ash was going to stay out of sight like the rest of my crew unless he was needed. I was hoping he wouldn't be. He disappeared in a puff of flame, my muscles tensing the instant he was gone.

"Get ready," Zula whispered. She pressed the button to let Maddox in.

The door slid open smoothly and Maddox stalked inside, his gait recognizable to me even in his spacesuit. He tore off his helmet and bee-lined straight for me, barely noticing Zula. "Jane," he snarled, "I can't believe it's come to this."

I ground my teeth together so hard my molars ached.

"Maddox. What a very unwelcome surprise."

"The powers you have—you'd just keep them from us—from your people? All because of what happened years ago?"

"They're not my powers. You don't understand."

"I gave you a chance to make me, but you refused—"

"And you were going to let them experiment and torture me! I know what we had was never love, but I at least thought you would care enough to not want to see that happen to me! Let's not forget how you also would have let me burn in that room. Burn alive! You were only worried about your damn self. Please don't tell me it's all because I shot you in the arm like a million years ago. I was just a stupid teenager."

He flicked his chocolate gaze to the ground. "We need protection, Jane. Sacrifices must be made." He sounded almost remorseful about his actions.

I tilted my head, studying him. "Protection from what?"

His gaze snapped back up to meet mine, and his white teeth flashed as he growled like some kind of rabid animal. "From the same bastards who destroyed Earth. That's what all of it has always been about. The splicing—the training ... They just never told us when we were kids."

"You mean the Denards?" I caught Zula's attention

with my eyes as she stood quietly by the airlock, ready to react.

"You know? You know and still you refuse to help your people?"

I threw my laser-cuffed hands up in the air. "Well fuck. It looks like you should have mentioned that little tidbit, too. I think what we have going on here is a huge miscommunication."

Ash flamed in dramatically to stand beside me. "She's right. We need to talk, Maddox. And you need to listen."

Maddox's hand hovered over his laser gun. He shook his head slowly. "You never intended to hand her over." Not a question but a statement. I just hoped he didn't try anything stupid because he now felt backed into a corner.

"No," Zula said. "We needed you here so you might listen to us."

"We're all on the same team." Ash stared down at Maddox; he was a good couple of inches taller than my ex. "The problem was that none of us knew it."

"Who the hell are you anyway?" Maddox's fingers twitched over his gun.

"I'm Jane's mate, and I'm a phoenix."

Maddox blinked rapidly, and his lips parted slightly. "I d-don't understand. Phoenixes were killed off by—"

"The Denards. Yes, most of us were. And the few of us left want revenge."

"You want revenge," Maddox mumbled as if on autopilot as he tried to process the information that was being dropped on him.

"As do the Gartians," Ash added.

"The Gartians," Maddox repeated.

"And me," Nina said softly as she strode across the floor, eyes riveted to Maddox. It looked like she'd been eavesdropping.

Maddox's eyes widened, and he paled as he stumbled backwards. "Nina?" He raised a shaky hand to scrub down his face. It was as if seeing her scars made him touch his face in reflex.

She notched her chin up even as her lower lip trembled. "Yes, it's me."

"Whaa-what happened to you?"

"I was a victim of the Denard prejudices as well. I was punished for not hating as much as the rest of them." Her lips pressed into a thin line as she waited for Maddox's reaction. Every muscle in her body looked to be locked with tension as she practically vibrated where she stood. I'd already figured out who he was to her. I had yet to put the pieces together about how they'd met, though.

"Jesus," Maddox finally muttered. He took a step towards Nina and stopped. Then he took another before halting again. He continued this process until he stood right before her. He raised his shaky hand to hover over her face. "Nina, I-I wish—" His expression abruptly hardened and he backed up, turning to face Ash. "I'm ready to talk now."

I could see the hurt in Nina's eyes even though she tried to hide it. She may have loved Ambassador Aralias on some level, but it was clear to me that her heart still belonged to Maddox. *Shit.* What were the chances that my ex-boyfriend would turn out to be Nina's human love from her past? The man who had caused her husband to disfigure her face? The Universe was a much smaller place than I ever realized. *Maybe too small.*

"Well, let's talk then," I replied before Ash could. "And, Zula, get me the hell out of these things … now." I lifted my cuffed wrists, waving them around demonstratively.

Ash touched my arm and helped me to flame out of the cuffs before Zula could reach me. Maddox's eyes widened slightly. It was probably a good thing to show him that we weren't bullshitting about the whole phoenix thing. Although I supposed he was instantaneously more open to us the moment he'd laid eyes on Nina.

"Come on." I headed off in the direction of the eating lounge. "We're going to have a full disclosure meeting." I paused when I passed one of the intercoms and leaned into it, pressing the button. "Group meeting in the eating lounge immediately. That means you Tamzea, Masha, and Dar, because everyone else is up here with me and already knows."

I continued on knowing everyone would follow me. By the time we got to the lounge, Tamzea, Masha, and Dar were already there. The three of them watched Maddox with suspicion.

"It's okay, everyone." I tried to make my tone sound carefree. Things were in a better place than when Maddox had first stepped onto the ship, but I wasn't fool enough to believe that meant everything was okay just yet. "Maddox is willing to listen to what's really going on. I—"

"What is he?" Maddox blurted as he stared in disbelief at Dar.

"That, my dear Maddox, is a Gartian." I pulled out a chair, flopped down in it, and propped my booted feet up on the table. "Have a seat, Maddox. As you can see, we really do have a lot to discuss."

He scrubbed a hand over his face, his gaze swinging wildly around the room to finally land on me. All of his hostility had finally seeped out of him. "Yeah, okay." Pulling out a chair of his own, he sat down.

"I guess I'll go first." I cleared my throat, meeting Maddox's dark brown pools. "It all began when I took the contract that the UGFS had out on Ash..."

IT FELT like hours since the impromptu meeting had begun. Maddox asked more questions than I would have ever thought possible, but finally, it seemed like things were wrapping up. Thankfully it also seemed like Maddox was now seeing things our way. We really were on the same team. Personally, I was shocked that New Earth was preparing for the Denards. They hid their intentions well. Maybe a little too well in some cases. That fact had almost resulted in me being experimented on for the 'greater good'.

"So how do you plan on getting the information on the

chip out?" Maddox asked Ash. "There are a lot of colonies that are off the grid, but they're no less important—"

"Before we can even begin to think about dropping that bomb we need to prepare the citizens that are ruled over by the UGFS. If we don't prepare them then we could do more harm than good. They must have protection in place. Even the more peaceful species need to be prepared with backup food or whatever it is that the UGFS could lord over them to keep control."

Maddox nodded, deep in thought. "We could use people like me and Jane who travel the galaxies to spread the word. It won't raise suspicion since it's what we've been doing for years. We can begin to spread the truth, prepare people, and when the time is right then we can let the information out."

"No one will believe us if we don't let them see the information first," I started to argue, but Ash didn't let me finish.

"More species have been learning the hard way, Janey. I hate to say this because I know you're going to make me pay for it later, but you were naïve. You were half blind to what was going on with everything you did and the things that were around you. Maybe you didn't want to see it because at the time you had no real way to fix it … but Maddox is right. We can't just drop the information without having a plan in place."

"That's what you meant before when you said things were more complicated than I thought, isn't it?"

"Yes." He squeezed my hand.

"Okay, but then— Wait! Does this mean I get to be a bounty hunter again?" I knew it was a bit twisted that with everything else going on I kept focusing on that little part of my life, but seriously ... I loved my job. Plus, I had no idea how else I was supposed to legally make the kind of money I pulled in as a bounty hunter.

"Focus, Jane," Zula said. Although I didn't miss the pleased tone in her voice. Zula had grown accustomed to a certain level of pay brought in by my bounties. She wasted most of her money on silly science-y crap, but who was I to judge?

"I am focused."

Maddox rose from the table. "I have a lot to report back to New Earth about." He met my gaze, and for the first time since meeting him again, his eyes softened towards me. "I'm sorry I thought ... I'm sorry I thought that about you, Jane."

I waved him off. "I guess it's okay. Although it would have been nice for you to have given me a little more credit than that. But whatever." He'd jumped to the conclusion that I'd been harboring secret abilities rather quickly. He'd also treated me like it was something right up my alley to do. I still couldn't help but wonder what I'd done to him to make him see me that way. Besides shoot him, which I wouldn't have done if he hadn't tossed me aside like yesterday's trash.

"I'll make sure the warrant is lifted and it's known that it was all a mistake. We do need you out there to help with this."

"Mmm hmm," I muttered as I drummed my fingers against the table.

Somehow I had ended up involved in this little rebellion slash uprising, or whatever you wanted to call it, despite my best efforts. I still wasn't quite sure how I felt about it. I wasn't even sure it had fully sunk in yet. All I knew was that I got to be a bounty hunter again. That part made me happy. I guess the rest I would just have to take day by day.

"We'll see you on New Earth soon," Ash said to Maddox as he stood and shook his hand. Maddox eyed Ash with something akin to respect. I suppose it was because Ash had gone to such lengths to get the information that would eventually bring down the UGFS, and therefore the Denards.

I studied Maddox from under my lashes as he readied himself to leave. He glanced over at Nina and gulped. He actually gulped. In that moment I saw a glimpse of the boy I used to know.

"Nina ..." He cleared his throat. "Nina, I—" She stood, reaching her hand up hesitantly to touch him. He watched it come at him as if horrified. As soon as her skin made contact with his, he jerked back as if he'd been electrocuted. "I better be going." He rushed off as if his life depended on it.

Nina stared after Maddox with utterly no emotions, the lack of them extremely creepy under the circumstances. Although, I was sure she had a lot of practice compartmentalizing from her time with the ambassador. I just hoped seeing Maddox, the man she actually loved, wouldn't push her over the edge somehow.

"Come here." Ash swept me up in his arms, and I squealed with delight. "No more serious thoughts for the time being. We need to have a little meeting of our own."

I heard Tamzea giggle, and Zula make some kind of snide comment, I was sure of it by her tone. But I couldn't care less. My time for embarrassment about Ash was over. I was proud to have him as my mate. Besides … the Universe was finally beginning to turn things in my favor like it should have been doing all along.

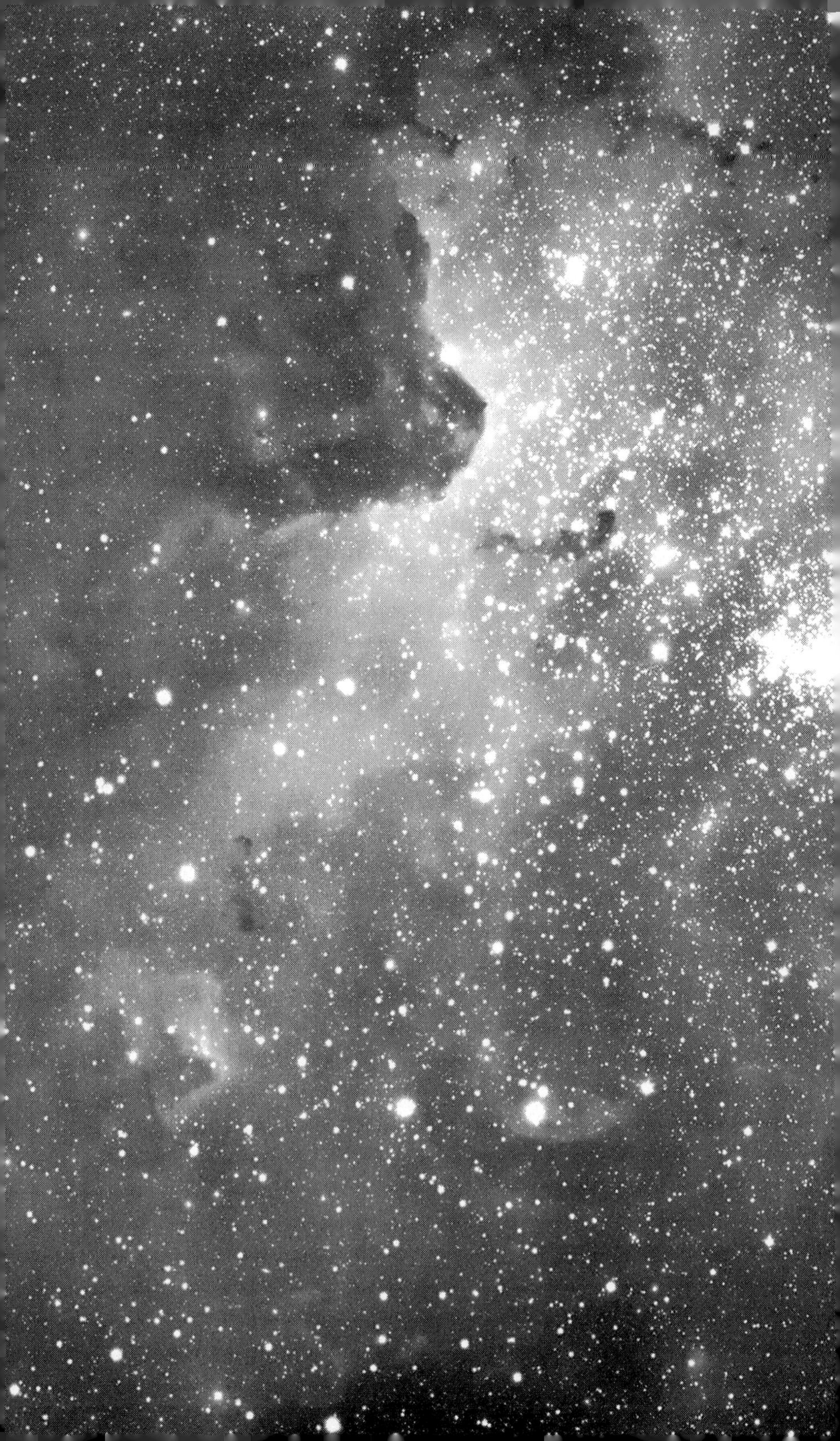

Chapter 30

"When did you have time to do this?" My gaze swept over my living quarters with a combination of awe and annoyance. It seemed like my reactions to things were like that often lately ... both positive and negative intertwined. It was like the old me was at war with the new me internally. Or maybe I was just afraid, on some level, of being happy. Because hitting any kind of high meant I had that much more distance to fall before I hit bottom.

"Dar and Masha did it. I guess Masha is feeling a tad guilty. Besides," Ash wrapped his arms around me from behind, "do you want to burn everything to a crisp every time we're together? Wasn't it nice not having to worry about that when we were on the Gartian planet?"

Leaning back into Ash, I inhaled his unique spicy scent. The not quite cinnamon note was rapidly becoming associated with home to me. "Yes, okay, I did say I needed to get me some flame retardant stuff, but it also would have been nice to not feel … I don't know, violated."

Rolling my shoulders, I internally scolded myself. Masha was my friend, one that had some explaining to do, but my friend nonetheless. She and Dar had done something nice for me. They didn't violate me, and I needed to stop being so touchy about such things. I forced my mind away from the overwhelming irritation. "And the Gartians really need to name their planet. It's kind of weird that it's just," I raised my hands to air quote, "The Gartian planet."

Ash nuzzled me, speaking against the side of my neck. "It had a name, once. But after the G-Pox it somehow didn't feel like home to them anymore. Or rather, it didn't feel like the planet that it once was. They felt it needed a new name and yet they didn't want to let go of the old. So they slipped into limbo with it, and now it's simply the way it is."

"I guess that makes sense. What happened to them," I shuddered, "their kind are true survivors." I reached up to lock my fingers around the back of Ash's neck so I was arched backwards. He took the opportunity to skim his long fingers up to cup my breasts.

"You're so beautiful," he rasped. "I'll truly never get enough of you."

My insides ignited just like they always did when Ash touched me, but it was more intimate this time. Maybe it was because of the completed mate bond. Or perhaps it was because I was finally giving him my trust. In the end, it didn't matter. Things had been off between Ash and me before. I wanted him, but I hated him. He made me burn for him, and yet the mere thought of my desire left me cold. Our relationship had moved too quickly, and at an awkward snail's pace at the same time. I needed and wanted him, but hadn't truly trusted him.

Now, finally, things felt like they were clicking into place emotionally. Quite possibly I'd been trying to fight my destiny all along, as corny as that sounded. There were still things about phoenixes that I didn't understand. Had Ash and I somehow been fated to be together all along? Were we meant to—

"You're thinking too much. I don't like it." Ash pitched me forward, and I landed face-first on my bed. He wrapped the end of my ponytail around his fist, tugging gently while burning away my clothes with the other.

"Hey, I liked that outfit!"

"I'll buy you another one."

He swirled his fingertips over the elegant pattern magically burned into my back. "You have no idea how happy it makes me to see this." His voice dropped an octave lower than normal as he rumbled, "I want to fuck you while I look at it."

He dropped his scalding lips to my back, trailing his tongue down my spine. "I want to be staring down at my mark on you—my claim—while I fuck you hard enough to make you scream. Then, I want to come all over it. Mark you again in a different way."

He released my hair, and I sank forward as he nipped

at my left ass cheek. "Then I want to clean you up and do it all over again." He palmed each ass cheek and lifted me up, spreading me. "But first I'm going to taste that very sweet pussy of yours."

Well, that seemed ... nice. "Yes. Do it." I urged him on by wiggling my bared flesh at him.

His low rumble of a laugh hummed against my sensitive flesh as he speared his tongue into me. I groaned in pleasure, clutching at the bed for some kind of leverage. Flames burst forth from my palms as he flicked my clit with his overheated tongue. "Come on, Janey baby, I can tell you're already on the edge. I need to taste your cum. Now."

"Dirty ... naughty ... phoenix," I muttered, undulating my hips back and forth against his mouth. Finally, I gave him what we both wanted, and I cried out as I burst into flames ... literally.

When my orgasm had run its course, I settled back into my human form. I had no idea that could happen. It felt damn good, though ... better than good. And I was ready for more. "Ash," I moaned, "I want the rest of what you promised."

Ash gripped my hips, sliding into me from behind in one hard thrust. "I think I can do that," he growled. His strong fingers dug into my skin as he pounded into me. The friction was delicious, just the right amount of pleasure mixed with pain. My muscles were already coiling tight again as Ash burned me from the inside out. "Tell me what I want to hear," he bit out. "Tell me."

"I'm yours."

"There's no doubt there. You belonged to me before we even met." He smacked my ass and ground his pelvis against me. "Tell me."

I tried to think with my hormone-addled brain what he could possibly want to hear from me. Obviously, I now knew what it wasn't. *Arrogant asshat who fucks like a god. What would someone like him want to hear? And do I even have enough brain power at the moment to figure it out?*

"Tell me," he demanded again.

"I-I ..." Quivering around him, I tried to think, tried to focus.

A millisecond of clarity barreled into me, and I gasped out, "I love you."

Ash burst into flames, taking me with him. We swirled around and through each other, riding out the bliss before we both settled back into our human forms.

"That isn't exactly what you promised." I play pouted.

Ash pulled me on top of him and kissed my temple tenderly. "Our emotions are still raw because everything's so new. I didn't think I'd lose control and burst into flames." He tipped my chin up so I could gaze into his beautiful golden eyes. "That's what you do to me, make me lose control."

I grinned smugly. "Good, because that's what you make me do. I suppose," I ran my fingertips down his arm, "we just need to practice—a lot—so we can control everything."

Ash flipped me over in a sudden burst of speed. "I

think I can get on board with that train of thought." He ensnared my lips with his, and I let my eyes slide shut as I once again got lost in all things Ash.

I LAY STILL with my eyes closed, too tired to move, but my racing mind depriving me of sleep. Ash wasn't having the same problem. His chest rose and fell evenly, his heartbeat thrumming steadily under my ear. It was soothing to be in his arms and to have him so relaxed. He was the missing part of my soul that I'd always been searching for. We belonged together like this.

Buuut ... I still had so many questions—questions about Ash's past, and all of our futures. With Ambassador Aralias dead and the warrant being lifted off of my head, things had settled back down, but for how long? Changes were brewing in the Universe, some good and some bad. I'd finally had the veil lifted from my eyes, and nothing looked the same anymore. There were secrets hidden behind what seemed like every star. I knew that rough times were going to come for all before things truly got better—*if* they got better. I was hopeful that our side would come out on top, but I was also a realist. Sometimes the good guys don't win in real life. Sometimes the bad guys conquer all and rewrite history so no one ever knows the truth.

Ash stirred beneath me. "I thought I fucked you

senseless, for a little while at least. You need to turn your brain off."

"I can't help it," I murmured against his bare chest.

"Well shit, I guess I'm just going to have to try harder this time." Ash spread my legs and slid into me from underneath. I moaned.

"That's my girl," he rasped.

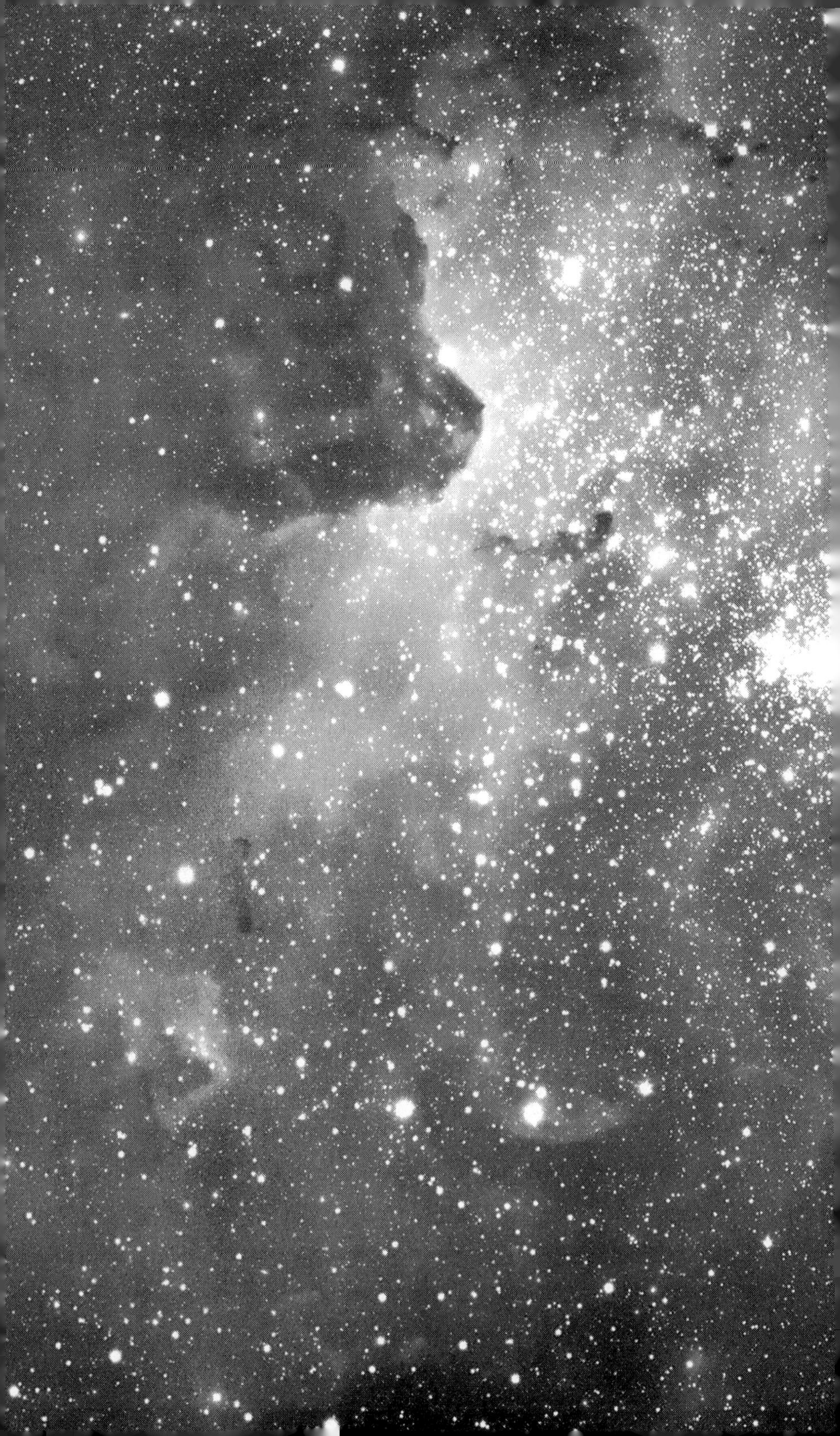

Epilogue

"Hey, you! Big, ugly, and slimy!" I stood with my feet shoulder-width apart, and my laser gun trained on the huge slug-looking creature.

The slug man slid around slowly to face me. Its huge black eyes regarded me with annoyance. No fear. Not good. "What do you want, hu-mutt?"

Seriously? My hand shook with the effort it took not to squeeze the trigger on my laser gun. I'd seen slug man's kind around before, and I still wasn't sure how they communicated when it looked like they didn't have mouths. And something like him had the nerve to insult me? At least I looked like—like something other than a pile of sludge with eyes.

"What I want is for you to come with me. I'm taking you in, Slime-o." My gaze roamed over him as I considered my options. How the hell was I supposed to contain him? The laser cuffs definitely weren't going to work. Maybe laser chains? Shit, I hadn't brought them off the ship with me. Maybe threat at gunpoint was good enough? Why did I never think these things through? I'd seen Slime-o's picture in the database, but the whole no arms thing hadn't really registered.

"Want my help?" Ash asked from just off to my right.

"No," I grated. "We talked about this. I'm the bounty hunter. You're just here so that you don't drive me crazy worrying that—"

"He's getting ready to attack." Ash quirked an eyebrow. "Trust me, you don't want to deal with what he can do."

I swung my gaze around to eye Slime-o. He was just standing there. Scowling, I fumbled for the PAER on my belt. I lifted it up just as it began to flash red. Not again. *Seriously ... not again!* "What the hell can he do? He's just a big ole' slug man!"

Ash crossed his arms over his chest, smirking. "I thought you didn't want my help?"

"Physical help! Tell me what you know." I kept glancing back and forth between Ash, Slime-o, and my PAER nervously.

"Nope. Information is very helpful, therefore if you don't want my help, I'm not giving you any information either."

"Ash!" I growled. He stared me down, letting me know he was willing to try and out stubborn me. He was learning entirely too quickly from me.

"Fine. Help me, puh-leeeaze." I ground my teeth together. I still hated the fact that Ash knew more about … well, most things in the Universe than I did. It was only because he'd been alive for such a long ass time. As a bonded phoenix, I would live as long as he did, and since he was immortal … well, when I was as old as dirt like him, I'd know plenty more, too. It also sucked because he always got this smug expression on his face every time I caved and actually asked him for help.

"Too late." Ash flamed forward and grabbed me, moving me back a few feet just as black sludge poured down in a sheet right where I'd been standing.

I stared at the black goo. "What would it have done?"

"Encased you in a cocoon. I would have had to burn you out. You would have been fine in the end. For most species once in there, it's almost impossible to get them out. It's usually a death sentence."

"He threw black goo of death at me? Oh, Slime-o is going down."

"You want these?" Ash produced a set of laser chains, the very ones that I thought were still on the ship. Mostly because I had stated that we wouldn't need them so I didn't have to be bogged down by them. And Ash had brought them anyways. I wanted to both kiss and hit him for not listening to me. *And ugh. He's right again.*

He winked. "You can thank me later."

I snorted. "Whatever." I snatched the chains from Ash and moved cautiously towards Slime-o. The entire time I had a huge grin plastered across my face. As much as it infuriated me on one level ... okay, having Ash next to me while I was on a hunt ... it was my happy place.

Or at least one of them.

Acknowledgments

As an overthinker, acknowledgments are quite an arduous task for me. I wonder if I'm being lackluster or too intense with the thanks. Or did I forget someone? Possibly I gave too much credit to someone and therefore slighted someone else who actually did a ton. A part of me doesn't want to include these in my books at all because the people I appreciate should know it already ... or do they??? No matter how I look at it these damn acknowledgments make me friggin' sweat.

But here they are anyways since if I don't include them then people will probably think I'm ungrateful and weird. I mean, I am weird, but I don't want people to think that. I am grateful though, so I'll just go-ahead and make this uncomfortable for everyone. Heh.

Okay, here I go. Right now. Actual acknowledgments to follow. Hopefully, they represent an appropriate level of gratitude to all the people in my life that deserve it.

(And yep ... I have totally copy & pasted what comes next from my *Replayed* book acknowledgments, which I originally took from *Virtual Reality Bites* acknowledgments. I thought maybe after *Replayed* that I'd come up with something better. Or at least something new. Obviously not. So this is now copy & paste edition #3. I'm thinking you should probably get used to it.)

My amazing Hubby! Words can't begin to explain how supportive and truly amazing he is. Hmmm ... I think I already used the word amazing. But unlike in books, when honestly applied to someone, the word amazing means something, well, amazing. And my hubby is all of the things that word implies. Romance heroes are nothing compared to him.

Lindsay Tiry ... what would I do without you? I hope I never have to find out. From cover design to interior graphics to logos, you do it all. Your talent is awe-inspiring, and I hope one day everyone else will be able to appreciate how you shine.

Melissa Ringsted ... my illustrious editor. Without you, this book probably would have gone straight into the trash. Thank you for giving me the confidence to publish when I convinced myself that I was the worst writer in the history of writers, and for fixing all the words.

Ren, Kristin, Shona, Ruty ... my O.G. chicas ... I wouldn't be here without you. I'm beyond lucky to know all of you.

And last, but certainly not least, thank you to everyone who has taken the time to read this book. Hopefully, you enjoyed it, but even if you didn't, I still appreciate the fact that with so many options out there today, you even gave my book a fleeting chance.

About the Author

Ava Wixx
Passion. Love. Chaos.

Ava Wixx escaped into books at a young age and decided to stay there. It was only a matter of time before she was driven to create her own fantasy worlds from fear of running out of places to explore.

Reader, writer, dreamer … Ava only toils in reality when absolutely necessary. She lives in North Carolina with her husband, and spoiled mini-poodle.

Made in the USA
Middletown, DE
27 August 2023

37276752R00191